Europe

A novel by Jesse Wilkinson

Copyright © 2018 by Jesse Wilkinson

All rights reserved, including the right of reproduction
in whole or in part in any form.

First paperback edition 2018

Cover art by Paul Smutylo

ISBN 9781541177314

In Memory of

Ron and Helen Wilkinson

And for

Don Wilkinson and Michele Lavin

John and Kathleen Lavin

Acknowledgements

Thanks to my family for all their support; to Harry Posner, Luke Wilkinson, Brian Barrie, and James Southworth for the crucial editing help; Frog Ponds Café for offering me a home away from home to write; and Sharon Von Etten for writing an album that was my soundtrack to this book. Lastly, I want to thank Mrs. Edwins who let me write stories in class as a kid and the Montessori school system for allowing children the freedom to be creative at an early age.

The mind is its own place and in itself
can make a heav'n of hell, a hell of heav'n.

John Milton
Paradise Lost

1

Leaving is always dangerous. It requires courage. But it's rarely thought of as courageous unless the motive is right. And the motive is never clear.

On separate days, fifty-six years apart, two men woke up and knew they had to leave the ones they loved. Something had changed for them and they didn't know why. Love and war can do that to a person. In fact, they always do. They bring people together and tear them apart. And these two things are not exclusive to one particular time or generation. They are no less innate to human beings than laziness or fear.

It was a Tuesday afternoon that Caleb Arthur knew he was going to leave. He was sitting alone at his living room window strumming his guitar and watching the rain fall on his red Volkswagen Jetta. Rivers of water poured down the windshield and pooled at the hood like tears building at lower eyelids. Leaves were pasted to the body of the car like stickers; the rain couldn't wash them away no matter how hard it came. He was killing time, waiting for his bar shift to start at Corrigan's Sports Pub and was reading a letter from his grandfather, Patrick, written during the war. The paper was thick and set in its folds, which made it difficult to keep open. It was yellowed and worn around the edges, and told of a town in Southern England that Patrick had visited during his leave. One passage described the colour of the water. Another detailed his walks through the cobblestone streets, where a Ferris wheel operated at the centre of town. 'It is a small piece of heaven in the hell that has surrounded me these last years,' he wrote in the closing. Caleb folded it neatly and tucked it back into the weathered envelope and into the drawer with the others. They had been given to him by his father a few weeks earlier after Caleb's aunt Catherine had rediscovered them cleaning out her basement.

Caleb had never left Piersville and so his experience of the world was contained and narrow, but deep down, he had always been spellbound by foreign places. As a child, it was for the forests behind his house, the abandoned buildings by the railroad tracks, the caves he frequented with his two younger brothers. As a teenager, it was for the mystery of girls' bodies and the parts they kept secret.

He saw what women kept hidden first in magazines he smuggled to the woods, fingering page by page, eyes glued to the mystery unfolding at each naked pose. Later it was in the abandoned buildings he frequented with his friends, a place that once housed wild imaginations, but later became a place to flip through magazines, smoke and drink beer with friends.

But the real mystery that came to him in his teenaged years was the furtive creation of the female heart, a sneaky machine hidden away behind the veneer of soft skin and woven with complex desires that developed far earlier than they do in men. It was this hidden place tucked deep inside a girl named Melanie Hazen that Caleb Arthur spent the years of his young manhood trying to understand. She was the ultimate mystery for him. But after seven years together, when he turned twenty-three and realized he knew her better than anyone else in the world, the quest for hidden places came back to him with intensity. The one that had always seemed out of reach was the continent his grandfather had traveled through during the war. It held the type of mystery that couldn't be captured in another person. It was the lure of adventure.

The letters he was given told of heartache, fear, and longing, but what Caleb couldn't read in each letter Patrick Arthur wrote home was the real weight of the war; the toll it took on Patrick's spirit after he returned. They were connected by one year on earth together, on the two sides of Jack Arthur's life, the man who knew the unspoken pain his father carried and the privilege his son would enjoy because of it. There was a darkness Jack tried his best to shelter Caleb from. There were letters that Jack didn't give him, letters that told too much, so Caleb grew up with an incomplete picture of what his grandfather's time in Europe was like; it had been romanticized when there was nothing romantic about war for those who lived it.

And because he believed his grandfather had been able to carry on with his life unaltered by his time in Europe, Caleb thought he too could leave his sheltered life and come home to it unscathed. He was not going to fight a war, but to seek adventure. He didn't understand that no one gets to have both freedom and comfort. No one gets to live two lives. He was young, and naive, and in search of something he couldn't name, a hazardous combination for a weak man. He didn't inherit the strength of his grandfather, who had also left a life behind fifty-six years earlier, but who was called away by duty to his country, not to his curiosity.

      Caleb knew that his trip would be a footnote in his life, one that began and ended in Ontario, but had one defining event that prevented anyone from saying he didn't truly live: real adventure - what every person seeks in their heart. And when the pull is strong enough, it can take them away from everyone they love because when choosing between contentment and freedom, there will always be times, at least certain people, who will choose adventure, and they are often deemed guilty of selfishness, but it isn't egotistical for a person to want to learn who they really are. They will find themselves, and they will also realize that every adventure must come to an end. Every adventurer must return home and find happiness in stillness.

2

He hadn't been to the gym in two months and his shirt, once white, had yellowed having been left too long in his gym bag. It smelled of old sweat and dirty socks. He lifted it to his nose quickly and recoiled.

The gym was quiet for a Thursday afternoon. He had hoped it would be busier. There were two women using the treadmills and an elderly man on a stationary bike. He pretended to fiddle with his Walkman and let his gaze fall on the younger woman as her ponytail danced back and forth in the pattern of her stride. When she slowed to a march, he stood up and walked over to a row machine and settled in. His movements were awkward at first, but he soon found a steady rhythm. He closed his eyes and imagined himself rowing across the water, a large expansive body where coastlines appeared out of the darkness. The water stretched infinitely towards the horizon and he could feel the waves rocking him slowly forward. He fell into a meditative state and forgot where he was. The sense of time vanished, but he soon felt the presence of a person close by and the slap of a hand on his back, forcing him back into reality.

"Hey fuckface! I guess they let anybody work out here," Charles McDonough said in high-pitched octave Caleb had never gotten used to.

"Oh, hey McDonough."

"Were you just in deep thought there, Arthur, or were you picturing Melanie bent over the kitchen table?" He let out a crude laugh. "Either way, I hope you reached nirvana."

Caleb had never considered McDonough a friend, but he was always among Caleb's group growing up, lingering and ready to call anything 'gay' that didn't suit his machismo.

"Melanie and I actually broke up a few weeks ago. Or at least I think we did," Caleb said and looked down at the machine to avoid eye contact.

"Shit, that's right. I'm sorry brother, I heard that. And you want to go backpack around the world or some shit, right?"

"That's the plan."

"Well, I wish I could go and do that. The city works me pretty hard though – don't get more than a week off here and there," he said and paused, distracted by the girls on the treadmills. "Just watch your ass over there, pal. Don't get mugged or raped or anything. I'm sure those European men love to prey on guys like you." He let out his trademark laugh and walked away.

McDonough always had a way of leaving Caleb feeling irritable, and just as he was about to get up and walk to the water fountain, he heard that same voice again.

"And you're having a going away thing at Corrigan's right? Hope it's cool that I go. Gonna be tons of chicks right? Mel and her friends?"

"Yup. Saturday."

Caleb watched him walk away and placed his headphones back on. He looked at his watch and realized he only had an hour until his shift started.

Two of Corrigan's regulars were sitting at the bar when Caleb walked in for his evening shift. They were watching baseball on the small televisions behind the bar, hands wrapped around their beer of choice. The middle TV was fuzzy, so they were both craning their necks in opposite directions.

Kenny, a middle aged, recently divorced contractor with thick, hairy forearms and thinning hair, was known around town to have lots of money and no where to spend it. He spent a good portion of it on Labatt 50, so Corrigan kept the fridge well stocked, knowing that if he couldn't get one there, he'd walk across the street to Chicago's. Men like Kenny in small towns like Piersville had to be known for something and next to working hard came the brand of beer they drank. Anyone who realized the importance of that would get along just fine with them.

Frank sat two stools down from Kenny in his usual spot that a few years back had been pasted with a sheet of paper with his name scribbled in black marker to signify it was his. Only a few times had someone decided to ignore it, sit down and was in turn ignored by the bartender out of honour to Frank. He owned a small used car dealership on the west side of town and had the habit of taking long, slow swigs from his bottle before sucking the small amount of beer that remained from his bushy, white moustache. It made a noticeable sound, but was such a habit that it eventually went unnoticed by those who knew him well. His forehead was large and extended beyond and back of where his hairline use to be until it was interrupted by a shock of white hair that he took extra care to keep patted down. When he had had more than his usual four bottles of beer, his hair grew messier until it eventually stood up on end in places, and everyone knew it was best to avoid conversations with him unless they wanted to be stuck for an hour talking about the reasons he never got married.

Both men acknowledged Caleb as he came in through the front door on his way to the staff room in the back. They were happy to see him. The day shift typically belonged to Norma, who had worked the job long enough to warrant efficiency, but had grown rather curt with the customers over time.

When he walked out to the bar to do his counts and change the till, he was instantly bombarded with a question from Frank. "How can you defend the Jays' pitching these days! What a disgrace!"

"At least they're above .500" Caleb shot back. "The Expo's will finish last in the National East the way they're playing." He made a few checks on his clipboard and looked up. "No fuck that, they're gonna finish last in the National *League* this year." He started to laugh and both Kenny and Frank noticed his mood had improved today. They were both happy to see this, but neither man showed it.

"Fucking Loria! Still doesn't have a place downtown locked up. They need a new stadium in the city."

"No, what they *need* is a television deal in English that'll get them some media coverage. If not, I give them three years and they'll be the goddam Washington Expos." Kenny chimed in and shook his bottle at Caleb as a sign he was ready for another.

Caleb made a correction on his counts sheet and pulled a 50 out of the fridge and replaced the empty. "Well, they won't be called the Expo's if they go to Washington."

"Good point. How about….the Washington Canons? Got a nice ring to it," Kenny said and took a swig.

"No, you gotta name it after a fucking bird, man. Jays, Cardinals, Orioles... you know."

"Or a sock," Added Caleb.

"Don't get me started on the fucking Red Sox."

"So, Caleb, you still planning to head away soon?"

Caleb looked up from his clipboard. "Ya, I'm leaving in two weeks. Corrigan's got someone lined up to take my place. I think he might give Kendra a shot at bartending. You guys should be happy about that."

"Ya, but now we'll probably have to start tipping for our beers," Frank said.

"So, you're just going to up and leave us are you?" Kenny said.

"Sorry, I didn't realize we were in a serious relationship, Kenny. I guess that puts me in the same category as your ex-wife...you know leaving you and all," Caleb said and smiled waiting for a reaction.

"Not really...I actually *want* you to stay. Heidi I could give two shits about. You're about the most serious relationship I've got right now, pal." They all laughed. "Get over here you pretty son-of-a-bitch and bend over. Let me show you how much I'll miss you!" Kenny stood up on his chair and started humping the bar, an act he was known for in Corrigan's. When the moment struck him, he would hump whatever was closest. Over the past year, Caleb had seen him hump the pool table, the television, a few chairs and even the Golden Tee golf game that sat at the end of the bar. Everyone in Piersville had something that made them unique, and Kenny's was to hump inanimate objects.

Kendra entered the restaurant and floated past the bar light as a feather, flipping her hair back as she often did. She smiled at Caleb but didn't stop to talk. She was wearing a short jean skirt and a tight, black t-shirt with the word *Ramones* splashed across the front, and the smell of her fruity perfume lingered in the air even after she disappeared into the back.

Both Kenny and Frank eyed her as she entered the staff room and then turned to Caleb for reassurance. Kenny made a face as though he were going to whistle but instead formed the word 'wow' silently with his lips and Caleb just laughed to himself as he picked up a glass beer mug and polished it.

Kenny looked over at Frank. "What I wouldn't give," he said.

"Ya, keep dreaming, pal. Too young for us," Frank said and took a sip of his beer. "Caleb on the other hand...I bet he's already given her the ol' 'how's she going, eh Caleb?"

"Jesus, guys. Give me a break. Mel and I *just* broke up. Am I the world's biggest asshole or something?"

"All's I'm saying is if I were you, I'd be going out and getting myself laid. That's sure as shit what I did when Heidi left me."

"And it only cost him 200 bucks," Frank chimed in grinning from ear to ear.

"I don't have to pay for sex, thank you very much. I've still got it. More than I can say for your over-the-hill ass!"

Frank just grunted and they both took a big swig of beer and turned their attention to the ball game. Caleb continued his counts and went to the back-of-house to get them okay-ed by Corrigan, who was chatting with Kendra rather intimately. Caleb tried not to interrupt but just handed him the clipboard and Corrigan nodded. Caleb walked away without saying a word.

The night was pretty slow and the servers were all sent home by 9pm. Kendra had been seating the bar fairly well, so Caleb had had a few booths on the go, but mainly just appetizers and beer. She came by to flirt with him a few times, but still didn't give him the same amount of attention she used to. After the servers were all cut for the night, Caleb told his tables he'd be back in a few minutes and decided to take a smoke break out the back before he had the whole restaurant to himself. As he walked past the office, he could hear some giggling that sounded like Kendra's voice and he stopped for a second to see if he could hear anything more. It was quiet again, so he continued outside for his smoke. The dishwasher, Sam, was out smoking a joint, so he chatted with him for a bit, turned down a puff of weed and just enjoyed the smell instead. He didn't feel like getting high tonight and so Sam just shrugged his shoulders and finished it himself. When he walked back in, he was in a hurry to see if anyone had come in the restaurant while he was gone and as he walked past the office again, the door opened and Kendra popped out. It was an awkward encounter, but Caleb ushered her ahead of him and peeked into Corrigan's office as the door was open slightly and caught a quick glimpse of Corrigan zipping up his fly as he sat at his desk. Caleb second-guessed what he saw for a second and at that moment dismissed it, but later when Kendra had gone home and he was sitting at the bar smoking a cigarette alone, he realized what he had seen, and it made him glad he was leaving.

The place was full of memories, but they seemed old. It had been his second home growing up, where he and Melanie had spent their special occasions, where he had learned to play pool, watched all the big games with they guys, and sat until two in the morning trading old high school stories. But it was also the place he'd worked the last two years, and so he knew the side of Corrigan's that many others didn't want to know: the politics, the hook-ups, the late night clean up, and the shitty tippers.

His close friends came in less frequently. Instead, there was a younger crowd that stayed until 2am. They had their own high school stories, their own inside jokes. Caleb knew their older siblings and often asked how they were doing and where they were living now. He always said to pass on his best. 'Tell them I said hi' he would say and they would always agree, but he knew it rarely happened. He wondered if they thought less of him for never leaving Piersville and often joked that 'he was living the dream' and 'there was no place he'd rather be' in an ironic tone.

The past year blended into one long shift serving drinks, laughing at jokes, and collecting money. He knew he had made the right decision to leave his job for a while, to leave Piersville, but he was less sure it was the right choice to leave Melanie.

He poured himself a shot of Sambucca and took a long, slow drag of his cigarette. He felt the ease of the smoke move down his throat and tickle his lungs. His muscles ached but his head felt light as air.

She had acted strangely after their fight on the stairs when he told her his plans. It had led to their break. She hadn't understood why he needed to go and things became complicated between them. That secret machine inside her chest seemed farther away from him than ever before. She was holding something back, a card that strong women hold, ready to play when they think they're losing a hand - an ace in the back pocket that isn't revealed until the time is right. Leaving a good woman, even for a short period of time, is always a risk unless the cause is noble.

3

The crowd inside Corrigan's was giving him a proper send off, but he felt uncomfortable being the centre of attention and snuck out the back door to light a cigarette. He was thinking about Melanie and whether he still loved her as much as he used to, and whether their break was a permanent one. It had been easy in the first few years: he had wanted to spend all his time with her. But slowly, her presence became a fixture in his life and he took it for granted. They moved in together early and some of the romanticism died. It became work at times and he didn't realize that all strong relationships take effort. He was just too naïve to understand it had to be that way in the long term.

His cigarette was almost finished when Kyle approached wearing his signature Red Wings hat pulled low over a mop of brown hair.

"Found you Arthur, you fucker. How long you been out here?"

"Not long."

"We've got shots coming," he said, "I wanna to make sure you're nice and hung over for your flight tomorrow." He grabbed Caleb by the armpit and pulled him up. They shot fake jabs at each other as they made their way back inside.

"Hey, did you invite Ferris Buckton?" Kyle asked.

"No, but he can come if he wants. Shit, I told McDonough he could come so anyone's welcome at this point."

"Buckton was here, but I think Tyler told him to leave. Poor kid."

"Ya, I feel for that guy."

"Remember when they threw him in the ditch and pissed on him in gym class? Fuck. Those guys were such assholes back then," Kyle said.

"Back then? What's changed?"

"You know what – I always thought Buckton was going to stand up for himself one of those times, though, you know. I wondered how much bullying a kid could take before he snapped and did something to…you know."

"Hurt people?"

"Ya, or himself. I always felt bad for not stopping those guys," said Caleb.

"I never really thought about it. Just glad it wasn't me, you know."

"I think he just wants to belong somewhere. I'm surprised he never left Piersville," Caleb said as they entered Corrigan's again through the front doors.

"Maybe you should ask him to come with you to Europe. You and Buckton – backpacking buddies," said Kyle and laughed, but Caleb didn't respond. He felt guilty. He knew how easy his life had been compared to that kid – the only thing they had in common was that they both wanted to leave their small towns, and now one of them was.

They moved past the crowd hovering around the foosball table and pushed through towards the bar, where Tyler was standing in front of a row of shots. He was well built and in mid-conversation with his girlfriend Kelly, a tall blonde. Caleb offered her a brief smile as she was called away by her friends.

"I found Arthur," Kyle said.

"Good," Tyler said. "This fucking world traveler is doing shots with us. Where's Stu the pervert?"

Stu popped his head out the crowd behind them and his hair flew into his face. His glasses had fallen down his nose and he pushed them up quickly out of reflex.

"Jeeesus man, I told you to stop calling me that. I don't even know where that name came from."

"It came from you being a pervert, that's where," Tyler said and looked around for laughs.

"Give me one of those shots, jerk. Why don't you call Kyle or Caleb that? Why am I the pervert?" Stu asked.

"That time I caught you jerking off to Reader's Digest."

"Such a dick sometimes, Tyler. Caleb was there and he never brought it up again. Why do you have to? And besides, I wasn't jerking off – I was just adjusting my boxers."

"Well, Caleb is a much better man than I am. Even though he is leaving his girlfriend behind to slay European babes by the buttload."

Tyler grabbed Caleb by the back of the neck and pulled him into his thick chest.

"So, cheers to Arthur for getting the fuck out of Piersville! It's about time man. Honestly."

Caleb laughed reluctantly. He looked around the bar for Melanie and saw her chatting with her friends by the pool table. She caught his gaze and shot him a smile. He always liked seeing her face light up for him. It reminded him of how beautiful she was. Her smile could do that. It always had. But she had learned to hide behind it and he should have known better than to trust it. On this night, his last before leaving for Europe, he took it as a sign that she would wait for him and they left his going away party early to spend one last night together, a night she knew might be their last, but for him a confirmation that she still loved him as much as she always had, and that their breakup didn't mean anything.

And in leaving early, they missed an event orchestrated by Ferris Buckton, the social outcast, who arrived again after being forced out of Corrigan's earlier by Tyler, the bully. While Caleb was leaving behind a life he took for granted, Ferris Buckton was ready to make sure that everyone in Piersville knew the consequences of the suffering he had endured most of his life. Piersville was a town that prided itself on hard work, stoic attitudes, and conformity. People who deviated from the norm often found life difficult. Some people just couldn't fit in no matter how hard they tried.

Ferris Buckton and his friend Tim Gerritson were two of these people. The cool kids, the farm boys, the stoners, the jocks – they all had their own form of bullying, some more aggressive than others, but all hurtful. And so the two lingered on the margins of their town as outcasts. Until they did something unheard of in Piersville, something that many others would do after them in small towns across North America - in bars, offices, churches, and schools. They fought back in the ugliest and most impactful way they knew how. They started a war.

4

As Caleb stood against the glass at the arrivals gate at Heathrow, he was thinking about his grandfather. He had snuck some of his letters into his pack without telling his father. It was foolish, he knew, in case they were lost or stolen, but he wanted them with him. They were, after all, part of the reason he was going to Europe.

His expectation of Europe was that it would be an extension of his life back home, a life in which he got most things he wanted, but a life he had grown bored by. He reached in his pockets for his calling card and found nothing but an airline ticket, a lighter and a broken cigarette. The sense that he had done something wrong had dissipated and he wanted to see Melanie's smile. He pulled out the only picture of her that he brought and found comfort in the symmetry of her lips. Surely, she would forgive him in time, he thought. Surely, their break would be over once he returned. He knew she was disappointed in the way he left. His parents and friends were too. But they would all forgive him in time. He was sure of it.

He looked around and felt the airport bursting with other people's lives. Each person had a history, a reason for leaving somewhere, a motive for seeking something new. He wanted to hear everyone's motive so he could know what brought them here. He wanted to tell everyone his.

The television above was breaking a news story about Bill Clinton and his aid, Monica Lewinski. The screen was split between their two pictures with scrolling text below describing a relationship of a sexual nature. It was difficult to follow without sound, and the split screen was difficult to focus on. He had very little vision in his left eye, a result of a small retinal detachment that was detected when he was a child, a diagnosis that came with no clear cause. Without the strength of his right eye, which was close to twenty/twenty and compensated for his left, he would have required glasses. He watched as the screen cut to a table of slick looking pundits talking excitedly about a possible scandal, but he cared little about politics, and dropped his gaze back to the lounge as people passed by with luggage and children in hand.

    He reached into the thin space between two telephones and wrote 'I belong here' on the glass. An old women watched him and their eyes met briefly in an awkward exchange before Caleb grabbed his stuff and moved over to the next set of phones, picked one up, pretended to talk for minute and then when he was sure no one was watching, casually walked down towards the exit and out into the grey, cold British morning.

    He asked a man in uniform how to get to the city. The man looked unimpressed with Caleb's curt manner, but turned to him in an open stance.

    "Well, see you got a couple options there mate. Your best, but dearest, is one of those taxis there in the rank. For a little less you can take the Connect right into Paddington; that's a train, and it runs every thirty minutes. There's the Express, too, but it's a little more dear. I'll tell ya kid, take the Connect and save your money for a bit of lager when you get to where you're going." The man let out a generous laugh through his oversized mouth and indicated with his posture he was done talking.

    Caleb nodded and said thanks. The ride into London was lonely and he spent it staring through the window at a landscape that was inked in purple dusk; at one angle, the window projected the reflection of his face and he looked closely and saw the resemblance of his father. He had never noticed it before. It was something around in his eyes. He shifted his focus back through the glass to the landscape but couldn't shake the feeling his father was watching him. Neither of his parents expected him to actually leave after the shooting at Corrigan's, so when he insisted he was still going to make his flight, his father helped load his stuff and drove him to Pearson. As his mother hugged him in the driveway for longer than she'd ever done, he could feel the warmth of her tears on his chest and he patted her back and said not to worry, but he knew she did.

    Caleb pulled out a letter from his pack and unfolded it gently. The edges were stained with cigarette smoke, and the creases were almost worn through. There was a picture tucked neatly in the folds, a man with a hardened gaze in a stance that was not natural - an enigmatic figure Caleb had only passed by in life. He had those same recognizable eyes as Caleb and his father, Jack. The hair was darker than Caleb's and tucked under a military cap. They had crossed paths for a year after Caleb was born and Patrick was leaving middle age.

He knew the letters well, and enjoyed the feel of them in his hands. They were something tangible that attached him to his past, to the person he was connected to by birth but so far away from understanding.

November 5, 1945

Dear Marie,
I'm on my way home to you darling. The war is over. I can't wait to leave this place behind and never return. They have postponed my departure, but given me a short leave to pass the time. I've come down to a town called Torquay on the southeast coast of England that Jack told me about. He said he planned to retire here and I can understand why. It's beautiful, quiet and peaceful. How I've longed to feel the calmness of the water. It's one of the deepest blues I've ever seen. Today, I sat and watched the boats come and go from the marina. There is a stillness in my heart here that I haven't felt since I was in your arms. How you'd love it here. I have missed your face, but your picture has brought me comfort in the darkest of places. The atrocities confound me. I can't even begin to tell you about the things we've come across over here. England's fairly bombed out too – what a horror. Being here in Torquay feels like I've escaped the war for a time, though. The Germans left this place alone, thank God. It's rather odd to see all the cobblestone streets intact, and every building erect. I do look forward to taking walks through town, and maybe even take a ride on the Ferris wheel in the centre.

How is our son, Jack? I haven't received your letters in some time as I've been moving too much, but I long to see his face as well. I think the idea of buying a cottage is a splendid one, and I can't wait to talk to you about it when I return. It could be a place we feel the calmness of the water together and watch our children grow. See you soon my love.

Yours always,
Patrick

Caleb tucked the letter away and fell asleep. He awoke in Paddington Station and was disoriented as he stepped off the train into the damp London air. The city was loud and intimidating. He had spent many weekends in Kingston and the odd night in Toronto, but neither city had prepared him for the intensity of London. It excited him.

He wandered the streets in search of a hostel and it didn't take long before he noticed a black and white sign overtop a stairwell, descending into a brick building off the sidewalk. It didn't look like some of the pictures he had seen of hostels, and it wasn't listed in his Let's Go book, but he was tired and needed a bed. He rang the bell and waited; just as he was turning to leave, a middle-aged woman popped her head out. A cigarette dangled from her coarse lips. They revealed darkly stained teeth when she spoke.

"Ah, you need bed son?" She said in a Russian accent and pointed to the sign saying twenty pounds. Her hair was wispy and grey at the roots. Caleb hesitated, but she ushered him inside quickly with her thin arm.

"Passport," she said. "I keep." When she had everything she needed, she dropped down behind her desk and grabbed a key and handed it to him.

"Room 5. It's down hall. Bathroom across from Room 8 and there's towel on bed. Check out 10am. No later, or you pay for new night."

The hallway was dark with low ceilings. An insect was buzzing stubbornly against a dim bulb. Caleb inserted the key into the lock and pushed the door open into a room with two sets of bunk beds against opposing walls. The translucent window at the top of the farthest wall softened the darkness with light from the alleyway. A small sink sat below the window dripping water from a rusted faucet. Both bottom bunks were open so he took one and crawled onto a worn out mattress that creaked loudly as he adjusted his frame supine. A spring stuck into his lower back.

He pulled out his flashlight to read some of his travel book on England and fumbled to get under the covers. While undressing, the flashlight fell and rolled over onto his pillow shining a spotlight onto the ceiling. A figure on the top bunk shot up and looked down into it – his eyes were fierce and wide on a skinny face covered in long greasy hair. He spoke quickly in a language that Caleb didn't understand. His voice rose and fell sharply and his tone was full of venom. He stopped and waited for a response. Caleb motioned an apology with his hands, grabbed his flashlight and shut it off quickly. The man rolled back onto his bunk, uttered a few words, and then fell silent.

When he was sure the man was sleeping, he continued removing his clothes and snuck under the covers. He wanted to listen to music but feared making any more noise. When he was still and everything was silent, his mind started to drift away.

A whimper from above stirred him and he lifted his head to listen. It turned to a sob. The man on the top bunk was crying and repeating something to himself. Each syllable was slow and heavy, broken up intermittently by moans of sadness: "nelepost" he said repeatedly and cried until it turned back to a whisper…'nelepost….nelepost…nelepost'.

    Caleb felt a sense of loneliness he didn't recognize. He had experienced the solitude of being away from Melanie before when she was in college, but it had never been more than a longing to feel her beside him. He wished she was lying with him now so he could snuggle up behind her like he always did, falling asleep in the spoon formation with the smell of her hair in his nostrils. He even longed to feel her cold feet on his legs. He wondered if she was missing his body beside her, as well, and for the first time since he could remember, he felt truly alone.

September 8, 1942

Dear Patrick,

Do you remember the first time we met? That afternoon in O'Malley's when your friend, Phenon, was being such a card? You walked in and saved me from his drunken shenanigans. You looked so handsome, Patrick, in your blue cap and that grey jacket with the collar flipped up. I was so nervous when you sat next to me. And you asked me about regrets – do you remember that? You asked me to dinner and said you'd regret it if you didn't? I'm so glad you did.

*   I don't regret our decision to court. I've never loved anyone the way I love you and I know it will only grow stronger. But I hope you haven't regretted your enlisting. I worry most of all that a feeling like that is eating away at you. It is a dangerous thing, regrets. I do know you miss Kingston, and we all miss you. It never gets easier. I know you're only a few hours away in Woodstock, and that I'll see you during leave in a few months for our wedding, but not having you here each day is so difficult. And once you ship out to England, you'll feel even farther away than ever.*

*   Have you given more thought to our wedding list. Your mother and I were making up the guest list and wondered if we should invite Thomas. Could you lend me your thoughts? My parents won't be able to come over for it but they send their regards from Ireland. They've heard so much about you from my letters. I write so many these days, but I also receive so many, which makes me so happy. My father approves of you, as you know and my mother thinks you're a brave man for enlisting. We all do, Pat. We're all so very proud of you.*

*   Please make sure to keep writing me often. It makes me feel less alone. Your parents have been wonderful at stopping by and keeping me company. Your father is very much looking forward to the wedding although he doesn't admit it. Well, we're off to the beach for an evening swim. It's been such a warm September so far.*

All my love,
Marie

5

Caleb could see signs for Hyde Park as he wandered away from the hostel. The loneliness and doubt that overtook him the night before had vanished with the return of the sun, which fell onto the street like thin honey stretched between spoon and jar.

He felt a sense of anticipation: he didn't know where he'd be sleeping, or whom he'd meet or even where he'd be eating dinner, and it was freeing. Back in Piersville, his days were scripted and he had just accepted it. How exciting, he thought, to be so free; it was strange how the rising of the sun could change one's thoughts so distinctly. As he strolled into the park and found a bench under the cool shade of the trees, he wondered why the night brings such despondency.

He set his gaze on a fountain a few metres away with a giant saucer spilling water into a large basin. Up from the saucer sprouted a statue of two bodies entwined in sexual bliss. People passed through his gaze but couldn't interrupt it. He tried to follow one of the streams from its origin, through its arc and back down into the basin. The particles of water couldn't be captured in a moment - they kept flowing no matter how hard he concentrated and it made him feel uneasy and released his gaze as a large frame dropped out of the shadows of the trees and onto the bench beside him.

"The Joy of Life suits you does it?" the man said.

"Sorry?" Caleb turned to see a thick, bald-headed man in his late twenties. His round head sprouted two small ears wrapped in silver rings up each side. There was a tattoo of a winged figure on his neck.

"Oh don't be sorry, mate. I take it you fancy it?" He pointed at the fountain. "So you're from Canada?" he said as he pointed to the flag on Caleb's pack. "I've been there." The man's face was plum red and he looked both delighted and tired. His black jacket was zipped half-way up a Billy Bragg t-shirt and it held a tall can of beer in the left pocket. "It's fairly cold there, but I liked it."

"Let me guess: Banff right?"

"Actually I moved to Sarnia for a year, mate."

Caleb couldn't keep himself from laughing.

"What's so funny? You don't like Sarnia?"

"Sorry. I could think of more exciting places to live, that's all."

"Hey, what are ya getting up to today? You look new. Why don't I take you around to see the sights of old London-town and all you have to do is buy me a few pints along the way?" His voice trailed off at the end making it unclear if it was a statement or a question. Caleb wasn't used to the idiosyncrasies of the British accent yet.

"My name's Mike, but my mates call me Skins."

"Mine's Caleb. I was actually just thinking of touring around on my own today. It's my first day here in London, so….."

"Ah bollocks! You're hanging with me today. We'll have some good fun."

Although he longed for a day to ruminate alone, he embraced the casual meeting with spontaneity.

The morning was filled with trips to pubs and museums. When they stopped to piss into the Thames together, it was a much-needed relief.

"Jesus Murphy Caleb, that's quite a cock you've got on you there, lad! You better be careful with that thing." Skins was pissing up into the air, his arc streaming far into the river and he was laughing with the glow of alcohol.

"Why don't you take a picture of it you fucking limey….hang it on your wall for all your buddies to see." Caleb turned and started shaking it in the direction of Skins, who did the same and they stood there, completely puerile, playing swords with their streams until there was no more beer to piss out.

The next pub was quiet, and as they entered, their laughter filled the room and the few patrons stopped talking and fixed their eyes on the two of them. The bartender was hesitant to serve them, but poured pints when they asked him to.

Caleb took a big drink of his beer. "So, I gotta say, Skins. I've had a great day so far."

"I told you, mate: stick with me and you'll never get bored," Skins said. His face was beginning to reveal a forest of thin red veins across his cheeks and nose.

"So, what would you have done today if you hadn't run into me?" Caleb asked.

"Probably, the same thing," Skins laughed. "But this way, I get free beer".

"You're not working?"

"Not right now. I'm in between jobs at the moment. Doesn't worry me, though. I just tend to let things happen as they should." Skins looked deep into Caleb's eyes forcing Caleb to look away uncomfortably. "I can feel something good is on its way soon. At least I hope it is. I've been in tough times before and made it back on my feet. But that's not to say that those times didn't come with some fucking dark thoughts. I'm not ashamed to say that I was close to ending it all a few times." Skins looked away for a second. "You know – shuffling off this mortal coil."

Caleb shifted uncomfortably and struggled for something to say. He had never heard someone talk openly of suicide.

The silence hung between them, thick and cumbersome. The bar smelled of old oak and rotten luck. Some men were at their worst hour after cheers-ing their way through an afternoon. Their eyes were half closed, heads hovering only inches above their glass. And some were still at the peak of their drunken glow smiling from ear to ear at the bartender's hyperbolic tales of womanizing.

Skins cleared his throat and continued. "It's kind of like getting to a point in your bloody life and stopping to look around. Is this whole thing worth it, mate? Is it something you want to be a part of? Blokes always speak about it with such disgust like the guy must have been depressed or full of demons or something, but what if they just get to a point, and said 'no thanks'? I mean we all have make that decision everyday. Most of us say 'ya, sure', but what's wrong with just not wanting to say yes after awhile. Fuck, I mean, it is pretty disgusting, this life we lead, don't ya think? So much anger, war, greed and lust - we're a fucked up species, mate, and I don't blame anyone for opting out of it."

Skins had become impassioned and when he stopped to collect himself, Caleb sensed the anger was brought out by the alcohol. After a short pause, Skins continued. "But that's the joy of living – knowing that you've made the decision to. Most people just carry on because they don't think they have a choice in the matter, and that ain't no way to live."

Caleb shifted uneasily in his chair. He couldn't think of a time he had ever considered life to be too much to take. There had never been anyone in his life who had told him it was okay to consider suicide. Skins' cavalier attitude caught him off guard and he just nodded and listened.

"I recognize my ability to end my own life, and that's what makes today so valuable to me. I'm choosing to be here with you, getting half-pissed in the middle of the day."

Caleb was interested but unsure how to navigate the conversation from there. He was pretty drunk, and hoped Skins would change the subject. He hoped he would ask why Caleb had come to Europe.

"Do you ever feel like time is passing through you?" Skins asked.

"That's an interesting way of putting it," Caleb said, slow witted from the alcohol. "I think I have been feeling like time's been passing me by lately. Partly why I'm over here."

"Well, cheers to you being here, mate." Skins reached his large forearm towards Caleb and they clinked glasses. Caleb set his beer down and Skins took a big pull from his glass, belched and set it down. "You didn't look me in the eye, mate." He belched again.

"Huh?"

"You didn't look me in the eye when you cheers-ed me just there. I don't know how you do it in Canada, but here we look each other in the eye when we cheers. And you didn't even drink after. Jesus, man."

They did it again, and Caleb got it right.

"I've been more conscious of time lately, but I don't know about it passing through me. I can't believe I'm twenty-three. It just seemed like yesterday I was graduating high school and thinking twenty-three would never come. I wish I could slow things down. The next thing you know, I'll be thirty."

"Nothing wrong with being thirty, mate. I'm thirty."

"I know. It's just that I spent my youth feeling great things were on the horizon, beyond the glorious box stores of Piersville." Caleb extended his arms to illustrate the sad, sweeping commercial landscape of his hometown, "and nothing ever came and now I'm twenty-three with nothing but a bit of savings, which I'm pretty much blowing on this trip, and a girl, who I think I've lost by coming here." He tried to laugh but failed. A feeling of panic took hold of him and he chased it away with a swig of beer.

"So, why didn't you make things happen, mate? No one's gonna do it for you. Beats having regrets about it now," Skins said.

"I know. I guess I was just focused on the relationship I've been in. I sacrificed my goals to stay there for her. She's had a tough go. She lost her mom when she was younger and then we've watched her dad slip into Alzheimer's the last few years. She's a nurse, right, so she's got a good job. We just decided to stay and make a go of it. I mean she couldn't really leave with her dad the way he is."

"What do you do for work?"

"Bartender. But my dad is waiting for me to start at his real estate firm. I guess it makes the most sense. I just keep putting it off, you know, like I'm not sure if that's my calling or not. Once I commit to it, that's it – I'll have to stick with it and take over the firm one day. There'll be no backing out."

"So why are you over here? Sounds like you've got a pretty comfy life back home."

"Well, comfort doesn't always mean you're better off," Caleb said.

"I think there are a lot of people in this world who would disagree with you. I'd give my left nut to be comfortable for a bit. Christ."

"I freaked out a little, I guess. Part of me wanted to have some fun, see some cool stuff, but I'm also over here to connect with my grandfather a little. He fought in WWII."

"Makes sense but you're never going to experience what he did. There's no war happening here anymore, except on the poor. And besides, all he saw was death; all you're gonna see is the inside of pubs and museums. Not the same kind of thing, mate. And I'm sorry mate, but I think most people would be happy to have a loving girl, and comfy job in daddy's company waiting for them. Shit, I think most people would be happy to just have a dad in their life. I've never had one," Skins said and paused to think. The alcohol was catching up with him. "So, this girlfriend you talked about - you're not sure about her?"

"She's a great girl, but I'm not sure if we're meant to be together long term," Caleb said and corrected himself. We broke up before I left, but I don't think she meant it."

He could feel Skins' large hand on the back of his neck giving him a gentle, understanding squeeze and it made him feel uncomfortable for the first time since they'd met. It lingered there too long.

"I guess I've just been really confused lately," Caleb said.

"Well, that's why you're over here, mate – new experiences. You made the right call there. You seem like a guy who's open to new things."

"Ya, I'm not sure what it is I want, but I'm hoping I'll find it over here."

A few more patrons wandered in chanting footy songs and slapping each other across the back. They filled the pub with noise and received a familiar nod from the bartender. They continued on to the back corner and out of sight.

"The relationship between a father and son is complex," Skins said. "I've only read about it. But I'm sure if I had known my dad, we would have had our difficulties. I tend to piss most of the people off in my life pretty royally."

Caleb finished his beer, stood up and signalled he wanted to leave. Skins followed. After three more pub stops and an hour at the Tower of London, their energy was being replaced by drunken lethargy. The large pack on Caleb's back was beginning to grow heavy and they were moving more slowly. Skins was having difficulty walking straight at times.

London Bridge could be seen from their resting spot and the city lights were beginning to shine brightly against the darkening sky.

Skins searched his pockets for a cigarette and was surprised when he found one. He placed it between his lips and it dangled there carelessly. His face looked more callous than when Caleb had met him that morning. Gravity seemed to pull harder on it the more he drank.

Skins pushed the cigarette out with his lips and raised his lighter to it. His gaze moved between the pavement and the night sky. A small cloud of smoke escaped his mouth, and he drew it back in quickly, before releasing it slowly as he spoke. "Well mate, should we head back to my place and have a few pints then."

Sitting down reminded Caleb of how tired he was. His feet ached. He longed for a place to lie down.

"I think I'll just take a room at a hostel." He looked at Skins. "Thanks for today, though. I appreciate the company."

"Well, it doesn't have to end here. I can keep you company over a few more lagers at my flat. Or you could sneak me into your hostel. I ain't ready for bed yet."

Caleb was growing more uneasy. "No, I just need to find a hostel and get some rest," he said and stood up.

"Ahhh, c'mon! Don't be such a pussy! The night's still got possibilities and plenty of good times. You said you were here for new experiences right? Open to new things?" His voice was tired and coaxing. It seemed unsatisfied. "C'mon, what did you think this was all about?"

Skins leaned in for a kiss. Caleb pulled back in reflex, and they both said 'What the fuck' at the same time. Caleb turned quickly and walked towards London Bridge, the only thing he recognized. Skins put his hand on Caleb's shoulder and slid it down to his chest to pull him closer. Caleb turned and pushed him with both hands, which caused Caleb to stumble under top-heavy weight of his pack.

Skins' face had turned a deeper shade of red and the veins throbbed in his cheeks. "Listen you bloody Canadian," he said in a tone so guttural it startled Caleb, "I've spent the whole fucking day with you and you won't even give me a bloody kiss?"

Caleb's mind went reeling backwards like a movie in rewind, stopping at certain moments that came to him in perfect clarity now. His heart was beating fast; even with the heavy pack, he started to gain some distance. He just wanted to get away. He could hear the sound of footsteps gaining on him and looked back to see Skins coming up behind but it was just a blurred figure. He had never been so conscious of the blindness in his left eye and tried to turn his head fully to gain sight with his right, but his legs were taken out from under him. He was able to brace his landing with his arms, and squirmed to get free from his shoulder straps, but they only fastened him further to his fate. Another blow struck him in the ribs. He began to crawl but knew it was futile. He pulled his knees up towards his chin and protected his face with his hands, but the boots kept hitting him squarely in places he thought he was covering. The last blow came to him in his lower back, and as he lay bleeding, he heard the words 'fucking tease' from a few feet away.

The attack was aggressive and humbling and for a second night in a row, he wanted to go home. He crawled towards the Thames and rolled into an empty crevice of dirty, damp pavement. He felt a warm sensation moving throughout his jeans; he let out a low groan and passed out.

He awoke with his cheek on the cold pavement and the sun hovering behind thin clouds like a dull coin, tucked into the pocket of the city skyline. He shivered at the cool breeze and heard the sound of feet shuffling on the sidewalk nearby. A child was crying.

He tried to move out of his foetal position but every effort caused lightning in his veins. His left eye felt swollen and his nose was throbbing. It hurt to breathe. When he finally hobbled down the steps to the river, it took all his energy. He lay down by the polluted water and rested his head on his arm. He was angry with himself for not being smarter. Why did he run, he wondered. Why didn't he stand his ground? He began to drift in and out of consciousness. He reached into the river for a fistful of water to clean the blood off his face and hands. He tried to make out his reflection in the water but the surface was disturbed by the breeze, and he couldn't make out a true image. His vision in his left eye was worse than before. When he closed his right eye, he could barely see anything at all. The water was a dark mirror muddled by the wind. It made shapes of his mouth as though he were speaking from some deeper face, beyond the mercurial window, and he lay staring through it with his hand outstretched so that it touched the surface. For a second, he thought he saw the face of his grandfather looking back at him, but he fell back asleep again.

September 15, 1942

Dear Marie,
How could I forget that day? You were wearing that beautiful yellow dress that I love so much. Your hair fell around your shoulders without seeming like it touched them at all. I've never understood how one person could look so beautiful.

In answer to your question, I don't regret my decision. It is important what we're doing here, and I know you understand that. I knew that from the way you spoke about your cousin, and how proud you were of him. I hope you're proud of me too. I never did tell you about the day I decided to enlist. I was sitting in the Kingston Public Library. Margaret had dropped off the newspaper to my table as usual, but on the front page there was a story of two young men, hell barely men, who were killed in Dieppe, and their eyes spoke to me. I knew that more boys like them would keep dying if we didn't make the effort to stop the German's once and for all. And Phenon tried to convince me not to go, told me it was stupid. But he didn't feel the same way I did. Maybe he's smarter but he didn't understand why I had to. Sometimes a man needs to do something he knows might destroy him, because it's bigger than he is, than he will ever be. We're a generation torn between love and duty my dear. I feel you understand that. I'm torn between my love for you, which is so strong, Marie, and my duty to stand up for what's right in this world. I trust I can do both.

The thought of marrying you in October keeps me going, honey. I can't wait to celebrate with all our friends and family (yes, please invite Thomas if you can). I wish I had a longer leave, but I know we'll make the best of the time we're given. Also, I wish your parents could make the trip from Ireland, but maybe one day I will get to meet them. I know it was important to have your father walk you down the aisle, but I know they must be so proud of you Marie. I hope they approve of your marriage to me. Know that my family is so fond of you. Who wouldn't be? You're such a wonderful, kind person. I'm the luckiest gent in the world.

Love always,
Patrick

6

Caleb found the hostel he had earmarked in his Let's Go by asking strangers for directions under a milky sky that threatened of rain and loneliness. It was located on a corner and the big, opulent glass doors signalled it was different than the one he stayed at the night before. Inside, it was bustling with groups of backpackers filling out forms, searching for passports and speaking broken English. A German couple was arguing at the front desk, while two blonde girls sat patiently on the couch flipping through maps. Kurt Loder was on the TV behind them analyzing Nirvana's sound and showing clips of Kurt swinging his guitar around violently with his hair draped across his face. It had only been four years since Cobain's death and Caleb wondered what kind of an impact it had had on Europeans. Had Teen Spirit come crashing through British television sets with the same impact as back home? He and his friends had been hungry for that sound and Kurt's suicide had left a void no one seemed able to fill.

"Looks like you've had a rough go," the attendant said scanning his bruised face. 'There'll be no fisticuffs in here, Tyson."

He had no witty reply.

"Are you alone or is there a lucky lady with you?"

"Just me."

"Sweet-as. Just need your passport and I'll get ya to fill this form in for me. Then we'll be good to go. By the way, the bruises make ya look tough, mate," she said sincerely before eyeing his passport.

"Hey, where can I go for a few pints around here?" he asked.

"I'd recommend the Waltzing Weasel. It's a good time – usually heaps of young people."

The room smelled fairly clean. There was a breeze coming through from an open window and a few bodies lying supine on white, clinical beds pushed against the walls. Someone was asleep on the bottom bunk by the window and had forgotten to take off his earphones. Another was reading an English magazine on a top bunk to his left. He thought about striking up a conversation but remembered about the phone calls he had to make; he placed his stuff on his bed and decided on a hot shower first. He remembered some advice about always wearing flip flops in the shower, and stuck a pair under his arm and wandered out the door down the hallway.

He watched the water drain below him, slightly pink from the small amounts of blood left on his body and in his hair. He felt happy to be clean, and as he walked back to his room, he felt confident to call home and lie about his first few days. If he had called them either of the last two nights, he might have told them he was coming home, but he had resolved to stay, out of some twisted duty.

It hurt to place the receiver next to his face. He hesitated, then pulled out his calling card and dialled the number to enter his code. It took a few seconds before it started ringing.

"Hello?"

"Hi Mel." He paused. "It's me."

"I know," she said indifferently. She had a way of sounding cold when she wanted to.

"Please don't hang up."

"I'm not going to hang up on you Caleb. I'm so mad at you, but I'm not going to hang up. It's good to hear you got there safely." The words came out flat. "Why did you do it?"

He hadn't expected her to ask him that so quickly.

"I'm an asshole, I guess."

"Bullshit. Don't give me that."

"If I didn't leave then, I never would have."

"Tyler's dead you know," she said and paused to let it sink in. "The funeral's in a few days. I don't assume you'll be coming back for it." She waited but there was nothing he could say. They both knew he wasn't coming back.

"Fuck, Caleb – what do I tell all our friends? You should hear some of the things people are saying about you. That you don't give a shit about any of us. People wondered why you were leaving in the first place....without me....and then you leave after one of your best friends dies. It was *your* going away party. Don't you even feel the slightest bit responsible?"

"Of course, but..."

"God. I want to defend you, but I can't. I tell people that I don't know why you left because I honestly don't. I don't know why you do anything anymore. You know, when you came home that morning after Kyle's, I knew things had changed between us. You never would have stayed out all night without calling before," she said, her voice quivering as she tried to hold back her tears. She had been able to remain cold and indifferent, but her emotions were taking hold. "Things weren't supposed to be like this," she said.

Then she cried.

"Mel, listen....."

"I have to go," she said quickly and composed her voice. "I hope you have a blast over there finding yourself while we all recover from tragedy."

The phone went dead.

When he entered the Waltzing Weasel, a pub that resembled the few he had visited with Skins the day before, he did so with the understanding that he'd be alone, that the only person he could be certain he'd speak with would be the waitress to order a drink. He walked out the back and found a large beer garden with old-fashioned picnic tables underneath lights strewn across birch trees. It was a place where people were forgetting the daily march of civic duty pint after pint. It was vacant of the pressing levy of life as Londoners chatted idly about footy. A few tables were singing in closed eyed merriment with glasses raised high.

The pointed finger of a tall, toothy waitress led Caleb to an empty seat on the fringe of the garden. A torn copy of Jack London's Call of the Wild stuck out of his back pocket and he pulled it out to shield himself from the crowds. It took two pints before the loneliness set in; on his third he grew tired of reading and looked up to watch a young couple sitting closely, planting light kisses on each other's faces. The woman was wearing the man's blazer. It resembled the one Caleb gave to Melanie the night they'd met when he saw her shivering at a field party.

They'd never talked much before that, but he offered it to her and she accepted. They spent the rest of the night by each other's side talking about their high school classes and friends they had in common. The conversation moved along without any of the awkward pauses he usually encountered speaking with girls, and he sensed that she was interested in what he had to say. He felt comfortable with her and eventually, when the night turned late and the party dwindled, they found themselves together in a poorly erected tent with the rain wetting the ground beneath them and the wind testing the stability of tent poles. While another couple beside them were grabbing at each other in drunken lust, Melanie reached over and slid her fingers inside his and held his hand until morning when the tent finally caved in from the rain and everyone had to evacuate with hungover groans.

It surprised him how good it felt to hold hands with her, and how nervous he felt to touch her. When they began dating, she was slow to open up. Her nervousness masked her vulnerability. In part it was due to the recent passing of her mother. Everyone in Piersville watched Jessica Hazen slip away from cancer, but they didn't know the intimate details, the daily heartbreaks, and conversations Melanie was forced to have with her parents about mortality. She told Caleb about the afternoon her parents led her into the piano room to explain that her mother was dying.

She told him there was a stillness to the room as the sun poured in on the white carpet, and what she remembered most was how sickly her mom looked now that she knew she was slipping away. The word 'dying' was like a bullet being fired into her tiny frame each time. Death had never been so close to her before.

When Caleb entered her life, she was starting to smile more, and everything in his life faded away behind her smile like the night behind the moon.

He was honest with her, and she learned to navigate his eyes. She always told him there was innocence to them, as she stared at him and pulled his thick hair back in play. He wasn't book smart but he was curious and eager to learn and he could tell she wanted that in a lover. School had come easy for her but she lacked curiosity about the world. She told him that other boys their age didn't possess his openness, and it wasn't long before she admitted she was in love with him.

He knew she was slow to let people in, and he waited until she was ready to physically give herself. When they did finally have sex, it was on her birthday and she initiated it. When he took her clothes off, he did so carefully, as though each piece were made of lantern netting and could fall apart with one false move.

He slowly kissed her body, until she was completely naked and full of desire and when he was inside her, he told her he loved her and her body filled with a glowing warmth, a reminder of how beautiful life can be when you're lucky and young and in love. She told him she loved him back, her face red with orgasm. Her whole body was numb and each time he kissed her skin, she shuddered with pleasure and when it was over, they ran their hands across each other's pelvis and fell asleep; when they woke in the morning, they knew they had a lot to look forward to.

He helped her forget the pain of losing her mother, until she had another conversation with a doctor when she was twenty-two. Caleb was with her this time when the doctor kept saying her father had an 'illness' as he leaned forward in his creaky chair. She later told him it felt like a knife in her side every time he said the word 'Alzheimer's'.

Caleb didn't want her to feel alone, but he knew she was retreating to that carpeted piano room from her youth where she felt helpless and confused. He knew there were places he couldn't reach, and when they walked outside to a beautiful, sunny day after the diagnosis, she turned to him and said, "the worst things happen to me when the sun is shining." For her, they did.

His stomach was growling, and he realized he hadn't had any dinner. He was almost finished his third pint and feeling light-headed. The patio was busier now and people who couldn't find a table were standing. He had placed his book on the table and decided to people-watch; he thought it would be nice to have someone to talk to.

He had been keeping an eye on a group a few tables down: a young man with three women, who Caleb assumed, after spying continuously with furtive glances, to be backpackers. He thought he remembered one of the girls from the hallway of the hostel, and stared for a second too long as she caught his gaze and spoke with the man beside her. Caleb should have looked away, but he let his regard last a few more seconds, long enough to lock eyes with the man who had turned his head to inspect the onlooker.

The moment someone's solitude in a crowded place is taken, their evening gives way to the romanticism of possibility. The freedom to be alone is set against the infinite actions of others. For every night that Caleb could sit alone reading Jack London until lethargy takes him back to his bunk, there is a night of chance encounters with people who will take him away from his aloneness. It is a toss of a dice down the alleyway of a man's desire to risk comfort for adventure.

People are always days and hours, minutes and even seconds apart; when someone is alone and free and waiting for good things to happen, a gaze left a few seconds too long can connect two people who may never have met, and who's encounter will change both their lives.

As the man on the other end of the gaze stood up and moved away from his table, the air seemed to move effortlessly around him. A strong figure with a thick chest and a smile that radiated across the garden, he walked with a subtle, patient gait that was akin to someone at a gallery; he eyed each person as though they were a piece of art, regarded with interest for a passing second but not given to distraction. When he passed a waitress, he stopped and uttered something quickly and she glanced Caleb's way and nodded.

Caleb eyed him suspiciously. He had been so far away all night and now he was close enough to see a smile that shone with great luxury on people as though it held something they wanted. His hair was short and tossed about his head in deliberate fashion, hinting at strawberry but with a deeper blonde that brought out some of the freckles on his face, which was round, with wide searching, blue eyes that seemed to pull at the corners of his mouth when he smiled as though attached by strings. His shoulders were wide over a masculine frame, yet his body was soft and gentle with hints of overindulgence. He walked with ease and had the confidence to approach, Caleb, a stranger and tell him a joke about two Scottish blokes in a pub and be so happy to tell it that laughter erupted regardless of the punch line.

"A South African told me that one," he said as he eased himself into one of the empty wicker chairs. "The name's Jason, but you can call me Kiwi-Jas."

Caleb moved his beer out the way to shake hands, and instantly found trust in his countenance.

"I'm Caleb," he mustered.

"Tell, me Caleb. Why are you sitting by yourself when there are so many boring people you could be sitting with?"

"I don't know anyone. I just got here."

"And you've already had time to get in a fight. Jesus mate. I won't ask about it, but I think you need a little company tonight. You're not wallowing while I'm around."

"Well, I just want to get this out of the way: I'm not gay. The last time a British guy invited me to hang out, he wanted a little more than 'company' if you know what I mean."

"Well, first of all, mate, I ain't British. I'm from New Zealand. That's why they call me Kiwi. And second of all, I ain't gay." His smile faded when Caleb didn't respond in kind. "Listen, it sounds like you don't have a lot of trust left, which is too bad. You might have been fucked with by some twat since you got here, but I'm offering you some good company and some pretty faces. I'll be sitting over at that table with those birds." Jas looked back again. "Come over and join us if you want. I'll tell 'em not to ask about your face either. And just so we're clear, I aim to have one of those girls keeping me company back in my room tonight, not some bruised up Canadian dude." His smile put Caleb at ease. He felt stupid for bringing up his encounter with Skins. "So what d'ya say – you want to come join us for a drink?" Jas asked.

"Sure, I'll head over in a minute. I'll just settle up with my server first."

"Already done, mate. I covered your pints…..figured based on the way your face was banged up, you've had a rough go lately. Come join us - those girls know nothing about footy."

"You mean, soccer?"

Jas rolled his eyes and laughed. "Yes, soccer you bloody North American."

"Well, then let's get this out of the way right now….I'm a Man U fan."

"Ah shit, I figured as much. I'm a Gunner. We can still be friends, though, right?" Jas stuck out his hand and Caleb shook it and stood up. Jas placed his hand on Caleb's shoulder and gave it a friendly pat. "At least you're not a Chelsea fan."

Kiwi-Jas made introductions at the table. Chantelle was American with short brown hair and a gentle face. Her eyes were small, warm and brown. She greeted Caleb in a deep Southern accent. The other two, Elsa and Linnea, were Swedish and had been traveling for a year, coming close to their return to Stolkhom. They looked like twins, but weren't related. They had met Jas in Berlin and spent the week going to clubs and taking ecstasy. What didn't come out in conversation, but what Caleb had assumed as he watched their body language, was that Jas had slept with them both at some point.

They talked about London for a little while, and about Texas and Sweden, because Caleb asked. The girls seemed bored to talk about their lives back home, and Caleb found the conversation more interesting when Jas had control of it. They all felt obliged to ask about Caleb's home and so he told them about Piersville. He explained about his bartending job, about his relationship with

Melanie, and in his nervous state, mixed with alcohol, he told them of his friend who had just died.

"Wait a minute. Your friend just died?" Chantelle asked excitedly and shot a curious glance to the others.

"The day before I left."

"Why didn't you stay?" Chantelle said in a tone that was much softer. "And be with Melanie?"

Caleb didn't answer, and after an awkward silence, Jas chimed in: "He came over here for the same bloody reason we all did: adventure," and began a story about streaking the Charles Bridge in Prague one night.

As the moon rose over The Waltzing Weasel and replaced the disappearing sun, the weight of the conversation remained light and the waitresses stopped by numerous times to inquire and to watch Jas' eyes light up as he agreed to another drink. His smile never seemed to vanish, only to dance across the spectrum of little enjoyments. He told jokes because he loved to tell them, and everyone laughed and it eased them into more conversation - coaxed them into more stories and more drinks. Caleb began to revel in the company and didn't want the night to end. They shared cigarettes and talked of their adventures. They all had reasons for being so far away from home.

By the time some people had exchanged emails, it was, by Caleb's account, getting pretty late and after the two Swedish girls excused themselves to use the loo inside, and it was rather clear they were not coming back, he decided to say goodnight. He didn't ask to walk Chantelle back to the hostel; she had clearly strategized to outlast the other two girls and be with Jas for the night.

Before Caleb could finish saying goodnight, Jas interjected.

"How drunk are you right now?"

It came with an earnestness disguised behind a smile.

"A little but I'm fine," Caleb said.

"Good. Listen mate, when I give the signal we're hoppin' this fence behind me and bookin' it."

Caleb was slow to understand, and a little surprised. "I thought you paid for my beers."

Jas shook his head. "They're on my tab, but we're bailing on it."

"I don't think I can do it," Caleb said. His memories of every single dine and dash at Corrigan's ran through his mind and how he hated having it happen to him.

"How long do you think I've been travelling now?"

"I don't know - awhile, I guess. It sounds like it's been a few years."

"Exactly. And how do you think I've been able to go at it so long? You need to learn a few things if you want to make this adventure of yours last longer than a month. I didn't ask you about your face because I have a pretty good idea why it happened – you're still new to this. You might know a lot back home in Canada, mate, but you still need to learn a few things outta the backpacker's handbook. Unless you want to be sitting in a train station in Brugge with your hand out and your bank account empty, and believe me mate I've been there, you'll learn to do this once in awhile."

Caleb was drunker than he had let on and didn't need much persuading. The real pressure was coming from Chantelle who was looking at him with cajoling eyes. He was caught up in the moment and didn't want to disappoint either of them.

"Alright – fuck it. Let's do it. Where do we go when we're over the fence?" Caleb was gulping down his last sip nervously.

"We'll go one way, you go another" Jas said.

Jas leaned over and put his arm around Chantelle, who gave Caleb a glance of approval; she was biting down on her lip and seemed anxious to dodge the bill like it was something too exciting to pass up. Caleb felt like an outsider, like this was some kind of club he didn't know existed.

"Oh, and since this is your first time, mate, you'd better take a souvenir." Jas placed the empty beer glass in Caleb's hand.

Caleb's heart was beating quickly. Kiwi-Jas gave a quick look for the waiter and seeing that she was out of sight, he turned, nodded to Caleb and grabbed him by the shoulder, his big hand wrapped tightly so as to paralyze him for a second.

"It's never not right now. Remember that."

Caleb shot him a confusing glance, and then Kiwi-Jas was gone. Chantelle followed instantly, and Caleb was left alone to watch the two figures dart hurriedly across the lawn. Someone pointed and yelled but Caleb was in a trance and couldn't hear. A few tables down, two male figures stood up, glaring at Caleb, waiting to see if he would follow. He did. He lunged over the railing and landed solidly with beer glass in hand and sprang across the grounds into the trees and away from the onlookers. He could hear them shouting as he manoeuvred his way towards the street, knowing once he made his way to a busy intersection, he was free. His heart beat wildly as he ran, but he felt free. The words 'It's never not right now' echoed in his mind. He didn't understand the gravity of them at first, but it would later become a mantra he could rely on when things in his life made no sense. For now, he smiled at his devious behaviour and kept running back toward his hostel, through the streets of London, forgetting the bruises across his body.

When he waltzed through the doors of his hostel, he passed the Aussie at the front desk and lifted his beer mug in the air shaking it triumphantly. "It is never not right now!" he bellowed as she rolled her eyes at him.

January 1, 1943

Dear Patrick,
Happy New Year, my husband (it feels so great to say that!) And with the turning of the year comes the most wonderful news. I won't delay – I'm pregnant! You're going to be a father, Patrick! I'm certain that it's a boy. Your mother thinks so, as well. I'm feeling so strange all the time and I keep craving the oddest foods. Just the other day, I ate a whole jar of pickles and then I wanted peanut butter! You'd find me so laughable right now, Pat. Oh, I wish you were here with me. I'm trying to stay positive, but I miss you. You should be here for this, but you should also be there, I know. I think the way you put it is fair: you belong to a generation torn between love and duty (I've been reading through all your letters and that's a favourite of mine). I know you'll make a great father, Pat. You have so much love in your heart. You're a good man and that's why I said yes so quickly when you asked me. I think it was darling that you were so nervous, but I wish you wouldn't be nervous with me, love. I'm yours always.

    My family is so happy I've found a man like you. I've just sent a letter to them informing them of the news. It seems all I do these days is write letters. But I do love receiving them, so please write again soon.

    When you left in October, I cried for days. The thought of you so far away in Halifax was hard on me, but your family has been so good to me here. Your parents are so supportive. I do miss my family, though. I wish my mother could be here with me during the pregnancy but hopefully one day they'll make the trip over. I read the papers everyday and think of you. Write me back as soon as you can.

Love Marie

p.s. we need to start discussing baby names. Lend me your thoughts.

7

The bus rolled into Salzburg as the morning sun crested its plain and lit the city on fire. It was still too early to rent a room at the YHA Hostel on the hill, but the bus unloaded its passengers regardless and moved onto Prague. More than half the bus shuffled off into the warm Austrian morning and waited to check in. No one on board could really say for certain they knew how long they were staying. That was part of the vacation from their lives. Routine was a ghost; it died the day they stepped on a plane and checked into their first hostel.

They only knew for certain where they'd been: for some on the bus, including Caleb, it had been Paris spending nights at the Three Pigs Hostel.

The two girls who had sat behind him for the last hour of the trip had hopped on in Munich and been chatting quietly with no interest in sleep. He hadn't noticed the girls get on, but when he heard them drop Ontario place names, he looked back through the seats and saw the small triangular face of a rosy cheeked girl with short, black hair, thin, plum lips, and large green eyes. She was talking with purpose to another woman, whom he could not see. He waited for her to finish her story before he poked his head over the seat to join the conversation. He was beginning to recognize the distinction of Canadian girls in Europe. They had self-deprecating charm and harsh wit; their faces were carved with winter.

He had listened to the one explain her family's transition from Meaford to Kingston. She had belonged to a military family and moved often; she had dated a guy in high school who grew too dependent on her and tried to follow her to Kingston until she made the break; she had to change her phone number and email account and finally leave on a flight for Portugal at the end of August. "It felt like I could breathe again," she said and took a long, natural pause.

It was then that Caleb turned around and said he couldn't help but overhear their conversation and it was nice to hear a Canadian accent. They stared blankly at him, unsure of which one he was speaking to, but the short haired one spoke up, introduced herself as Joss and asked him where in Canada he was from.

"Piersville," he said and searched their eyes for a reaction.

"No way! You guys just had that restaurant shooting recently. It's been making headlines everywhere. Some dude brought a gun into a public place and started firing," she said and paused before asking the inevitable question: "Did you know anyone involved?"

Joss was leaning forward showcasing her green eyes and sharp nose. Her hair was cropped cleanly around her face. She looked childlike; her countenance only hinted at features of adulthood. Caleb had expected the question, but stared into her face awkwardly; he lied and said he didn't.

"I try not to read the news too much over here," he said. "I should probably call home though."

"Yes, you better call home!" she said excitedly and ruminated for a second. "What would make a person shoot up a crowded place?"

"I don't know. Small towns can be pretty ruthless places to live if you don't fit in."

"You think it was a bullying thing? Jesus, seems a bit extreme," said Joss. "It was probably a love triangle or something." She paused for a second. "Love or money – those are usually the reasons people kill for."

Caleb decided to change the subject and asked them what their plans were for the day. Joss told him they were planning to visit the Hohensalzburg.

"That's the castle on the hill," the woman beside her said matter-of-factly. "I'm Miranda by the way." Her tone signalled a maturity that seemed out of place amongst the backpackers he'd met. She had a skinny, handsome face.

The bus had slowed to a low rumble outside the YoHo hostel, and a loud, spasm of exhaust signalled a final stop. The exterior of the building was plastered in yellow stucco with national flags sticking out above the main entrance like stick fingers on a snowman. Caleb searched for the familiar red maple leaf to see if his country was among them.

"Mind if I join you today?" he asked.

Miranda hesitated, but Joss said "sure" enthusiastically and shot him a smile.

The hike to the Hohensalzburg was long and the incline pained their calves, but by the time they reached the castle gates, the sun had emerged from behind the clouds and warmed the morning air. Caleb's head was glistening with sweat as he paid the attendant and entered the gates with his head tilted up to the height of the castle.

He let Joss go ahead of him through the archway that led out to the parapet and put his hand on her lower back as though guiding her safely ahead. When they stopped to look out over the city, he put his hand on her shoulder to get her attention and pointed to the building he told her was their hostel. She laughed and moved his arm a few degrees.

He pretended to fix his gaze over the landscape, but he stole glances of her when he could. He thought of all the ways she was different than Melanie – she didn't speak much or use her words with an agenda. She just spoke what came into her mind and her words had no intention of provoking a response. He often felt she was talking to herself more than anyone else and she often giggled after the things she said. She was self-aware but not in a confident or phony sense; it was as though she were embarrassed of it. He didn't always find her words funny, but the way she said them and the way she laughed afterwards drew him to her. She had a way of making typical expressions sound new. Her excitement grew easily and inconsistently so Caleb couldn't put his finger on the type of conversation that might arouse her. Some people were easy to figure out – there were things that made them laugh, made them silent, and made them upset. The people who had clear response patterns were easy to understand. There was something comforting in knowing how they operated but there was no mystery to them. With Joss, he couldn't find a pattern, so he just came to enjoy her laughter when it happened.

The three of them took a rest on the parapet facing east to watch the sun rise over the hills. It broke through the clouds intermittently and warmed their faces as they rested. Caleb lay supine on the ground and covered his eyes with his hand.

"So you guys just met in Munich?" he asked.

"Ya, we were staying in the same hostel," Miranda said.

"What do you do back in Canada?"

"Hmmm, what do I do? It's a long story."

"We can't check into our hostel until three. We've got time," he said and laughed.

"Ya, you haven't even told *me* much about your life in Toronto," Joss chimed in.

"Well, there's not much to tell. My marriage ended and now I'm trying to pretend I'm twenty-one again backpacking through Europe. I'm such a cliché," Miranda said.

"I don't think that many people have the spirit to come and take on such an adventure at your age. And you don't even seem that old. What are you like, mid-twenties?"

"Twenty seven"

"Shit, I'm twenty three," said Caleb.

"I guess I'm the baby then – twenty-one," said Joss sheepishly.

"I don't *feel* that old," Miranda said. "And actually, my husband and I were supposed to take this trip together. We both saved for it, but after I found him cheating on me, I ended it. He gave me the savings and told me I should go," she said and forced a smile to her lips. "So here I am."

"Why do guys do that? Why do they have to ruin things by sticking their dicks into everything?" Joss said angrily. "What a douche."

"He's not a douche," Miranda said. "He just didn't love me anymore. I've accepted it. We didn't have a forever together. It was bound to happen sooner or later."

"I think anyone who cheats is a douche," Joss said. "He should have talked to you first and told you he was interested in someone else. He didn't. He cheated and then tried to clean it up afterwards."

"Can we head back to the hostel?" Miranda said to change the subject. "I'm getting chilly up here. The sun keeps dipping behind the clouds"

They both nodded and stood up to brush themselves off. The descent was quick and when they reached the bottom, Miranda said she was heading back to the hostel lobby to take a nap on the couch until they let her check into the room.

"Want to keep walking?" Caleb asked Joss. "We could find a coffee joint or something."

"Sure. I'm game. You can get back alright Miranda?"

"Oh ya – I'll be fine. You kids have fun."

As they walked on, Joss battled to keep her hair in place as the wind tossed it about. She pulled an elastic out of her pocket and tied it back into a small pony tail.

"So I couldn't help overhearing your conversation on the bus this morning," Caleb said. "Did all that really happen?"

Joss' eyes narrowed. "How much did you hear?"

"I was sleeping for awhile but I woke up when you were telling Miranda about your high school boyfriend and how he couldn't let things go between you. I mean, I can't blame him for not wanting to lose you." He knew it was odd to say, but he felt bold.

She seemed reluctant to let her guard down. "It's nice of you to say that, but you don't even know me."

"I know a little bit about you."

'We just met this morning," she said with a hint of agitation.

"I know that you play with your hair when you feel awkward and that you close one eye when you're thinking really hard about something."

Her hand let go of her ponytail and he regretted telling her, realizing how strange it must have sounded. He was trying so hard to make some kind of impression, to be different, but it came across as far too brazen for two people who had, in fact, just met hours earlier.

He didn't feel in control as he stood next to her, like the vibrations of her body compromised his will.

"Let's talk about something else, okay?" Joss said looking at her watch. "Which direction should we head for a coffee?"

His compliments still hung in the air as they searched for a café. When they found it and took a seat inside the front window, she seemed distant.

"I'm sorry if I made you uncomfortable," he said and took a nervous sip of his coffee. It tasted bitter.

"I just don't like when people compliment me, okay. It makes me feel strange. Especially people I don't know that well."

"I don't want to come off as creepy or anything. I just think you're pretty cool. I won't say anything more."

"I'm just kind of tired of guys saying one thing and meaning another. Compliments are never just compliments with guys."

"Well, if it helps, I think you have ugly ears."

"What?"

"Your ears, they look weird. You have no lobes."

"Well fuck you very much," she said and punched him in the arm.

"I think you smell funny," she said. "You're stinky."

"I should be. I gave up on using deodorant over here."

"Well lucky me then. Should I get used to having your smelly self around from now on?"

"If you're lucky."

"I'll buy you some deodorant then," she said and tried to hide her smile by putting her mug up to her face.

When they got back to the hostel, there were backpackers arriving in steady streams, looking exhausted but happy. The energy was electric and everyone used their national flags as conversation starters. Light filtered in through the windows as the sun hung low in the sky. It was warm and Caleb sprawled out languidly on a couch by the pool table with his Jim Morrison biography held close. He tried to read but was distracted by people passing by him towards the pub, disappearing through the entrance behind the pool table. A group of American teens passed wearing baggy jeans and speaking with perfect sarcasm; a French couple held the wall up looking too apathetic to be anywhere but half-naked smoking cigarettes in their room; a few Germans made sporadic dance moves as they caught a burst of music from the bar and laughed as they walked by; a lone Spaniard stood by the oversized map on the wall and smiled at everyone he saw, a smile that could make the knees of most girls weak. The atmosphere was right for a party.

Joss and Miranda eventually appeared and sat down next to Caleb on the couch. The scents of shampoo and fruity soaps entered his nostrils. He noticed Joss' hair had been done neatly with a thin braid down the side. She looked different: arranged, he thought. He decided that it had been done for him, and smiled at her. They joined the trail of people heading into the pub and took a table in the corner. When the waitress came by, they ordered beers and nachos, and both arrived fairly quickly.

"So what was it like to grow up in Piersville?" Miranda asked.

"Well, I haven't lived anywhere else, so it's hard to compare. We didn't have too much to do growing up besides sports and parties but we didn't feel like we were missing out much. It's only been recently I've realized Piersville isn't the centre of the universe." Caleb laughed and counted the bills he had pulled out of his pocket. "I had a good group of friends growing up who made it fun."

"Have you talked to anyone back home about the shooting?" Miranda asked. "They just did a story about it in the Toronto Star – I was reading it on the hostel computer this afternoon. It said the shooter was a kid named Ferris

Buckton who had been a misfit. Bullied a lot. Apparently, he did it out of revenge. You were strangely right about the bullying thing."

"Mhm…..so weird," Joss said with a mouthful of food. "What are your friend's saying? Did you guys know him?"

"I haven't really called any friends since I got here. But ya – I remember that guy from high school. Everyone picked on him, especially a few guys I know. They did some shitty things to him."

Joss and Miranda shared a puzzled look.

"They listed the people that died too. Tyler something, and a girl named Kendra," Miranda said.

"Do you know any of *them*?" Joss asked.

"Fuck," Caleb said and looked despondent for a few seconds until he felt they were satisfied. "Ya, I knew Tyler. He was in our group of friends."

"Aren't you sad? I'd be on the phone all day if that happened in my home town," Joss said. "You really need to check your emails and call home."

"Will you guys come with me to the Internet café tomorrow?"

"Of course," Joss said and Miranda nodded in agreement.

"So you mentioned your ex. You don't have a girlfriend back in Piersville?" Miranda asked.

Joss looked up from her plate of nachos.

"Do you think I'd be here if I had a girlfriend?"

"I guess not. Stupid question," Miranda said.

Joss smiled.

The place was filling quickly and the symphony of conversation was rising to match the music until the bartender noticed and cranked the knob a few notches higher.

"Who wants Tequila?" Joss asked and her question was met with nods. She spilled out of the booth with a reassurance that it was on her. She moved through the crowd towards the bar.

"So you like her," Miranda said plainly.

It wasn't clear to Caleb if it was a question or a statement.

"You know, she just had a fucked-up experience with a guy. If you just want to hook up with her for a night, then that's all she's looking for right now. I wouldn't suggest falling in love with her or anything like that," Miranda's tone was akin to a concerned parent. Caleb took offense to someone giving him advice as though he were a teenager.

"I saw the way you were looking at her today at the castle. I know that look."

"Well thanks for the advice, Miranda." Caleb understood the dynamic well – Joss attracted the attention and Miranda acted the parent, making sure no boys took her girl too far away from her. She was reliant on Joss to make this trip more interesting, to make sure there was some excitement.

He had no problem defending himself.

"Listen, I do like her – you're right. But it's not a big deal. I'm sure we'll part ways very soon and I'll have never got to tell her that I think she's beautiful or even get close to fucking her, so don't worry, and it's really none of your business anyways."

She gave him a penetrating look as Joss approached with three shots placed vulnerably onto a plastic bill-fold.

"Are you guys ready to get drunk?" she said as she carefully set the shots down. Her voice lightened the atmosphere again and they both shrugged and took a shot glass. "Don't be so excited," she said sarcastically and eyed them suspiciously. "To Salzburg!"

A few drinks later when Miranda was distracted by a tall, lanky man who was harmlessly slurring his words, Caleb said he needed some air and casually, as soberly as he could muster, asked Joss if she wanted to join him.

She said 'okay' and her braid fell from her ear as she moved out of her seat. He had no idea what he would say to her when they got outside. He wanted to pause time and think of all the perfect sentences, but they were outside before he could think of anything interesting to say.

They stood awkwardly looking up at the stars, happy to be free from the loud music. The night was clear and still and the moon hung in a soft, waning glow. He pulled his hood up onto his head and turned his face towards her and stared for a few long seconds and then turned away. The seconds seemed to slow down as his heart sped up.

"Time moves differently over here. I can never seem to remember what day it is," he said.

"I think it'll take you awhile to get used to it. I remember feeling that way when I first started travelling. It's not a way of life that's propagated by routine; you have to accept each day's absurdity."

The word 'absurdity' rang through Caleb's ears like he'd heard it recently. Joss continued, "And be ready for deviation at any moment."

"Deviation?"

"Yeah, deviation," Joss said. "You have to be ready to accept the possibility that your plans might change in a moment. You can't be a slave to your route, so to speak. If you want to truly experience Europe, you have to be open to listening to the stars instead."

"Listening to stars? Jesus, how many shots did you have in there?" They both laughed.

"Okay, for the record, I don't listen to the stars, but what I mean is that it's important to let fate guide you sometimes and leave your experience up to chance. I've seen people that stick to a schedule and it makes me feel sorry for them. They're brave enough to come all the way over here but they're too scared to give themselves to it fully. They plan out every hour of every day and shy away from letting anything or anyone change their plans. This experience should make you hurt sometimes. It should make you follow somebody somewhere you never would have gone alone. I deviated from my plan. I wouldn't be here right now if I hadn't."

He turned to look at her but she turned away; she stepped back and sat on the stone slab entranceway to the hostel. It was cold on her hands and she brought them together for warmth. Caleb was still looking up at the night sky.

"We're all in the gutter, but some of us are looking at the stars," she said.

He gave her a puzzled look. "There are no stars tonight," he said. "But it's a nice line."

"It's Oscar Wilde," she said. "Sorry, I'm kind of drunk."

"Tequila will do that."

 "Listen, I'm going to tell you something that I probably shouldn't," she said. He turned to see her sitting in a pose reserved for classic photographs. He tried to capture it in a memory, but all he could see was her hair blowing gently under glow of the streetlamp. The light fell on her cheek-bone at an angle that deepened the valley of her face and danced against the light as she spoke.

"I noticed you in Munich when I got on," she said. "I could see you on the bus through the window. I was talking to Miranda on the curb, but I couldn't keep from looking at you. I don't think you noticed me. Anyways, I sat behind you on purpose because I thought maybe you'd talk to us. And you did. But I kind of wish you hadn't, you know." Joss was standing now with her gaze fixed on him. He gave her a puzzled look.

"Don't you ever see people in a crowd that you can't take your eyes off like you know them somehow, intimately from another time. You just want to watch them from a distance because if you spoke, just once, it would ruin everything?" Does that make any sense?"

She paused and looked at him. He nodded.

"Words just get in the way sometimes don't they?" she said.

Caleb shifted his feet, and erased the distance between them.

"Well, I feel like that sometimes and I felt that way when I saw you. So, on the other hand, I was kind of hoping you wouldn't talk to me," she said and turned her face to his. "But I'm glad I'm here with you now." She embraced the slow movement of his mouth onto hers.

    Caleb's heart was pounding. He hadn't kissed anyone other than Melanie for seven years. Joss' lips tasted different, her mouth moved in strange ways but he liked it. They turned their bodies into each other until a group stumbled out onto the street talking loudly and pointing in all the directions they thought the night clubs might be.

    The group was soon gone and they were left together under the streetlight. Joss wrapped her arms around his waist. As she rested her head against his cheek, a thought occurred to him that he and Melanie would not spend the rest of their lives together. It was fleeting, and soon his mind returned to Joss and he kissed her forehead. Piersville was too far away to be real anymore.

January 12, 1943

Dear Marie,
I'm going to be a father! That makes me happy beyond belief. I couldn't ask for better news. I wish I could be there with you to watch you eat pickles and peanut butter! It is possible this war will be over, though, in time to watch our son be born (I have faith in your intuition about a boy, but I'd be just as happy to have a beautiful baby girl in our lives). There isn't a day that goes by that I don't wish I could see your face. I carry your picture with me and take comfort in it always, and know that you're carrying the next generation of Arthurs inside you. That will fill me with warmth no matter how cold things get. The training exercises can be quite numbing in this February weather, but I imagine England will be warmer at least. This mechanics training is pretty far over my head. I'm not worrying, though – I'm no mechanic and they know it!

I took my platoon on a long route march today and it rained all day, but we'll go out again tomorrow. We've been doing seven miles and that's enough for one day. We also spent some time firing mortar bombs, but I don't want to bore you too much with my day. I'm in the mess now watching a crap game and thinking of going to bed. We saw two good pictures tonight in Halifax: "Bittersweet" and "Blossoms in the Dust." It was good to get out of camp for awhile.

I was told I was 'steady and dependable' and I've been recommended for Sergeant. I won't hesitate to accept the position should they offer it. I have much respect for the Queen's Own and the men I am in company with. They are a rather different breed than my classmates at Queens, and I'm still learning how to communicate best with them. I didn't expect to see so many French Canadians, but I've been placed with the Chaudieres and so I'm doing my best to remember my French. Well, the boys are getting loud in the mess tonight and I'm having difficulty concentrating. I'll write again soon.

All my love,
Patrick

8

The bus snaked its way along the winding ascent of the Swiss Alps towards Jungfrau campground. The road was narrow and Caleb felt nervous every time the bus corrected itself along the cliff side. The campground sat below a jarring cliff face spilling a singular stream of water from two hundred feet. A layer of wet snow covered the ground, but the air was warm. The campground, sprawled over three acres, consisting mainly of small cabins fit with bunkbeds. The small village looked vibrant and accessible. They checked in at the front lodge while people tossed Frisbees and drank beer on the lawn behind them, tall cans resting in the inch of snow that covered the ground. Their cabin was in the back corner of the grounds and they each claimed a bed before taking a short nap. Joss and Miranda took the two bottom bunks. It hadn't been a long drive from Salzburg but it had been an anxious one. The air was damp, and sleeping was easy.

    Caleb awoke first. He leaned over his bunk and threw a dirty sock down at Joss, who threw it right back.

    "Ssshhh – she's still sleeping," Joss whispered and gave him the finger playfully.

    "It's alright – I'm awake," Miranda said opening one eye and then the other. "Caesar's anyone?"

    The campground had a romanticism that was fitting for Joss and Caleb's courtship and they began to be more open about it. They often walked into the nearby town to buy wine and food and while Miranda often walked ahead to let Caleb and Joss be alone, sometimes she and Joss walked arm in arm and let Caleb trail behind. On their way to buy supplies for a spaghetti dinner they had planned, he couldn't resist the urge to gather a little snow and toss a snowball in their direction initiating a battle that enlisted a group of teenagers and a middle-aged couple with kids. It wasn't until the teenagers enlisted more friends that Caleb and the family realized they were overpowered. They threw their hands up, but Caleb, too proud to admit defeat, was eventually surrounded by teens and pummelled until Joss broke through and drove a snowball down, under his shirt and rubbed it into his back. After some high-fives and jokes in broken English, everyone waved goodbye and went their separate ways. They continued on to town and through the doors of the small grocery store, laughing and re-enacting scenes from the battle.

The tasks for gathering groceries were assigned by Miranda, who was slowly becoming the matronly figure. She instructed Caleb to find some wine.

"I'm going to make us all a feast tonight," she said and grabbed Joss' arm in jest to pull her away.

After finding the wine section and choosing the largest jug available, insurance that there would be enough for drunken decisions to be made, Caleb went looking for the girls, stopping suddenly at a row of condoms at the end of an aisle. He stopped, looked around, and then set the jug of wine down at his feet. He reached up and then hesitated for a second. The next twelve hours played through his mind and the final scene involved him and Joss lying next to each other in one of their bunks. He thought for another second and then slowly reached again to grab one.

"We're all set," Miranda said. Her voice startled him and his hand shot back to his waist as he turned. They looked at each other and Miranda smiled and said, "Well, I guess we'll leave you alone to make *that* decision, then," and walked away laughing.

He met them again at the checkout counter, red faced but with time to concoct a cover story.

"So when you guys caught up to me back there, I was just killing some time – I wanted to see if they have the same types of domers as they do back home, you know with all the crazy things they're doing with them now. A friend of mine told me about these ones that actually warm up on their own or something like that – crazy eh? It seems like the Swiss are pretty sensible – not too much variety," Caleb said and looked at them, curious for their response.

Joss smiled and replied, "I wouldn't know anything about that. I'm a virgin," and looked at Miranda.

"Ya me too," Miranda replied and they laughed and left Caleb holding his oversized jug of cheap French wine. Joss looked back at him and winked. He was becoming helpless to her wit and easy social graces.

As he hoisted the wine up onto the counter, Miranda turned, looked at the jug and then at him. "Do you think you grabbed a big enough bottle of wine there Mr Arthur? Jesus – we're all going to be in for a long night if you expect us to finish that off!"

"Relax – I'll make up for what you two lightweights can't handle. I grew up in Piersville, remember – we drink this much for lunch." He paid a few Francs to the cashier and with two hands, lifted the jug off the counter and carried it like a trophy all the way back to the campground.

Miranda prepared dinner while Caleb and Joss claimed a picnic table. The area was enclosed on one side by a low hanging shelter that extended out over the kitchen but left the picnic tables open to the elements with full view of the towering cliff face. He pulled the table underneath the shelter where Miranda was boiling the pasta and took Joss on a walk to find napkins. When they returned, they could smell the spaghetti sauce heating on the stove.

"Dinner's almost ready," Miranda told them and handed them utensils and plates. Caleb let the girls go first as he poured wine into plastic cups for everyone. When they were all seated, they raised them into the air, ate, and watched the sun disappear behind the mountains.

The jug of wine was getting easier to lift as the evening went on, and the stories and jokes and playful jabs were increasing and seemed to be funnier with a head full of wine. When Joss said she had some Swiss chocolate for dessert back at the cabin, she poked Caleb in the side.

The night was spotted with cabin lanterns and the further they walked the more surrounded they became. Each light represented a camp and it was difficult to determine which cabin was theirs; he couldn't remember if they left the light on and as they wandered up mistakenly to what they thought was their cabin, they were startled by two figures at the entrance sitting in the dark. One stood up, tossed his cigarette to the ground and spoke quickly in German: he was asking a question. It was followed by silence. Caleb apologized in English, hoping that would ease the tension. The German spoke again, harsher this time.

Joss stepped forward, releasing Caleb's hand and said: "Wir dachten, das war unsere Hutte. Mein Freunde ist betrunken"

Caleb stared at her in amazement and turned to see the Germans laughing. They said: "Ja, wir sind zu betrunken"

As they walked back onto the pathway, Caleb turned to her.

"I didn't know you could speak German. What did you say?"

"I told them that you were looking for a big German penis tonight. They said they weren't interested. You're not cute enough for them."

"Haha, very funny. But seriously?"

"That's what I said. I guess you'll just have to make do with me tonight," she said and grabbed his ass. She pulled him into a light jog. Her hips swung seductively, and her thin legs moved nimbly in front of him as she cut into the darkness. They reached their cabin out of breath. Their hearts were beating quickly. As they kissed, their hands fumbled for the door. They spilled into the small cabin like a gust of wind, bodies entwined and moving slowly, awkwardly backwards towards Joss' bunk. As they fumbled with their belts, there came a quiet rustle across the room and both turned to see a mound underneath a sleeping bag sprouting dreadlocks.

They both froze as the figure shifted in his bunk, and poked his head up; he stared at them like a raccoon startled in a tree, and then went back to sleep without saying a word. Joss rested her head into Caleb's chest in defeat. They quietly slipped out of the cabin and back to the light that hung over Miranda's figure drying dishes; her body looked old as she faced away from them, hunched over the dishes. She looked lost in her thoughts when they approached and was surprised to see them so soon. She turned and gave Joss a confused smile.

They fixed a fire and sat up late and finished the jug of wine. The subjects of sex and ex-partners weren't discussed. Instead, they shared stories about other travellers, disgusting hostel rooms, and favourite historic sites: stories they could laugh at together or wince at knowingly. Caleb told them about his first hostel in London, but he didn't tell them about Skins; his bruises had healed and he wanted to forget the whole day had ever happened. All that remained was a cracked rib that he did his best to hide and reduced vision in his left eye. He wondered if he was slowly going blind in it and it scared him but he didn't let on.

As the fire crackled before them all, the wine had done its part in bringing emotions to the forefront and as the conversation died down and each was left to their thoughts, Miranda began to cry – softly at first, but soon in audible sobs, loud enough that Joss noticed and went and crouched down beside her in a comforting embrace. Caleb came over for support but lingered awkwardly beside them.

"I just miss him so much," Miranda said. "Coming here hasn't made it any better."

Joss signalled to Caleb that she had it under control, so he turned, and as he left the fire, he heard Joss say: "Distance never changes anything. Only time does that."

July 28, 1943

Dear Marie,

They've promoted me to Sergeant! I'm honoured, and now it's my job to keep moral up. It's difficult at times since most of the men in my squadron are French Canadian and can't understand me much of the time. My French is rusty but I'm trying. I got my revolver today. It's a .38 and quite a little honey. I was the only one of the sergeants to get one, and I'm not sure why exactly. I think you'd like the way it hangs my figure.

    I met an interesting fellow from the RAF the other day named Jack. He was commenting on the pistol dangling by my side and we struck up a conversation. We ended up quarrelling about the nature of our involvement over here but he is an intelligent man and he stands his ground. I respect that, even if we don't agree on things. He's told me about this place in the South of England called Torquay and says he goes there during his leaves and urged me go there, as well. He says the water is blue as the sky, and there's a lovely beach and even a Ferris wheel! Can you believe that, honey? Just like the one we went on at the Kingston Fair during our courtship. That was a swell time. Remember how hard you were holding onto me when we reached the top? God, I miss your arms around me, sweetheart.

    How are you feeling? Are you still waking up often during the night? It sounds like our son is ready to get out into the world with all that kicking. I wish I could be there to watch him born, but I'm glad my family will be there to help. My mother is almost as excited as we are. I think she's ready to be a grandmother, although she'd tell you she doesn't feel that old.

    We are training hard, and I feel we will be well prepared when the time comes. I'm in the company of fine men here. I've come to know a few especially well – Paterson is a Canadian fellow I sailed over with. I think I've mentioned him previously. Poor chap broke his leg when a barrel of spuds rolled portside on him during the voyage over. Not one of the lucky ones. And there's Jack I mentioned previously. It's good to have a few friends over here to help the time pass. I've told them all about you and our boy and they would love to meet you one day. Such a thought. They do enjoy the care packages you send. The honey is a hit, and well, the cigarettes are always handy. And the stamps ensure that I'll always be able to write to you my love.

All my love
Patrick.

9

What he really wanted was to have two lives: one where he had Melanie and a family and a career, and one where he was free to travel the world with Joss. He imagined each of these lives playing out as he lay in his bunk alone. A small bird was inspecting him from the window. It pecked at the glass and twitched its head until it fixed one eye in a judging stare. Caleb looked at his watch and wondered where the girls were. It wasn't quite noon and a silence hung over the campground. He was upset he had slept through the morning, a sleep that brought strange dreams. He figured it must have been around 6am back home and knew she'd be getting up for work. He rose from his bunk and wandered to the common area. Finding the pay phone unoccupied, he took the opportunity to call her.

"Hello?" a sleepy voice sounded through the telephone.

"Hi. It's me," Caleb said and waited a second. "Sorry for calling so early."

"No, that's okay. I was getting up for work anyways."

"Ya, I figured I could catch you before you headed off."

"What's up, Cal?"

"Nothing. I just wanted to hear your voice.

"Well, it's my raspy morning voice. I'm barely awake."

"It's just good to hear it."

"Caleb, don't be cute. What do you want?"

"How was Tyler's funeral?"

"Horrible."

"Was everyone there?"

"Caleb, I'm not going to discuss it right now. You should have been there. You weren't. End of story."

"Do you miss me?"

"Yes," she said flatly. "How could I not? I still love you. That's what makes this so fucking hard. But I'm getting used to things without you. Did you read my email?"

"Not yet."

"Of course you haven't. That would require you sitting at a computer for longer than thirty seconds. Well, I wrote that in a daze anyways, when I was scared I'd never see you again. I'm not sure I still feel the same way. You've probably slept with someone else by now anyways. Isn't that why you really wanted to go away? To sleep with other girls? Actually, don't answer that. Listen I have to go to work."

"You're getting used to life without me? That's great, Mel. Thanks, that makes me feel really great." Caleb's heart began to quicken. His skin felt hot. He regretted calling.

"Is that what you called me for? To make you feel good? Come on Caleb, what did you expect?"

"Well, I thought you understood why I left. It wasn't to fuck other girls, Mel."

"Sorry I shouldn't have said that." She let out a sigh and paused. "It's just that I've been doing a lot of thinking lately, since you've been gone. Just about whether I could be okay without you in my life. I've surprised myself. I'm finding new ways to be happy. I still love you, Caleb. I'm just not sure about us, you know? Maybe you're not the one for me long term. Anyways, it's too early to be having this talk. I wish you would call me at a normal time when we can actually have a real conversation. I'm still half asleep."

"But you still love me, though?"

"Yes, of course I still love you. I'll always love you, Cal. I'm just not sure if it's the way I've loved you in the past." Her voice was starting to crack. She composed herself quickly and said "Listen, I have to get ready for work. We'll talk again later."

Before they could say goodbye, Caleb desperately said "I love you too!" and the words hung awkwardly in the silence between them.

She paused. "I know Caleb."

He put the receiver down slowly. He had been so involved in the conversation he'd forgotten his surroundings. He hadn't noticed Miranda standing a few feet away waiting for the telephone. Her head was turned away towards the backdrop of towering Interlaken peaks. He felt a sense of panic as he quickly measured the distance between them and knew she was in a dangerous proximity to hear his conversation.

"All yours" he said sheepishly and went to move past her.

Miranda eyed him neutrally; her eyes narrowed. "Thanks" she said and let him by.

Caleb was sitting alone at a picnic table in the beer garden when Joss and Miranda approached. He looked up and set his book down.

"Hey loner! Whatcha readin?" Joss asked playfully.

Caleb laughed and reluctantly lifted his book for them to see.

"Siddartha, eh?" Joss said as she eyed the cover.

"Ya, I traded my Jack London for it. It's an interesting book, and look - I can fit it in my back pocket."

"Stupid me - I brought Infinite Jest," Joss said but neither Caleb nor Miranda understood the joke.

The late morning turned to early afternoon as they sat conversing about the places they still wanted to visit and flipping through their travel guides. Caleb kept his eye on Miranda for signs that she might have overheard his conversation with Melanie. He couldn't get comfortable.

Joss got their attention when she noticed a figure approaching the bar with his eyes down and his hair hanging over his face in long dreadlocks. His hands were sorting through the bills and coins from his pockets, separating the used tickets and sundry items. Joss explained to Miranda that he was the one who was in the fourth bed and Miranda nodded and looked at Caleb with a blank stare.

"I think it's him anyways," Joss clarified.

"Well let's invite him to sit with us, then" Miranda said.

They both looked at Caleb, who hesitated when he realized they wanted him to do it. Joss pleaded and he gave in.

"Alright, I'll ask him" Caleb said as he stood up and walked over to the bar. He returned with four beers and a tall, skinny guy he introduced as Ryan.

There was something melancholic about him, like he was wounded in some way, and just as some women are drawn to a wounded bird, found helpless and without flight, they are affected by the injured spirit of a man. There is a decided willingness to fix the wing and be the one to watch as flight takes place again, knowing that it was by their hand; knowing that they had done some good by caring for something that had been damaged by the injustices of the world. Ryan had been hurt, they could tell, but they couldn't quite locate where the damage had been done, so they searched with words. In response, he said little and gave only subtle hints of his past. The conversation was stilted, but Caleb liked having another male in the group.

His dreadlocks covered half his face until he swept them away and excused himself and said he was going back to the cabin for a nap. He did it politely, and they watched him as he zipped up his sweater and place the hood over his big hair.

Miranda said something to Caleb about growing dreadlocks, but Caleb was watching Joss' gaze. It was fixed on Ryan.

"Don't you guys find something odd about him?" she said.

Miranda agreed and Caleb didn't care for the topic and excused himself to use the washroom.

The wash-house was filled with damp air that stuck to his skin. As he stood at the urinal, he stared at the drops of condensation falling slowly from the handle onto the ceramic and pushed hard to piss. He hadn't had to go very badly. When he stepped to the sink, he noticed his cheeks were flush with afternoon beer. The metallic bang of a stall door took him by surprise and he looked away from his reflection. It was Ryan. They accepted each other carefully as two men do in a washroom – a nod and a brief hello.

"You left pretty quickly back there," said Caleb.

"No offence – you guys seem really cool and all, but I'm really just here to get some boarding in. I was put in with you guys because it was one of the only beds left. I don't want to mess with whatever you guys have going."

"Well, we all just met back in Salzburg, but we get along pretty well. They're pretty cool girls."

"You're fucking one of them I assume," Ryan said with indifference, which caught Caleb off guard. He laughed awkwardly but Ryan was still waiting for an answer. "That was you and that Joss girl last night in your bunk wasn't it? When she was ready to give you some cinnamon? Sorry if I ruined your plans."

"Well, to be honest – you did kind of surprise us last night, but…what the fuck are you gonna do right? It's not your fault."

Ryan nodded and went to dry his hands. The dryer was placed low and he had to bend down awkwardly to get his hands under it. When he finished, he turned to Caleb. "I'm gonna head back and smoke a J, but I'll catch up with you later."

"Mind if I join?"

Ryan hesitated and said "sure" and Caleb followed him out of the washhouse and back to the cabin.

The smoke spiralled around them in lazy coils dissipating into the cabin air. Caleb adjusted himself on his bunk in a position that suited his new frame of mind. He passed on the third round and sat back and closed his eyes.

"Weed's not that great. Picked it up from a British guy a few cabins down this morning – mostly just shake."

Caleb wanted to act like it wasn't affecting him much, but he hadn't smoked in awhile and he forgot how it had a way of letting in paranoid thoughts. The more he tried to shake them, the more they took grip and he began to regret getting high - the weed was taking him places he had been trying to hide from.

Ryan coughed and put the joint out on the top of a pop can, placing the roach meticulously back into a plastic bag. "So how long will I be bunking with Three's Company here?" he asked.

Caleb took a few seconds to register the question. "I don't know how long we're planning to stay here. We might catch a bus to Prague. We all want to go there. What about you?"

"I think I'll stick around for a little while. Supposed to meet a friend in Paris in a few days, but I might just tell him to come meet me here."

A minute passed without conversation.

"My brother died – that's why I'm over here," Ryan said to break the silence.

"I'm sorry, man," Caleb said having little capacity to accept such a heavy confession in the state he was in; he let the words bounce around in his head and searched for someway to respond. Each time he considered offering a sentiment, he analyzed it too much and lost confidence in it. Nothing seemed like the right thing to say. A few minutes passed until Caleb sat up, startled by a thought.

"Shit – I just remembered that the girls think I went to the washroom. They're going to wonder where I am."

"I'm sure they'll survive."

"No, I better head back – I've got half a beer waiting for me"

"Okay."

Caleb rubbed his eyes and put his feet on the ground and used the bunk post to leverage himself up. He turned before he opened the door. "Hey man, I am really sorry to hear about your brother. If you ever want to talk about it…you know."

Ryan looked over from his bunk and nodded his head. He put his earphones on, and lay back in his bunk.

As Caleb walked across the thin snow, he squinted at the sun reflecting from it. He had forgotten his sunglasses at the table and cursed himself for it. He was thinking about death and how Tyler had spent his last few minutes. Did Ryan's brother know he was going to die? He forgot to ask him. As he came upon Joss and Miranda, the thought of death melted away and he just wanted to kiss Joss on the lips, so he did.

Snowflakes fell around them as they waited for the bus to arrive. Caleb was still surprised Ryan had agreed to come with them to Prague. Joss had made a strong case - that the architecture was out-of-this world, and while it was still under the relaxed fist of the Soviet Bloc, it was not yet a tourist trap. She said it was now or never to see it still relatively un-touched by Western tourism. She also told him about the currency exchange - a nice meal at a restaurant with a bottle of wine would likely be about five Canadian dollars. They could live like kings for weeks. And then Caleb chimed in that Czech girls were supposed to be pretty damn good looking, which provoked a punch in the arm from Joss. She didn't let up like other girls might. Even though she was never angry with him, she put everything she had into it.

    They settled into their seats and prepared for a long bus ride. Melanie was far away again – in a part of his life that no longer seemed real. He was learning how to separate his two lives. He slipped his hand into Joss' and she placed her head on his shoulder. It was a different kind of happiness.

"So you must have had a good night, did you?" Melanie said without looking up.

    "Sorry, Mel. I just passed out at Kyle's. We all went back there after work. Got a little crazy," he said, trying not to look at her.

    "Ya, looks like it," she said as she turned to him.

    "Listen, I knew you'd be mad. I'm sorry." He fumbled around for his wallet and placed it on the table. He looked back to gauge her anger. He could see the fire in her eyes and decided to get defensive. "Oh, don't give me that look. Jesus, let's not make a big deal out of it," he said. "You know you're always welcome to come hang out with Kyle and those guys after work."

"...and girls," she replied.

"Oh, so that's what this is about! You think I'm hitting on the girls at the restaurant. Jesus, Mel, they're like 18! Do you really think I'd do that?"

"Well you're not having sex with me, so you must be fucking someone!" It was not in Melanie's nature to swear, so the word 'fucking' came out charged like from the mouth of a child and her face erupted in tears. He watched her cry and wanted to comfort her. He knew she had cried too much in her life and he always prided himself on being the one to make her smile, but it wasn't as important to him anymore. He blamed her for feeling trapped. He blamed her for their boring sex life. And he hated himself for blaming her.

"I'm too tired to fight, Mel," he said and made his way to the stairs. She caught him halfway up with an embarrassed look on her face. She had made her hands into fists and pushed them into his body, pinning him against the wall. It forced a few pictures to tumble down the stairs until they smashed at the bottom. He grabbed the windowsill to keep himself up and pulled his body around her using the bannister She looked wild with words unsaid.

"Tell me *something* – tell me you don't love me, tell me you're sleeping with someone....tell me *something*."

Caleb was caught off guard. It scared him to not recognize her.

He was about to yell at her to get herself under control but he could see in her eyes she too was startled by her own outburst. She had always flaunted a strong character, but he needed her to be weaker than him sometimes. The truth was that he had, in fact, wanted to kiss another girl and that was part of the reason he had not come home; he entertained the idea of kissing Kendra Taylor, one of the tall, big-eyed, hostesses from Corrigan's. He wanted to be around Kendra more than he wanted to come home and he wasn't sure how to tell her. So he didn't. He just looked at her and prepared to be silent. But as he looked at her, she made an unusual gesture with her face where her eyes stopped all accusation; her eyebrows lifted from their furrowed spot and she just looked puerile and concerned - scared for what they assumed to be the death of something that was once easy, but now hid in surreptitious places that they no longer had access to. Their love had fallen into the corners of their lives.

He decided to give her what she needed. "I'm not screwing anybody else for fuck sakes. Do you really think I'd do that?" She was looking up at him with her fists resting against his chest. The tears had slowed down leaving thick, wet tracks that shined against the morning light from the window. "We've definitely lost something, but there's..... I'm...just," he stopped and hesitated, not sure if he was choosing the right words.

"I'm just tired of," he paused "being here. Piersville...my job...I'm starting to go crazy."

"How long have you been feeling this way?" she said as she lowered herself onto the step.

"Let's get out of here for a little while. We can come back and start a family after a year or two of traveling. Don't you want to see the world?"

"I can't leave my dad. You know that. Alzheimer's doesn't take a year off."

"Why can't your sister come home to care for him? Heaven forbid she leave her stressful job as a house-wife in Kingston. If your mother were here, she'd want you to live your life too."

Melanie's brown hair covered her face and spilled onto her knees. She wiggled her toes as she listened. When he mentioned her mother, she looked up at him wildly and then put her head back down.

Tears rolled down her face onto her knees, and she wiped them into her shins. Caleb pulled her into his shoulder and felt the dampness of her cheeks through his t-shirt.

"He's been starting to forget the simplest things, like when the garbage goes out. He doesn't even know what day it is sometimes. I had to take him in to see Dr Lekman again and of course Lekman doesn't know how fast he'll deteriorate or how bad things will get. He just says to rely more on the support workers. He says I should just enjoy the times when he is lucid. God. I guess I'm just waiting for everything to fall apart. I don't know what I'm going to do when he's gone. And you're gone. I'll be alone." She pulled away from him and wiped her cheeks clean. "Listen, if you want to go travel, then do it but I'm not going with you. I can't leave my dad right now. Besides, I don't really understand the draw of sleeping in dirty hostels every night. I like my own bed."

"It's more than that for me. Remember when I told you my aunt Catherine found all those letters. Well, I've been reading through them and realizing there is this man that I know nothing about. He traveled all through Europe in World World II and I thought if I went over there, I could connect with him somehow. I know he went to Torquay after the war ended. The way he describes it in his letters made me curious for places like that. We've never seen the ocean, Mel. Doesn't that make you feel sad?"

"We can take our kids to see it one day. That would make me happy."

"It's just that if I don't do it now, I don't think I ever will. I work at a goddamn bar and grill for Christ sakes. I have nothing keeping me here."

He panicked for a second and knew it would be too late but he said it anyway. "Except for you, of course." But it was too late.

Melanie broke away from him and sat upright. "You don't even *want* me to go with you, do you?"

"Don't be silly."

"I knew it. You feel like you're missing out on things," she said and narrowed her eyes on him. "We moved in together young and I know we haven't really led an exciting life, but we've been happy together, haven't we?'

He nodded.

"I want to keep building a life together. But I can't go anywhere right now."

"I'm not leaving you forever, babe. I just want to go away for a little while. I have to do this now or I never will. I'll come back. I promise."

He ran his fingers through her hair as her head rested back on his shoulder. No one spoke. Melanie had stopped crying.

"I could tell you've been unhappy the last few months but I didn't think it was us."

'It's not you, Mel. I just haven't been myself lately."

He put his arms around her and rested his chin on her shoulder; his lips sat close to her cheek and he could feel the warmth of his breath reflect from her skin. They sat together in silence until she went upstairs alone.

A week later, she moved in with her father. Caleb asked her to return home, but she refused. He had expected her to be weak and tell him she missed him but that didn't happen.

He tried not to let his biggest fear creep in – one he had not anticipated when he was making this decision to go: that she was finding life without him tolerable, even suitable - that she had found something deep inside her, an inner strength. As the weeks went on, and she didn't contact him, he showed up at her work one morning and demanded she talk to him. She got angry and walked him back home like a lost child.

"Cal, I'm sorry to hear that you're feeling down, but you know why I moved out."

"I miss you. I'm not sure I can leave you. What if things aren't the same when I get back?"

"You might not feel the same way when you return. Maybe you'll never return," Melanie said and her eyes fell to the ground as though she had already accepted that was a possibility.

Caleb couldn't figure out how this girl, who had just been crying and pleading with him a few weeks ago, could be so reserved now. He wondered what tool was she using.

"Why don't I just stay here, and not go. My heart is really hurting right now Mel. I'm really confused"

"I know, Cal." She wiped the tear away from his face and resisted the urge to cry herself. "But I want you to go. You are going to have the time of your life."

"But I don't want to lose you."

"That's not something we can talk about right now. All I know is that you need to go. I need to figure some things out on my own, too. I can't be with you right now."

Those words rattled around in his head for the next few days and he tried to remember which part she put the stress on. Was it the *I*, or the *can't* or the *right now*?

August 10, 1943

Dear Patrick,
We've got a healthy baby boy! 7 lbs 9 ounces. We still need a name, so please help me decide between Mackenzie, Robert or Frederick.
 I'm sorry to hear you're still training, but to be honest, my love, that's exactly where I want you. The longer you're in England, the less I worry. I read such awful reports of the goings-on in the continent. I've stopped inviting Phenon over unless he promises to be more hopeful. He's just started seeing a new girl, Margaret, and she's just lovely. I don't know what she sees in him, though, and I tell him that! I'm glad you are enjoying the honey and cigarettes. I also put more stamps in this one so you have no excuse not to write to me. Not that you need one – you've been very good about writing back to me and to your parents, but I feel things will change when you head into action. It'll break my heart not getting those long letters from you, but I know you will try.
 The ladies at the Church put out a collection for you even though I said your father would gladly cover the cost of the care package. He is so proud of you, but I'm sure you already know that. He and your mother stop by to spend time with me often. Your mother has so much advice during this first trimester. Honestly, I don't know what I'd do without her, but I do wish my mother was here in Canada right now. I feel so tired all the time and I get hungry for the strangest things, Patrick. I wish you were. I miss you dearly.

All my love,
Marie

10

It was close to noon when they saw Prague through the bus windshield.

They had reserved beds at the Boathouse Hostel, which sat on the outskirts of the city along the Vltava River. It was a square building raised on thick white pillars overlooking the riverbank. A long balcony stretched across the west side with tables arranged around a large checkers game. A ramp led up to the main entrance at the south end. The hallway to the check-in was covered in names and comments left in black marker, which dangled from a string on the wall tempting guests to use it.

The pathway from the road was long and wound through bushes and overgrowth in an empty lot behind a driving range. The hostel grounds were secluded and quiet, which made it a rare find for those who knew of it. Two matronly women took the foursome to their room, but first showed them the common area, set with square tables around a small bar with three taps of Czech lagers. They explained the services they offered, which included laundry and home cooked meals.

Some nights, the four of them lazed around the television room watching old movies or sat out on the balcony talking with other backpackers and playing checkers. Caleb and Ryan got to know other guests by chatting over cigarettes in the evening, and the girls made friends in the TV room and on the riverbank in the evening.

They often gathered in the common room, playing cards and drinking beer until someone made the call to go into the city. It always took awhile to get everyone on the same page, but they eventually all left together down the path to the tram stop. They laughed and carried on like old friends. The two Aussies, Tim and Marshall, loved to tease the Canadians, and they expected it right back, so Caleb played along, but kept his eye on the two of them around Joss. Ryan got along well with an American named Greg and found he could talk to him about music rather effortlessly and even jammed a little on the balcony some evenings using the hostel guitars. He tried to include Miranda in their conversations, but her knowledge of music was limited and she shied away from him when he talked to Greg. Caleb watched her make attempts at conversation with the others but they were all younger and she struggled to find a connection. She often referenced the time they had shared in Interlaken; Caleb knew she felt more powerful then.

When they all boarded the tram into the city centre, they were drunk and loud. They talked vulgarly as the train cars became an extension of their hostel and the waxen commuters turned their heads to the windows with dead stares waiting for their stop, listening to stories that were so far from their own: lives that didn't hold the luxury of tramping through other people's backyards to escape the tediousness of life.

Caleb led the group to the Underground, a club he had read about that was across from the Astrological Clock. They entered through large wooden doors that led down stone steps into to a cavernous bar with Gothic stone pillars separating the dance floor from the lounge. The bar extended across the back.

A girl was dancing half-naked on the stage, her finger pointing seductively across the crowd. She was slim with small breasts and long blonde hair, and as she danced, she slowly removed her clothes and threw them into the crowd. By the time they had ordered their drinks and found a hightop, she was down to her underwear.

It was too loud to talk, so anything that needed to be said required leaning in. Their only communication was to clink their glasses together and look each other in the eyes.

The girl on stage was now entwined with a male partner, a boy with short blonde hair, Hawaiian shirt and cargo pants. She was pulling him into her aggressively and he was throwing his head back in laughter as his friends looked on.

The place was warm and sticky; condensation dripped from the pillars. Joss excused herself and returned a few minutes later with shots of absinthe. There were spoons and a sugar bowl on a tray between the rocks glasses. As the bass pounded in the background, she gave them all a spoon. The small container of sugar was placed in the middle of the table and they waited for Joss to go first. She took a mound of sugar, then dipped the spoon into the glass of absinthe and lit it on fire. They all followed. A thin blue flame melted the sugar down to a gluey caramel. Everyone's gaze was fixed on the small lick of fire like an ancient ritual. Then she extinguished it, stirred it into the rocks glass and drank it back. She winced when the bitterness kicked in.

    Caleb was last to drink; he had declined at first.

    "I've heard bad things about this stuff," he said.

    Joss urged him on. "Try everything once," she said. "You won't regret it."

    He acquiesced as he looked around the table. Joss blew his flame out and before putting it back, said "Here's to Europe, then." It tasted like nothing he had ever had before. It burned his throat, but the saccharine taste of the sugar helped the unpleasant flavour.

    The girl on stage was now fully naked and wrapping herself around the body of the blonde kid, who was down to his boxers. He had his hands in the air, laughing, looking down at his friends in the crowd, who were all yelling at him in ritualistic envy. He tried to pull someone on stage with him but a large man in black appeared from the corner of the stage and prevented it with one smooth motion. It was a sobering reminder of control.

    The girls wanted to dance, and Joss tried to convince Caleb to join them, but he told her he wasn't in the mood. He wanted to wait until the absinthe kicked in. He pulled out a cigarette and lit it. Joss turned to Ryan and grabbed his arm, pulling with all her might in exaggerated fashion until he gave in and followed her and Miranda to the dance floor. Caleb inhaled a lung full of smoke and squinted his eyes suspiciously. A pang of jealousy hit him, followed by a wave of intoxicating joy.

    He could feel the music reach beneath his skin. The absinthe was starting to kick in. He began to notice small traces people left as they moved. Every body melted into one continuous sense of flux. The buzz was sharper than weed but exciting and inward in a way that alcohol wasn't. He liked it and went to order another.

    His body was tingling as he went to find them on the dance floor. It was crowded with bodies gyrating in the darkness. The girl had left the stage and in her place was a slideshow of funkadelic images transposed onto a backdrop. Colours moved in and out in rapid, undulating movements: red swirls formed into blue circles and then broke apart into yellow waves before melting back into flecks of green light. He was transfixed by it.

    He felt the urge to dance and wandered through the crowd, bumping into strangers as he searched for a face he recognized. He saw Tim and Marshall dancing with three girls and he grabbed Tim's shoulder and asked if he'd seen Joss. Caleb couldn't hear his response through the music, but his body language said no. The deep beats of the house music had everyone in its grip; it was transcendence through movement and wormwood. He pushed his way into the middle and saw Ryan's dreads before he saw Joss and Miranda. They were tight together in a closed circle and Ryan held both their hands as he moved smoothly around them. He was happy to find them, and didn't notice their hesitation at first. He felt good. He put his arm around Joss' neck and pulled her close forcing her to adopt his rhythm, which was just out of step with the beat. He witnessed Ryan and Miranda shoot each other a look that he wasn't meant to see and the smile that appeared on Ryan's face was subtle. He reached down and kissed Joss on the lips. She kissed him back and they broke off into the crowd together, bound by their waists and a need for something comfortable. He felt far away from himself.

 When they realized it was 4am, they slipped out of the bar together and boarded the tram. They were alone. Joss pressed her body into his against the railing as the tram jostled and shook along its track. They were forced to grip the railing after nearly falling into the seats. The absinthe still had its grip on them but was weakening, so their affection was tender – more genuine. Caleb's skin tingled when she touched him.

 There was nothing to interrupt them but their destination: an inevitability. Wherever there's movement, there's destination; wherever there's a means, there's an end. He would have given anything to push the destination far into the future, but the train ultimately stopped where it was destined to stop and they stepped out to the platform dimly lit by one red street lamp.

 They walked towards the hostel hand in hand. When the gravel road ended and the path emerged and eventually forked, they chose the trail that led into the woods instead of to the Boathouse. They passed the cement foundation of an old dwelling with rebar protruding from the ground like the old, rusty fingers of a buried palm.

 The path skirted closely, and cut between it and an old house, still fully erect and abandoned long ago. Caleb directed them until they were close to the exterior wall, tagged in graffiti; he coaxed her body up against it and in one quick decision, they gave into desire. He pressed his body into hers and explored her neck and chest with his lips until Joss pushed him away. She propelled herself from the wall and, keeping her hand closed tightly onto his, pulled him with her as she struck out into the woods.

 She didn't seem to have a destination in mind but when she stopped, they were in a small clearing, an opening where the moon could be seen through the trees. She pulled him into her and they kissed again until they were both on their knees. Their movements were clumsy and the sex was quick but satisfying. They lay naked and dirty and Caleb felt her hand across his chest.

She was lying beside him, just as he had dreamed many times, her legs stretched delicately into his; her small, round breasts lifting with each breath as her hand caressed his pelvis and inner thighs. He had been inside her and the scent of her was stuck to him. He had wanted this since he'd met her, and now that it was over, he felt vacant and tired.

They dressed again and walked back to the hostel. Caleb held her hand tighter than before. Her cheeks were flush, and felt warm when he pressed his lips against them. She had a complexion after intercourse that seemed unique to dark-haired girls of a northern climate, as though sex were a healthy way to keep warm in the cold. It radiated in her countenance; she was glowing when she asked him for a favour on the steps.

"Can you kiss me good night when we get back to our room? I mean, before we go to sleep? I guess it would help me to feel..." she paused. "I don't want to feel like a slut."

When they got to the door, he kissed her goodnight and held his mouth to her warm, red lips trying to stamp the moment into his memory. He was closer to the secret machine inside Joss' chest now, closer to understanding how it worked; and there was something familiar about it.

August 28, 1943

Dear Marie,
I hope this letter finds you well…and finds our son well! I hope you are showing him pictures of me so he can see my face. I long to hold him in my arms, to hold you both. Please rely on my mother as much as you need; she is eager to help.

      Things here are just fine. I've been training for what seems like an eternity, and the company of men I'm among, while they do seem to like me, have rather narrow views of the world and I've been hoping to find someone who will make a satisfactory companion. I think I've found it in Jack. He is earnest and honest; a respectable Irishman who has had to work for everything in his life. He has not been afforded much, and I admire that, as I have had it pretty easy in life – loving parents, a great girl, and a good education. He lost his parents when he was quite young and he's lived a poor life. But you wouldn't know it by the way he carries himself. He is very intelligent, so I value our conversations. They are helpful over here. You'd like him Marie. Who knows, maybe you'll get to meet him someday if this awful thing ever ends.

      I've been able to take a few short leaves here and I've seen some good movies that I think you'd like. I don't remember what the British one was called, but the American film was "Louisiana Purchase" and it was quite good.

      I like all your choices for our son's name and I'd be happy with Robert, but if you are open to it, I would suggest 'Jack'. Think on it, Marie. I wouldn't suggest it if it wasn't something I've thought a lot on myself. He embodies many things I want for our boy and he's been a good friend over here. Well the boys are starting to get loud in the mess and I'm going to head off to bed now.

Love always,
Patrick

11

Caleb spent days wandering the streets of Prague with Joss. He felt alive with her, but he knew there was a danger to being so open. He couldn't stop the nagging possibility that someone from back home would see them - that Melanie would find out.

They crossed the Charles Bridge every day to take in the music and merchants and beautiful Czech people that seemed to live life effortlessly. Life in Europe seemed more vibrant. The four of them took in soccer games and spent afternoons in cafes people watching. They found comfortable spots by the Vltava River to read and lie on the grass and let the afternoons pass lazily. He wanted to stay forever, but all good things end one way or another. They have to.

He noticed Miranda and Ryan becoming much closer in Prague as well. They would often spend their evenings in pubs playing pool, and while they all got along well during the day, alcohol and games brought out the competitiveness between Caleb and Ryan. Miranda and Joss often worked diplomatically to keep them from arguing too much over their viewpoints on war, social welfare, and sports. Caleb was learning that they didn't have much in common and the only thing that kept them together was the girls.

When Caleb asserted that people should have to apply for a licence to have children, Ryan disagreed.

"That's bullshit. Who's to decide who can have children and who can't? The very notion of it screams Maoist China to me" Ryan said.

"I don't see why anyone can just decide to make the biggest decision of their life, one that affects the rest of the world, and not have to demonstrate they're ready and competent. There are so many fucked up people in this world that are not fit to raise a kid and are doing a horrible job at it."

"I don't disagree with you," Ryan said. "But that doesn't mean we can just control people's ability to procreate. The world is always going to be full of fucked up people – it's a matter of ethics, really. We can't just take the things we don't like about the world and apply some dictator style solution to them. I mean, who would get to decide this? How do we decide who's fucked up and who's normal? I think many of the people we say are normal are really the ones that are fucked."

"Okay, now you're losing me. I don't think we need to decide who's deserving, but just make sure people are ready, you know? Apply for a license to have a kid to make sure the basics are going to be met. So many people have kids for the wrong reasons – they have them to get looked after by the government. I see it in Piersville all the time. Girls have babies so they can collect government support. And then these kids grow up and do the same thing. It becomes a cycle. There's something wrong with that."

"Well, there's something wrong with the way you want to fix it, man."

Joss took the opportunity to interject. "Who wants another round? On me....as long as we change the subject," she said and laughed nervously eyeing Miranda for support.

"I'm game," Miranda chimed in and gulped back her last sip.

"And let's play pool!" Joss said as she jumped and took them both by the hand and yanked hard.

By the third game, their tempers had subsided, but their competitiveness hinted at undercurrents of anger.

Overall, they felt happy together in Prague. They absorbed other travelers from time to time, but never let anyone seep into their group for longer than an evening. Miranda had worked hard at opening Ryan up a little and it worked. He seemed to trust her and in turn, she was beginning to understand him.

Caleb asked Ryan one night whether there was something going on with him and Miranda, but Ryan shrugged it off.

"I don't know man. She's just a cool girl. You should get to know her more."

"I've gotten to know her. I've been hanging out with them since before we met you."

"Ya, but you spend all your time with Joss. You barely speak to her. I think she feels it – feels a bit neglected by you two sometimes."

Caleb had noticed Miranda's tone was changing when she spoke to him at times, and was nervous she had overheard his conversation with Melanie in Prague. He could sense her discomfort at the relationship he was forming with Joss, and he grew uneasy knowing that he had let slip the one thing that could unravel everything. He still didn't know if she heard him on the phone in Interlaken and began to suggest in subtle ways that he and Joss spend more time alone. He wanted to split from Miranda and Ryan and devised ways he could initiate it. When Joss resisted, opting constantly to meet back with them, Caleb grew restless. He became dangerously vulnerable around her, which manifested in blatant attempts for her attention.

Ryan's strong, silent personality drew the women's attention more and diminished Caleb's value in the group. Ryan's indifference to the affairs of others belonged to his sense of respect for privacy, but Caleb assigned it to his habit of smoking weed throughout the day, which seemed to Caleb as an unfair way of seeming aloof and cool. Caleb had decided not to smoke around Joss, so he could absorb her completely, feel without any filters on his reactions. Alcohol was a better enhancer of his mood and one he could participate in with her; she didn't smoke weed. She had told Caleb in passing that she hadn't liked when her ex-boyfriend smoked and so he believed that applied to everyone.

After one of their usual walks across Charles Bridge, Caleb had convinced Joss to have dinner alone but when they ran into Ryan and Miranda, they decided to all eat together at a restaurant Miranda had scouted earlier that day.

He became sulky and resentful. He could have insisted, but he worried he would sound too reliant. They wandered the streets, and while the girls bounced from window to window, pointing and eyeing the expensive looking items laid out plainly and with hints of communist sensibility, Caleb and Ryan were forced to labour for long stretches in silence. They were both realizing how little they had in common.

Their stilted conversation was cut short by Joss' small frame bursting between them. She spun around, stopping them both with a hand on each arm. She had a wild look in her eyes.

"Let's get tattoos!" she said.

Caleb gave her a confused look and Ryan smiled at her spontaneity.

"Look." She pointed at a glass storefront with a large image of a woman's back with the words 'Bloody Blue Tattoo.' The word 'Bloody' was in red.

"I don't know. Let's think about it and come back tomorrow," Caleb said.

"No. It has to be now. Or we'll never do it," she said.

"We don't even know what we'd get."

"It's easy – Europe."

"I'm in," Ryan said and she high fived him aggressively.

"Come on Caleb, we're all in. Just say yes."

"Miranda?" Caleb looked to her for some sensibility.

"I know – it's crazy. But try saying no to this one," Miranda said and shot Joss a smile.

The parlour smelled like iodine and weed. The man behind the counter had one arm covered in ink and only half his other arm detailed. His neck was wrapped in images of flames and headless motorcyclists and there were a few words in Czech on his hands. Joss spelled out the word she wanted. She pointed to her foot and the large man took her money.

They waited on a couch underneath a wall covered with pictures of previous customers showing off their images inked over red, raw skin. Caleb wasn't concerned about the pain, but he didn't want to make such a quick decision on something that would stay with him for life. What if he got it in the wrong place? What if it he didn't like it after it was too late? There were too many things to regret.

"Where are you going to get it?" Joss asked and turned to him on the couch.

"I think my back."

"You should get it on your chest!" she said.

"You think so? Just the word 'Europe'? Won't it look weird there?"

She shook her head. Her eyes were wide.

"Where are you guys getting yours?" Caleb asked Ryan and Miranda.

Ryan pointed to his forearm and Miranda to her hip.

Caleb panicked for a second and felt like escaping. When his time came, he paid the large man and stepped over to the chair and laid down with his shirt off and pointed to the spot on the top of his chest beside his shoulder. The woman nodded, took out a razor and shaved his chest hair. She set the paper with the word 'Europe' on the chair beside his supine frame and went to work. The ink pen buzzed below his ear as he looked away, out the window into the street. He watched two young boys run away from their mother and play fight on the sidewalk. They both made their hands into guns and pretended to shoot each other from a short distance while their mother tried to gather them. One of the boys reacted to the play by grabbing at his chest and falling to the ground.

The first contact on his skin felt foreign, but it didn't hurt. He would describe it later as a tickling sensation. It moved across his upper chest in a deliberate motion until the buzzing stopped and she wiped away the blood and ink with her gloved hand and signalled for him to look. He craned his neck to see it and his first reaction was that he had made a mistake. He didn't like it. But it was there, glistening in fresh black ink over raw skin. Joss stepped up to see it before the bandages went on and she smiled in encouragement.

"I love it," she said. "Do you?"

"Love it," he said and put his shirt back on.

"Miranda's having second thoughts. I think we're ready to go as soon as you get your cream."

"What?" Caleb said, angered. "She's not getting one? I thought we were all...."

"I guess it's just you, me and Ryan. Oh well. We can't force her. She doesn't want to."

"But I wasn't sure and I did it anyways," Caleb said, his temperature rising. He wondered why he hadn't just said no, too. A strange anger welled up inside him. He walked past them into the street and Joss followed and put her arm around his.

"I think yours is sexy. Do you like mine?"

He wasn't in a mood to be cheered up but smiled and said he did. He was angry with Miranda, but respected her, at least, for voicing her concern and standing up to the pressure. He had been weak, and that's what bothered him most.

They walked along the streets for an hour and when Caleb stopped to sit down, Joss joined him, knowing he was still upset. Miranda came back and told them the restaurant was just around the corner and to look for the name 'Bertoldi's'. Joss comforted him for a little while by stroking his arm until they started walking again. When they turned the corner, they could see an older couple sitting in the window eating pasta. The sign was barely noticeable but held the name in a faded green above the entrance.

When they stepped into the restaurant, they were greeted warmly with a broken 'hello' and a smile. The hostess, a young woman with a soft face and pinned back hair, showed them to their table in the corner where it was dark. She proceeded to light a small candle that offered enough radiance to read the menus. Miranda chose the wine, and Joss joked in a snobby British accent that it was an excellent choice.

The conversation was sharp and funny and tense at times. They started to feel loose from the wine and Caleb was trying to let go of his resentment. He watched Joss try to peel back the bandage on Ryan's forearm until he stopped resisting and let her. She made a shocked face at the sight of his tattoo and laughed. Caleb reached down to find Joss' hand and squeezed it lightly to let her know he was there; it caught her off guard and she smiled in a gesture her eyes didn't fully support.

Another bottle of wine arrived, and then a third. Caleb's sips were becoming more frequent and he received a look from Joss when he filled his glass again.

"Can you save some for the rest of us?" Miranda said in a joking tone, but he felt embarrassed for being called out. He was not used to drinking so much wine but he needed it to lessen the grip of regret. It made him feel good, but it loosened his tongue.

He didn't know when the balance of the group had shifted. He knew he looked weak in front of them at the tattoo parlour, but he resented them for putting him in that position.

The exchanges between Joss and Ryan seemed too frequent for his liking. They began their own conversation and while Caleb spoke to Miranda across the table, he was only half present in the dialogue, much more aware of the words being spoken beside him.

When Caleb interrupted their conversation with a laboured, unnecessary cheers, Ryan laughed and continued speaking to Joss about his adventures snowboarding in Whistler. Caleb realized his rash, foolish act and felt stupid but it was too late to salvage his composure so he went ahead with his provocations.

"So, you lived in Whistler eh? Did you actually board or just sit around and smoke weed all the time?" It was meant to sound witty, but no one took it that way. Ryan didn't care for it and laughed again, which angered Caleb even more.

"I've heard Whistler's a great place for stoners. Never been there before, but I'm not rich…" Caleb burped. "….like you".

Miranda called him out. "Caleb – I don't think that's fair. Listen, why don't we grab the bill and head back to the hostel. I think everyone's getting pretty tired."

Joss nodded and shot an irritated glance at Caleb like a displeased wife.

"Ya, go sleep it off, pal," Ryan said.

"It's jus' you can't hide behind weed. You're brother's gone. Pain's always gonna be there," Caleb said.

"What the fuck do you know about pain, man?" Ryan bellowed at him, and stood up.

Miranda decided she wasn't interested in the direction things were going and stood up to open her money belt to pay the bill.

Caleb turned and said. "Oh, what the fuck, Miranda. You're leaving?"

"I don't like the way you're acting. You're drunk. Anyone who wants to come with me is welcome to," she said, looking at Joss and Ryan.

Caleb eyed her angrily. "Well, at least pay the whole bill. You've got a lot more money than we do since you *didn't* get a tattoo." He looked to Joss and Ryan for support.

"Maybe you shouldn't have gotten one. We all saw how red your face was afterward. It was embarrassing."

"Miranda," Joss interjected.

"I'm not interested in this tonight. If he wants to get drunk and act like an asshole, that's up to him. He's been in a bad mood ever since we met up with you guys today."

Caleb had lost control and everyone knew the wine was partly to blame, but it didn't lessen the gravity of the words he then said at half volume almost to himself: "Jesus. No wonder your husband left you."

Miranda didn't react immediately. She had also had some wine, but in a level-headed response to something she could have easily slapped him for, she focused her attention on Caleb in an exacting stare and said simply: "And which reason will your girlfriend choose to leave you when you get home?"

Joss turned to Miranda and then to Caleb. "Wait. What Girlfriend?"

"I don't have a girlfriend," Caleb said. "Easy Miranda."

"I heard you on the phone that day in Interlaken. I've been struggling with it. I wanted to think it was a family member, but I knew deep down it was your girlfriend. I should have told you Joss, I'm sorry. He's got a girlfriend back home. He told her he loved her on the phone."

Joss looked at him. "Tell her she's wrong." She waited. He couldn't look at her. "It's true isn't it?"

"Hmmm, kind of," he said, and poured himself another glass of wine.

Miranda laughed and said "Ya, that's a real good idea. Drink more wine."

Joss just shook her head in disbelief. "Unbelievable" she said and walked out ahead of everyone. Ryan and Miranda looked at each other and Ryan put some money on the table. "Nice work pal," he said, and walked out with Miranda.

Caleb gave them the finger as they left and drank the glass in one gulp. He reached into his pocket for some money and found an old train ticket and his passport. He shrugged and went to fill his glass again.

When the waiter returned to the table to collect empty glasses, Caleb pulled down the collar of his shirt and revealed the white gauze on his chest.

"Look what they made me do," he said.

"You are....wounded?" the waiter asked in a confused tone.

"Something like that," Caleb said and wandered out of the restaurant.

He walked until he found a payphone. The booth was plastered with pictures of naked women, phone numbers and foreign words scrawled in black marker. The light inside flickered unnervingly revealing cigarette burns in the black plastic. The only sound was the faint rumble of tracks vibrating in the distance. Caleb fumbled beneath his pants with his right hand in a perverted struggle to find his money belt and held the receiver to his ear with his left hand. He pulled out his calling card and started dialling – slowly at first but the rhythm increased until all twelve numbers were inputted. He waited.

'Hello?' Melanie's voice sounded sexy to him when she was tired. It was raspy though the cadence was still graceful.

 "It's meeee."

"I thought it might be," she said flatly.

"Bad timing?"

"No, it's fine. I'm just watching ER – I taped it."

"Ah, I see....I didn't mean to interrupt your Clooney time!" Caleb laughed awkwardly.

"It's okay. Are you drunk?"

"I wish I was there watching it with you," he said and hiccupped.

"You're drunk."

"Yup," he said and hiccupped again. "I remember when we used to curl up on the couch and watch TV. Those were the days."

"Don't start that Cal. You can't just call me up drunk and get sentimental. What do you want me to say?"

"What, I can't tell you I miss you now? I do miss you so much."

Melanie didn't respond.

"I was jus' thinking maybe it was time I came home," he said.

"What would you be coming home for? You've already missed Tyler's funeral." There was a long pause. She sighed. "You made it all the way over there. You should at least spend some time traveling. Who knows when you'll get to take a trip like that again? I think you'd regret it if you came home this early."

"Fuck regrets. What, you don't miss me anymore? I thought you of all the people would convince me to come home. Jus' think, I could take my real estate courses, like you and my dad want me to do. We could talk about starting a family. Maybe look into houses. Maybe it's jus' time for all that now."

"I don't know, Cal. When you left the way you did, the part of me that thought I would always need you...well, it kind of went too. I guess it might have been the last straw for me. I realized that I don't deserve to be treated like that. Not even by you. What I'm saying is...I don't think we should talk for awhile."

Caleb hiccupped abruptly, and tried to hide it by speaking quickly. "Can't you forgive me for that? I know I messed up bad, Mel, but I want to make things right with us."

"Forgive you for what exactly, Cal? I don't even know where to start. Plus, I'd rather not talk to you when you're drunk."

"I was jus' out with some friends. Well, they don't really like me right now, but..." Caleb let another hiccup go. "I miss you, Mel. I want to come home." He ran his fingers down the pictures of half nude women in the telephone booth. "How's Tyler doing? I mean his family." He paused. "Not him obviously."

"They're doing horribly. They don't leave the house. We try to stop by as much as possible, but you know...people start to move on with their lives. But how are they supposed to? He was in the prime of his life and now he's gone. It's all so weird, like we're living in some movie right now. There are reporters all over town trying to interview us and we just want things to get back to normal. I've really just needed you here, but I've gotten used to you not being around. I don't care if you come home or not at this point. I'm over the worst of it. I really feel that way right now. I don't know – I don't know what to say to you. I guess it doesn't matter – you probably won't remember it in the morning anyways."

"I'll remember. I will. Jus' tell me what you were going to say."

"I don't want you to call me anymore."

Caleb didn't respond. The words affected him physically.

"Listen, Cal. I have to run. I've got someone coming over for dinner, and I have to get ready. Can I ask you one question, though?"

"Ask away," he said belligerently.

"Have you even reached out to Tyler's family since you left? A phone call, an email? Have you at least done that? I mean it's one thing to treat me like shit, you know....maybe I deserve it, but his family was always good to you. His parents loved you. I have nothing to tell them when they ask about you."

"I've been trying to, but I've just been moving around so much. So much has happened over here Mel. I want to tell you about it. You're the one I want to tell all about it. Don't you see that? That's why I'm calling you. I want to start making things right."

"Oh, Caleb." A deep sigh escaped her lips. "Well, they've stopped asking. I really have to go. I hope you find what you're looking for over there. Goodbye Caleb."

Caleb hung up without saying goodbye.

He wandered out of the phone booth and into the streets of Prague. He had nowhere to go. There was a mist hanging over the Vlatva River so he sat down on the river wall and stared into the fog. He had always had an innate urge to jump whenever he approached an edge. He had had it since he was a kid. It was a harmless feeling, but one that he didn't understand. Sitting along the river, with his legs dangling like a child, he looked down to the water below and considered releasing himself into it. He didn't want to die; he just wanted the shock. He wanted to feel the cold water surround him. He wanted to see if he could survive it. But he didn't fall. He lay on his back and looked up to the night sky.

"We're all in the gutter" he said, "but some of us are looking at the stars."

September 25, 1943

Dear Patrick,
God, how I miss you. You last letter arrived and I keep reading it over and over. It sounds like Jack has become a good chum to you. I think it's important to have someone to confide in, someone to call a friend. Maybe I'll get to meet him one day. And yes, I agree that Jack is a fine name, and I would like to honour the man who's become such a confidant to you. If our son grows up to be brave, kind, and intelligent, then I believe we'd be very happy.

I'm sending a care package from the ladies at the Church. I don't think there will be cigarettes, but there should be a jar of honey and some of Hannah's fudge, which I'm sure will be a hit with the guys. I'm also sneaking a few pictures of our son in the package. Jack is getting bigger every day it seems. He's a heavy boy and testing my strength. He looks so much like you. Even your parents said when they came to visit last.

You wouldn't believe what Phenon said the other day in conversation – the most horrible thing – that he'd rather invest in the Germans than fight against them. I almost slapped him. He can be so insensitive sometimes. He knows how much my heart hurts right now as you're over there. He still thinks you should have stayed home, and sometimes, I do too. I know it's selfish, but I do feel that way sometimes. This war has gone on for too long – Phenon was right about that. At least now that the Yanks are involved, it might speed things up. I keep reading positive accounts in the newspapers. I think about you all the time. Stay safe my dear.

All my love,
Marie

12

When Caleb awoke, it was close to noon and his body felt depleted. He wasn't used to the type of headache red wine brought.

Scenes from last night flickered through his mind – the restaurant, the phone booth, the river - but everything was dark after that. The last thing he remembered was having a cigarette on the patio; then someone trying to help him up and another coming out to scold him. He turned over onto his stomach and buried his head under his pillow. He wanted to sleep forever.

Why hadn't he been able to keep Joss at a safe distance? When did he become the vulnerable one? He went to the patio for a smoke and ran into Tim and Marshall.

"Bloody miracle you're alive mate!" Tim said as they both laughed and Marshall punched him in the shoulder on his way by. Caleb raised his eyebrows indifferently and grunted.

He only finished half a cigarette and went inside. When he found Joss, she was reading on the couch and wouldn't look at him. Her eyes had stopped moving across the page. He sat down next to her and she finally glanced at him quickly, inconvenienced by his presence. She turned her book over and placed it gently on her lap. Her hair had fallen down over her face and she made no attempt to fix it.

"Melanie," said Caleb.

"What?"

"Her name is Melanie. We've been together since high school. We did break up before I came here....actually, *because* I came here. Then we sort of got back together. I think. I don't really know."

"You love her?"

Caleb thought for a few seconds. "Ya, I think so. "

"Why did you leave then?"

"It's complicated" Caleb winced and averted his eyes. She wasn't satisfied and looked at him deeply. He raised his chin and scratched his beard. "I felt trapped. I wasn't ready to settle, so I freaked out and left."

He pictured Melanie caring for her father alone, just the two of them in a lonely house where Caleb had spent countless Sunday afternoons watching football and trying to make conversation with a sick man.

"I just needed to get away for awhile and experience something new," he said.

"Like having sex with me?"

"Yes, like having sex with you," he said. There were no more lies. It was clear to him that whatever they had was over the only currency he had left with her was the truth.

"I saw myself as this husband and father, working some job I hated, trying to convince myself I was happy, ignoring what else was out there. Here. Whatever this is. I didn't plan on meeting someone like you. She did ask me not to hook up with anyone, and I promised I wouldn't, but we were broken up."

"Because she wanted things to work out when you got home. And deep down, so do you"

"Maybe. Although I'm pretty sure she hates me anyways for leaving when I did. My friend died the day before I left." He snorted.

"Jesus. So you *were* there when that shooting happened? Why did you lie?"

"I don't know. I didn't want to think about it, I guess. I was far enough away."

"That's not a healthy way of dealing with things, Caleb. You left your girlfriend for a trip to Europe after your friend had been killed? What kind of a person does that?" She pondered that thought. "Why didn't you just bring her with you? Why didn't you guys both come over here....together?"

"Her dad's been sick. She lost her mother when she was young, so she takes care of him." Hearing the words leave his mouth filled him with self-loathing.

"I don't know what to say, Caleb. I would go back to your girlfriend if she'll still have you. It sounds like she's a pretty understanding girl if she's still talking to you."

"But maybe I'm supposed to be here, experiencing Europe with you." He unconsciously touched his tattoo on his chest. It was still itchy and raw.

"That's the thing Caleb, I feel like we have a connection too. I feel comfortable around you. That's why this is so hard. But part of that comfort was assuming you were single, that what we were doing wasn't based on bunch of lies."

"But I wasn't lying to you, Melanie and I aren't really together.

"But you're still in love with her."

"Listen, you told me that deviation is the most important thing when traveling. Well, I've deviated from my life completely – I've left it behind."

"Have you told her about us?"

He could sense this question was important to her.

"No," he said.

"So, you haven't even been honest with her either?"

"I'm kind of living for myself right now."

"I can see that. Maybe you're not the person I thought you were," she said and paused. "I came on this trip to un-complicate my life. I'm confused about you right now and it's not where I want to be. I just don't trust you." There was another long pause. "I think we should go our separate ways."

Caleb knew those words were coming and it hurt him more than he led on.

"Can you answer me something honestly?" he asked and looked her in the eye.

She nodded her head in a movement that loosened tears from her eyes. They stopped on her upper lip and quivered there until she moved her mouth and then they ran down into her mouth. She tried to wipe them off and smile stoically.

"Do you have feelings for Ryan?" he asked.

She gave Caleb a sad smile. He had made it easy for her to run away the previous night, but there was nowhere to run this time.

"I think I do."

His heart sank. He felt a sudden distance from her.

"It came on suddenly when I realized I was jealous of the time Miranda was spending with him. But I was enjoying my time with you so much that it didn't matter. I know Miranda likes him a lot so things are getting a little weird between us. And I don't know why she didn't tell me about hearing you on the phone. I'm worried that when you leave, nothing will be the same. Our little group is falling apart. What a mess."

Caleb sat in front of a quiet Japanese couple and pulled his shoes off and curled his feet up under his day pack in the empty seat beside him. He rested his head against the bus window as water streamed down the pane. The rain seemed much more violent now that they were moving. He knew there was a safety to standing still but it was stillness that made him numb in the first place.

'Was it possible to be in love with two women at once?' he wondered. They both lived in different dimensions of his life – they belonged to different continents, one attached to movement and one attached to stillness. Would he love Melanie if he met her over here, living this life in flux? Would he feel the same about Joss if they moved to Piersville and stood still? Maybe love for a person had to be combined with love for a place. He loved Melanie at a time when he loved being in his small town. He met Joss while being seduced by Europe. But in this new space, one of struggle between movement and stillness, he felt attached to them both.

The bus was gently rocking in the arms of the wind as it eased its way south along the E50 highway, and put Caleb's thoughts to rest for awhile as he tucked his feet up into the empty seat beside him and rested his head against the window. He needed something to hold onto. He pulled out his bundle of letters and noticed the rain had reached one of the envelopes. It was wet along one side. He removed the letter and it too was damp along one crease line.

January 1, 1944

Dear Marie,
Happy New Year! I hope the New Year brings you what you want, which is everything isn't it? Well, maybe just for the war to end and for me to come home. That is all I want – to see your face again. I received the package you sent. Thanks for the honey – it has been nice to take a spoonful of at the end of the day. And don't worry about the cigarettes - everyone here is pretty generous. There is a certain type of camaraderie that I never experienced with my classmates at school.

Prime Minister King came to visit the Canadian Army over here to rally the troops, but I don't think it worked quite as he hoped. The men here are looking for action, to fight the Germans, not protect the south of England and train constantly. I hope we ship out one of these days, but I know you want me to stay put my dear. I love that you think of me, but please don't worry about me darling. I'll be coming home to you soon enough and we'll get to finish our honeymoon. We'll make up for all the lost time by spending every minute together.

Anyways, it's getting too dark, so I better call it a night. My candle is flickering, but my love for you is strong. I'm sorry for the short letter, but I'll make it up in the next one. I'm feeling lonely tonight and want to head off to sleep and dream of you.

All my love,
Patrick

He lay staring out the window thinking about these two figures who had kept their love strong with so much distance between them. Did they ever question it? He wished he could talk to them now, to find out what they found strength in, but their lives were so far from his own. He had only known his grandmother until he was twelve, and his grandfather died the year he was born. There was so much to ask him. How did he handle the pain of being so far away from home for so long? Caleb had learned a lot about himself in Europe, but felt no closer to his grandfather. Maybe he didn't need to come all the way across the ocean; maybe he could have found more connection at the cottage he built after the war, the cottage Caleb grew up visiting. His father took them there every summer for weeks on end, but he never realized how important it was to his family. His grandfather's handprint was everywhere – the walls, the chimney, the deck, the trails he blazed around the lake. Yet Caleb had never stopped to notice. Instead, he flew across the ocean to find him in the place he spent his years missing home and losing hope. It occurred to Caleb that Europe might not be able to close the gap for him. If he didn't find some connection in Torquay, he thought, he would return home having gained nothing but a perspective on how much the continent had changed, and how lonely life can be at times.

He fell asleep and dreamed a long dream: he was sitting in a café in a city he didn't know. The book in his hands had a comfortable, familiar shape, but it wasn't clear what story he was reading. Across the café there was a woman he recognized, a scarf wrapped around her neck and cloaked in long flowing jacket. She didn't look at him, but he kept his gaze on the side of her face. The way she crossed her legs intrigued him. He put out his cigarette and carried his coffee with him to sit beside her. When she looked at him, it was with a curious stare. He said hello, but she said nothing; she looked sad. He asked her name but she wouldn't tell. She said she had to go, and as she turned to leave, he noticed a smile cross her lips. She was gone, but her book remained. He opened it in search of a clue. Her name was scrawled inside the back cover. He repeated the name to himself and loved the mellifluous sound it made when he spoke it out loud. He repeated it to himself over and over. He waited for her to return but she never did. He walked through streets he didn't recognize. He saw her ahead and called her name; she turned to see him and smiled. She told him she knew they would meet again. He gave her the book and she told him she left it for him. She led him to her loft apartment, up a long wooden flight of steps. He could smell the coffee grinds of the café below. She took her clothes off and they made love on her large bed. When she left the room, she never returned and he went to find her. She was sitting alone at the bottom of the steps crying. He wanted to comfort her but he stepped over her and walked out into the rain. His father pulled up in a van and told him to get in. He looked back to say goodbye but she was gone.

    The pressure of cold metal on his skin woke him from his dream.

    "Vake up! Passport……Passport"

February 10, 1944

Dear Marie,
I've just come from the nurse's station where they've stitched me up after some card tossed a piece of a shell in the salvage yard. Hit me square in the head. I had some choice words for him, let me tell you. Jack went and gave him a piece of his mind as well. Some of the privates are rather careless and it worries me for when we're deployed.

    Paterson came by my bunk the other day and asked to borrow my sergeant's jacket for a dance he was going to. Don't worry – I told him no. Some of the men think they'll have a better chance with a sergeant's jacket on, but I told him to just be himself and be a gentleman – a bit of a paradox for Paterson! I asked Jack if he was going to the dance, but he's been writing to a sweetheart at ▮▮▮▮ (I can't say what that is but you may have read about it in the papers) I've been warned not to say much in these letters and I don't know what you're reading at home. But Jack is quite smitten with her and she seems like lovely woman. I'm happy he has someone to write to. It makes a world of difference.

    It's been hard to sleep lately. We sure do hear the moaning of the bombs over here but they say that if you can hear them, they're not very close. I guess if one hits, I'll never hear it coming! I'm sorry to kid about these things, dear, I know you don't like me to. But it helps to joke about things sometimes. You should hear some of the jokes the guys tell – I'd never heard any of them before and to be honest, I don't imagine I'll repeat any of them to you. I'm amongst a good group of men, though. They all want to see action and get this bloody thing over with so we can all return back home. Some of the men have no one to return to except their mother and father and I'm glad I have you and our son to come home to. I look at the pictures you send all the time. I can't wait to feel you in my arms.

All my love,
Patrick

13

Birds fluttered from table to table pecking at day old crumbs and sugar packets as Caleb stepped onto the patio with a coffee in his hand. It was a quiet morning and like all quiet mornings, the coffee tasted better in measured sips. A matronly woman was working on a crossword a few tables over and a young couple sat silently sipping tea at another, but Caleb preferred his table on the edge of the terrace. The coffee was strong and too hot to drink right away. He chased the rising steam away with his breath, and cupped the mug in both hands and the warm ceramic eased the morning chill.

    He had slept well, and for the first time in days showed no signs of a hangover. The bus had rolled into the bucolic green estate the previous night revealing a Viennese view soaked in gothic beauty.

    It had been a long bus ride and Caleb had fallen asleep soon after checking into his room. When he awoke, it was alongside the rising sun - a sight he wasn't used to. He wandered the grounds in a reflective mood and drank his coffee overlooking a city painted in crisp, pastel brush strokes. Each one represented a rooftop or a park or a set of manicured trees. He felt like he could reach out and take each building in his hand like a piece of Lego.

    Now on his second coffee of the day, he was happy to watch people come and go for breakfast. He opened a letter to keep him company, but his attention was quickly taken by a young man walking across the patio. He was too young to be traveling alone, and Caleb watched his mother greet him with a warm embrace. Her hand graced the top of his head as she fixed his hair. He resisted and tossed it back across his face.

The woman said something to the couple a few tables down and they laughed, which caused the teenager to slump further down in his chair and open his book.

Each morning, Caleb watched him join his mother in this fashion. He recognized the slow, sluggish movements the boy made; it reminded him of the way he, himself, felt in the morning. His soul was not of a balanced kind that communed with the sunrise and morning dew. The chirping of birds was not something he usually revelled in, but was often a thing of annoyance when he was trying to sleep late after a long night. It became such routine that even when he hadn't had to work, he had just stayed up late in servitude to the habit. Melanie had often chided him for not coming to bed with her, but he had always, in truth, enjoyed the late hours flipping through channels with a beer in his hand. There was a comfort to it.

He was only now beginning to understand the attraction of the early morning and the serenity that came along with rising before the sun. His senses seemed heightened – every sound seemed clearer, every smell sweeter and every face more earnest. It was a new kind of comfort, one that carried on throughout the day. He was much more self-possessed because of it.

He only said 'good morning' to the woman and her son, but that somehow equalled a full conversation with someone he might meet in a pub at night under the influence of alcohol where words are full of hyperbole, emotion, and irony. The two words spoken in his morning encounters were earnest and carried more truth than whole conversations at night.

When he said good morning to her on the third occasion, she did more than just glance up from her book, smile warmly, and wish him a good morning. She had been waiting for his greeting and placed her book down and followed him to his table, introducing herself as Franny. Her presence was palliative. Her hair, pulled back in a ponytail streaked with grey, fell heavily down her back. Her clothes flowed elegantly across her body, and a scarf that was wrapped carefully around her neck, spilled down over her chest. Her smell was familiar, like incense – something that had wafted through his nose many times but could never attach a word to.

She pointed to the birds pecking at crumbs on the lawn. "Do you know what type of birds these are?" she asked.

"No, actually. Do you?"

"No fucking clue," she said and laughed. Her eyes were soft and knowing. A smile still seemed to convulse at the corners of her mouth ready to turn into laughter again. She was a handsome woman, intelligent looking. Her attractiveness had been hardened by age with a face full of hidden fossils that were dug up each time she talked. The juxtaposition of her stature and her language hinted that she was easy to confide in.

"Can I ask you something?" she said and continued without a response. "I've seen you down here for the last few mornings looking like your dog just died and then you mope around the property on your own. Why aren't you partying with all the other people your age? Where is the beautiful woman in your life?" Her tone was direct and her words could have come off as offensive, but Caleb was comfortable responding.

"I think I've done enough partying lately. I think it's what's caused the beautiful women in my life to leave me."

"*Women?* – you've got a few of them do you?" When she laughed, her eyes squinted and her upper lip retracted, uncovering her teeth. It was a facial gesture that would have caused men in her youth to desire her. Caleb looked closely at her face and couldn't tell her age.

"Ya, there's two of them. Well, none now, but there were two"

"Let me guess – one at home and one over here. Where are you from? Michigan…New York?"

"Ontario. And yes," he said. He trusted her like she was his parent. But she wasn't and so he didn't have to worry about the guilt of letting her down.

"Hmmm. Well, sometimes a man needs two women in his life to make him realize that he can truly only have one," she said and tossed some crumbs for the birds.

As they talked, Caleb noticed her son following their interaction, having folded his book neatly in his lap.

"Daniel and I are on an adventure. I pulled him out of school this spring and we've been traveling Europe. He was born in Holland so we've been staying with my family," she said and looked back in the direction of her son "he needs some real-world experience before he goes back to school."

"Was he struggling?"

"He wasn't prepared for the workload and pressure and all the people in academia who didn't give a shit about him. He's a fragile boy. A mother can say that about her son."

Caleb looked over and thought his boyish good looks and wavy hair must afford him some attention from girls his age. But he could tell there was a sadness about him, something that made him seem vulnerable.

"He's a sweet, curious kid," Franny continued. "I've put my doctorate work on hold to bring him here. Maybe college isn't for him."

"It wasn't for me. I could never figure out what I wanted to take, so I didn't want to pay all that money for something I wasn't sure about."

"What kind of work have you been doing?"

"Well, there aren't too many options for someone with a high school diploma, but bartending works just fine for me. I make decent money, I work with fun, outgoing people and I never have to wake up early."

"What does your girlfriend do?"

"She's a nurse," Caleb said. He remembered how clear of a choice it was for her after her mom's cancer. She always told him how good the nurses were with her. They had made the ordeal easier and she knew she wanted to do the same for others. For Caleb, there had never been anything in this life that had been as clear for him until the thought of traveling Europe entered his mind.

They watched a group of people wander onto the veranda with menus in their hands and take a table near the railing.

"Does he have a girlfriend?" Caleb said and nodded at Daniel.

"Why don't you ask him yourself? Join us this afternoon. We're planning to go to the Schonbrunner Gardens. We could meet for lunch at noon and then take a bus out. I know Daniel would enjoy having someone other than his mother to talk to for awhile, especially a cool, young man like yourself, and you can do without a day of moping around ignoring everyone."

Caleb hated the thought of being regarded like Ryan and he agreed to the offer. He was beginning to get lonely in Vienna on his own and he had enjoyed chatting with Franny. There was nothing pretentious about her. He could let his guard down and stop performing for a while.

"Schonbrunn means 'beautiful spring,'" said Franny as she took an available seat near the front of the bus. Caleb and Daniel stood above her and clasped the railing. "I think it refers to a nearby spring, or possibly the Wien River." She looked up at them. "Are you guys excited?"

"I am" Daniel said. "I've read the Baroque architecture is mind-blowing!" He opened his travel guide and pointed to the picture of the Palace overlooking the gardens and then closed it quickly to steady himself on the handrail as the bus rattled around a sharp turn. "What's your favourite thing so far in Europe?" Daniel asked Caleb eagerly. He was young and curious, a slender boy, whose face was handsome but with no signs of ruggedness.

"Well, it isn't exactly a tourist attraction," said Caleb, "but I really enjoyed Prague. It was very different from any city I've ever been to."

"How so?"

"Hmmm, I guess it just had a really cool mix of old and new. I enjoyed walking along the Charles Bridge," he said and leaned in close to whisper, "and the women." He glanced at Franny to see if she heard. She did, and she smiled.

The bus arrived at Schonbrunn just after one o'clock and everyone shuffled off into the sunshine.

As they wandered into the maze of gardens, Daniel stuck close to Caleb. He was never a few steps behind even when Franny stopped to take in an eyeful.

"Do you have a girlfriend?" Daniel asked as he hustled to his side.

"I did." Caleb said and turned to him smiling faintly. "I didn't treat her very well. I don't think she wants to stay together."

"Her loss," Daniel said.

"What about you?"

"There was one girl at college. Did my mom tell you I went to college?"

"Ya, she mentioned you did a year."

"Well, not a full year." He looked lost for a second as he looked up at the giant archways. They both stopped and marvelled at the Roman brickwork, still structurally sound after two thousand years. They waited for Franny to catch up. She was much more interested in the intricacies of the garden than they were. She was still far behind them buried in her tourist brochure.

"I didn't finish my exams because I got run down. My mom said it was for my health."

"Well, that's none of my business, but we all get run down sometimes. I would like to hear more about this girl that caught your eye. What was her name?"

"Vivian. She was in my biology class. She was *really* smart. I told her she should have been doing a pure maths degree."

"What was it about her?"

"It was everything. She would always come to class wearing this red beret. She sat in front of me, so she was pretty difficult to miss. I would go early just so I could watch her walk into class. I think she knew. She wore these tall boots that went up to her knees." He placed his hand at his knee in a chopping motion. "And she always wore a long rain coat, even when it wasn't raining. She was very interesting. But she was so pretty. Most of the other guys made fun of her. They couldn't see past the strange outfits. But she didn't care what other people thought. I found that out after we got to know each other. I think that was the part about her that drove me crazy." He stopped and grabbed Caleb's arm. "In a good way."

"The ones worth spending time with are the ones that you can never seem to understand. I don't think I ever really got to understand Melanie – that's my girlfriend's name."

"Your ex-girlfriend. It's best to start saying it that way. Believe me. I learned that with Vivian."

"So, what happened then?"

"Well, it's a long story, but let's just say I messed up," Daniel said as Franny caught up to them.

"Is he telling you about Vivian?" Franny asked.

"Yes, mother. Please don't belittle her. She was important to me."

"I know dear; she was a part of your life for a month and she's become more important to you than your own mother," Franny said eyeing the Neptune Fountain and suggesting they stop for rest.

"It's only you who needs a rest Mother," Daniel said. "Why don't you sit down for awhile, and Caleb and I can keep walking for a bit. We'll come back and meet you here."

Franny agreed.

They walked on and circled the fountain before turning left along one of the garden's neatly cropped walkways. A group of schoolgirls passed them with their schoolmaster walking sternly behind shouting something in German to the unruly group.

"It drives me crazy thinking about her with some other guy, revealing herself to him in little ways until he understands her in a way I never did," Daniel said.

"So, I'm assuming you had a tough time getting over her?"

"The last thing she said to me was that I was just a boy and I would never understand what a woman needs and then she went inside and locked her door. That was the last time I saw her. I didn't go to class for the exam review 'cause I wanted to avoid her and then my mother made me quit school right before exams. I don't really remember that time very clearly."

"Can I be honest?"

Daniel nodded.

"I don't think you want to be involved with a girl like that – sure, she's interesting, but it sounds like she needs to figure some things out herself before she can be in a relationship with someone. When you build a relationship with a girl who's ready to be with you for who you are, you'll realize how good it can be – what love really is. And it will happen, believe me, and you'll have to work hard at keeping it good, but you will. You're going to have some great relationships with girls in your life. You have a lot of things that other guys don't have and girls will realize that. You're a European traveler now."

Daniel blushed and thanked him.

Franny was back in their sights as they turned the corner and faced the Neptune Fountain again. She was sitting calmly on the same bench where they left her. She didn't notice them until they were only a few metres away.

"The men are back from their adventure in the Gardens….and they look hungry. Let's go eat!"

The café was busy and the waiter was taking a long time to come by for their order. As they discussed the highlights of their day, they took turns gazing out over the serpentine paths of the grounds.

"You're stuck with us now, Caleb. I hope you don't plan on ditching us," she said.

Caleb laughed "Where would I go?"

Daniel stood up and excused himself to use the washroom. "We'd love to keep hanging with you." He said and he tucked his chair in.

"It's nice for him to have another man around," Franny said as her son was out of ear shot.

"I wouldn't worry about him too much. He's going through a tough phase, but he's just trying to figure himself out. Life can be tough for sensitive guys."

"I can see similarities in the two of you. I noticed that right away when we met. I think you're going through a tough phase too, Caleb and I hope you find someone to talk to about it. Someone who helps you figure out who you are. It can't always be a woman. Sometimes it takes another man – a father figure. Do you have a father in your life?"

"Yes."

"Can you talk to him?"

Caleb didn't answer right away. "I could. I don't, but I could. We have a good relationship, but we don't talk about what's going on in our lives. I'm not sure we understand each other sometimes."

"I'll tell you a secret – no father and son really understand each other. There's not a more complicated relationship in the world. I get so frustrated with the way Jonas and my boys communicate sometimes….or don't communicate - that's really the problem."

"I guess guys aren't that good at talking about their feelings."

"It's more than that, though. There's something preventing them from it that I've been trying to figure out. I've tried incorporating the idea into some of my seminar courses over the years. I've been taking a series of courses on constructs in our modern world. The modern man is a fascinating one. A lot has to do with the gaze and how it falls on the father. Every man can look at his father and see himself in certain ways – the paternal-reflective gaze, I call it. It is important for every man to see himself in his father. It helps him understand who he is, but conversely, who he can avoid to become if he chooses. But the father is not only a reflective agent; he is also a gateway to the other side of paternalism."

"What's that?" Caleb said, struggling to follow.

"The other man – the grandfather. The even more distant one, but the one whose connection can be more accessible. The son can see through his father to his grandfather, as well. And that's where it gets interesting – when the son becomes a father and then grandfather. He moves from being on one side of the glass to the other, and in between he is the reflective agent. It's one long cycle and by the time he has become the grandfather, he can see himself in his son and see through his son to what his grandson will grow up to be like. But it takes that long for a man to truly understand himself and be able to discuss his feelings truly."

"I never got to know my grandfather. He died when I was young. I don't even have memories of him, just pictures and a few letters. But I'm not sure if your idea about older men being able to open up and discuss their feelings is right. My dad said grandpa never wanted to talk about his life, especially the war."

"Interesting – so you never really got to know each other, your grandfather and you?"

Caleb shook his head.

"That's where my theory really seems to fit, because the only way to access him is through your father – you have to look to him to understand who your grandpa was. And your grandfather had to use your father to understand who you might become – which aspects of his son you might embody."

"I hope not – he'd be pretty disappointed," said Caleb.

"Don't say such things. That's part of the problem. Men are always comparing themselves to other men. You do not need to prove anything."

"That's just something women don't understand," said Caleb.

"What?"

"That men *do* have to prove themselves. Ask any man. If he's honest, he'll tell you - there is something inside him, driving him to prove himself. It comes in different forms, but that's what it is to be a man."

"I think you're confusing the pressure you feel with the actual innate desire. Some men just want to be loved," said Franny.

Caleb laughed.

"Is something funny?" she asked.

"It's just that if my friends back home were listening in, they'd find that funny."

"But they're not here. You are. And I can tell this stuff makes sense to you."

"It does. I think you're onto something there. I like the idea of the glass because it does have that ability to reflect like a mirror, and also see through to the other side," he said.

"Yes, the father is such a powerful figure in man's life because he gives access to the self in the present, the future, and the past. And that's why a relationship between a father and son is so complex. It always will be," said Franny.

The food arrived as Daniel returned from the washroom and the three ate lunch in a comfortable silence.

The next morning came with a slight chill, which made sitting outside uncomfortable, and Caleb excused himself from their company to go in. He settled on the couch in the lobby with his book and his last, cold sip of coffee. He was tired and felt like going back to sleep, but noticed the computer in the lobby was free. He hadn't checked his email since arriving in Europe, and he knew there would be at least one from Mel on the day he left and expected there would be more. He hadn't embraced the emerging use of email like many of his friends had but knew it was an easy way to communicate.

He stared at the screen in a Zen-like trance trying to remember his password. He thought back to the last time he signed in and spread his fingers across the keyboard to feel his way to the words. The screen was slow to load, but as each segment of his inbox unfolded in pixelated words, he recognized names in bold running down the left side of the screen. He scrolled past many of his friends' names to find Melanie. Her email name, they had decided, should be 'PurpleHazen@hotmail.com', one that she had originally protested, but Caleb insisted was too cool to pass up. Caleb clicked on her subject line: *please read*. It was dated the day he left.

Dear Caleb,
When I think about my life, I realize you've been my only real friend. I don't think anyone knows me the way you do and I don't want that to change, but I'm so confused about us right now. I really feel like I don't know the person you've become over the past year. You've slowly drifted away, so when you told me you wanted to take this trip, I freaked out a little. Maybe I shouldn't have moved out. That might have been a little drastic, but I needed you to see what your life would be like without me. And then you freaked out. I was actually worried about you for a while, Cal. I had never seen you that low before. But it was then I knew you needed me, like I needed you. I'm so mad at you right now, I can't believe you left us all here, but I don't want to let it drive us apart. I still think there's a future for us, but you have to promise that you'll come home soon. The funeral for Tyler is tomorrow and I can't believe I have to go alone. You know everyone's going to ask where you are and why you left - it's Piersville after all. They've arrested Ferris Buckton. What a mess. I miss you. I hate you right now, but I do miss you. Don't kiss anyone over there or I'll kill you. Seriously.

Love Mel

He closed the message and went to log out of his account, but a recent subject line caught his attention: 'mug-stealing canuck'. It was sent just a few days ago. The name was one he never expected to see again: JasonCahill88@hotmail.com He had a vague recollection of writing down his email on a beer coaster and placing it in Jas' big freckled mitt.
    He clicked on the message.

So, I've informed the bobbies that there's a mug-stealing canuck on the loose somewhere in Europe. 'He's most likely got the evidence with him and he's bound to repeat his crime now that he's had a taste of lawlessness. He may be found sitting alone in a café or bar reading Jack London.' If they haven't found you by now, then that means you're safe somewhere and hopefully reading this. Listen mate, I want you to make your way to Paris to meet me. I've been hired at the Village Hostel to work the front desk in exchange for free accommodation. It's a fair gig, and I can hook you up with the same deal. Come soon, though or they'll hire someone else. I told them you're on your way so get your ass here. Paris is Paris and there are beautiful women everywhere. I've even scoped out the hostel talent for you, mate and I'll think you'll be happy here. Unless you're still tangling with your lady from back in Canada, but I advise you leave that behind. There are so many more boring people you can give your love to – especially French women. They're boring but they hide behind cigarettes and politics and never shave their crotches....and they're asking about you, Caleb Arthur. Get over here!

Kiwi Jas

He closed the screen as though it were evidence in a crime he was about to commit. He knew he should stay in Vienna – the pace of life suited him. But the excitement of spending time in Paris with this enigmatic figure blinded him from the benefit of another week with Franny and Daniel. Caleb had never met anyone like Kiwi Jas back home and wanted to be part of his world again if only for a few weeks. When the next morning came, he had already reasoned his way into another adventure leaving Franny and Daniel on the patio in their usual morning routine waiting for him to join them for coffee. Caleb boarded the bus to Paris, leaving only a note at the front desk to explain.

Franny,
I'm sorry for leaving like this. I wish I could have said goodbye to you both in person, but this trip was unexpected. I'm off on another adventure, but I want to thank you for the last few days. I've had a great time getting to know you two. Daniel is a great kid – you should be proud. I see a lot of myself in him. Hopefully he makes better choices than I have in life. I've been thinking a lot about our talk at Schonbrunner the other day. I have been trying to figure out who my grandfather was and I think you've helped me more than anything else over here. I haven't been trying very hard to find him lately. I guess I wasn't sure where to start or how to go about it. Hopefully I'll have more luck in Holland or back in England.
I'm not a writer or a poet or anything like that, but this is something I wrote down after our talk. Maybe you can use it for one of your papers or something:
Every man has a gaze and every father is a window.
Enjoy the rest of your travels and give my best to Daniel,
Caleb

June 1, 1944

Dear Marie,
I can't say much of anything at this point, but trust that I'll be thinking of you and our boy. All my training -19 months - has led to this. I don't know what we're to encounter, but I'm ready. My legs are still sore but a good rest tonight should put them at ease. God willing, they'll need to be ready in the weeks ahead. ▬▬▬▬▬▬▬▬▬▬▬▬▬▬▬▬▬▬▬▬▬▬▬▬▬▬▬▬▬▬▬▬▬▬▬▬ *We all feel confident, especially the Chaudieres. We're a proud bunch. I'm sorry for the short letters of late but I don't have as much time as I used to. I bet I've looked at your pictures a hundred times the last few days. Yours and Jack's.*

The weather's been horrible here and the food even worse. They serve us bland porridge, weak tea, and hard mutton. They have promised better to come and I hope that's the case, but let's just say I miss your cooking dear!

In other news, my French is getting better. I can sit and talk more now with my men, which is important for me. I'll write you a letter in Francais one of these days. But regardless, I'll write you as much as I can. I promise you that. I've had some really good, long chats with Jack about our lives and the nature of this war. He understands politics very well and we agree on many things. We have some disagreements on the reasons for this war, but I respect his opinion on the matter. We've had different experiences and I know we've both been shaped differently by them. I'll write you another letter soon my dear.

All my love to you and Jack,
Patrick

14

The last time Caleb had seen Kiwi Jas, there was a feeling of lawlessness between them and Caleb wondered what adventures were awaiting him in Paris. He was nervous but excited.

He didn't learn much about Jas that night in London, but he imagined life had been easy for him, even though he knew it was wrong to think that way. People assumed Caleb's life was easy because it was comfortable, but he knew there were cavities of darkness in him, as there are in everyone, which can eat away at happiness if ignored too long.

Those who accepted the world with all its idiosyncrasies, often had an unshakable and annoying confidence. Caleb was aware of these people, they were often marked by smugness – they shot condescending looks and spoke pedantically. He rarely encountered the ones on the other end of the spectrum, the ones with a quiet confidence about the world, radiating beautifully and hidden by an approachable countenance. Franny had exhibited this, and Caleb imagined Jas lived on this end of the spectrum, as well. He felt he was leaving one of them for another.

He knew the The Village Hostel on Rue D'Orsel was close to Sacre Coeur, so when he exited the bus and flagged down a cab, that's where he asked the driver to stop. He hadn't seen The Basilica before. When he got out, he was impressed by the humbling stature of the Roman Catholic Church and almost forgot to pay for his taxi. His eyes followed the incline of lush, green hills and fortified walls of white Travertine stone leading to the Byzantine monument overlooking all of Paris. Caleb had not been that impressed with the Eiffel tower, finding it rather contrived and pretentious, but the opulence of the Sacre Coeur impressed him. The growling taxi driver snapped him from his gaze and he quickly paid the fare.

Kiwi Jas was working at the front desk when Caleb walked through the door, and he greeted Caleb with his famous smile before moving quickly from behind the desk and embracing him with a strong hug and slap on the back that extended into a firm shoulder grip.

"The crazy Canuck is here. Finally. I'll show you to your room. I see you didn't bring any cute little side-kick with you. I guess you and…." Jas put his hand up and rotated it around with two fingers in the air searching for a name.

"Melanie," Caleb said.

"Yes, Melanie! I guess you and Melanie are staying faithful to each other. That's admirable," said Jas and smiled coyly like he didn't believe in fidelity.

"Well, I'm not sure what's going on with me and her. Actually, there was this one girl I was traveling with for the past few weeks. Two girls really, but I kind of had this thing going with one of them. It's a long story."

'I want to hear about it….tonight! Over a few pints on the balcony. We'll talk about you working here as well, mate. I've got you all set up. You just need to fill out this form and get it back to me. Just don't mention the job to anyone else yet, alright pal?" Jas eyed him for a second "Hey – you're looking good! The bruises are all gone. I trust you've learned a few things about avoiding beatings then, hey?"

Caleb laughed sheepishly and Kiwi Jas left him with a slap of the arm and walked towards the door. He pulled it open and before exiting, turned back and pointed.

"Tonight!"

Caleb responded with a thumbs up and instantly felt stupid for doing so. He sat down on his bunk and felt good to be back in Paris. He was becoming more comfortable moving from place to place, and wondered if he could ever commit to a life of travel as he eased onto his bunk. He wondered if Jas ever missed his family, or ever went home to see them. He thought of his own parents and decided it was a good time to call home. He wandered down to the lobby to find a phone and Jas pointed him in the right direction.

The phone call with his mother left him feeling cold. It was clear she was still concerned about him and he couldn't convince her to feel less anxious. She reported that the police had formally charged Ferris Buckton with three counts of first degree murder, and three attempted murder charges, among a number of crimes associated with the act of opening fire in a public place. The town had been turned upside down by reporters looking for stories. She had been approached by CBC, The Star and the Globe for quotes about her family's connection to the victims. It had become apparent that Caleb had had a connection to both the victims and the bar, and that it was his going-away party the massacre happened at, and so not only were the press requesting to speak to him, the police had expressed interest as well. They had contacted her about Caleb's whereabouts and were not happy to hear that he had left the country. But since he was not a witness in the shooting, they couldn't formally request his return.

"Nothing has ever happened like this in Piersville," she said. "I just wish we could go back to normal here. It's all anyone talks about now. And your name comes up Caleb, I won't lie. More people are asking about you and where you are. We all just wish you'd come home." She sighed

"I'm working at a hostel in Paris for awhile. If I can make some money, I could stay for longer than I planned. And I still haven't visited Torquay yet. I won't be home anytime soon, Mom."

"I understand," she said and paused. "I ran into Melanie the other day. She looks good."

"I'm sure she does, Mom. Tell her I said hi if you see her again. I don't think she really wants to hear from me right now."

"You guys are fighting?"

"Not really fighting, but just kind of...having troubles. You know."

"Because you left?"

"Ya sort of. Listen, Mom I have to go. Tell the police that I'm not coming home to give a statement. Melanie has already told them I was with her when the shooting happened. We didn't see it. I didn't even see that Ferris kid that night. If they really need to talk to me, they can put my face on Interpol and take me down in a Parisian standoff at the Arch de Triumph," he said and laughed.

"Caleb."

"I gotta go mom. I'll call again soon."

It was close to six thirty by the time he returned to his room and he had to go meet Kiwi Jas.

There was a warm, southern wind that was blowing across the terrace as he stepped out. A glass of dark rum was waiting for him at the table. He sat down and grabbed a can of cola from the grocery bag on the ground and snapped open the tab. He filled his glass and poured a little in Jas'. He felt the warm sensation of the rum and coke in his belly.

The terrace was decorated with small tables placed awkwardly next to large plants and latticed fences. Their view of the Sacre Coeur was partially obstructed by scaffolding that looked forgotten about – a paradox of idleness and human ambition. Only one other table was occupied with two women sitting comfortably drinking wine and reading. The streets below were busy, and the sound of traffic filled the spaces between conversation.

"What are your first impressions of Paris, Cal?" Kiwi Jas said as he glanced over at the two women. He reached across and took Caleb's cheap plastic glass and filled it up with more rum. Caleb usually hated when people he didn't know well called him 'Cal', but when Jas said it, it didn't sound patronizing; it sounded genuine and it made him feel warm as though he were a part of Jas' close circle of friends.

"Actually, this isn't my first time in Paris. I spent a week here after London. It was a bit of a blur," Caleb said and paused. "But I didn't get beat up at least."

"So, if you don't mind me asking, what *did* happen to you in London?"

"It's embarrassing. I'd rather not talk about it."

"Fair enough. So then what have learned about yourself on this trip?"

Caleb took his time. "Well, I've definitely learned how easily I can be conned by people. I guess I'm pretty naïve when it comes to the world." There was a slight pause that hung in the air, and Jas afforded him the opportunity to continue. "Which is strange, because back in Piersville, I'm pretty good at recognizing the bull-shitters."

Kiwi Jas chuckled as he took a sip of rum and coke.

Caleb continued. "I'm surprised by how little I miss home right now. There are so many interesting people over here. It's great to find all these other people who aren't living the life they're expected to. It kind of gives me permission, you know?" He paused. "I'm learning a lot over here. A lot about life."

"There's a lot to learn. Life is just a series of moments, and they drag you along for the ride whether you like it or not," Jas said.

"You know, that reminds me of something you said to me the last time we saw each other. Actually, it was the last thing you said."

"Oh ya? What's that mate?"

"You said 'It is never not right now. I thought a lot about that afterwards. I don't think I understood what you meant then, but it makes more sense to me. I think I was so caught up in the next place I was going or what would happen when I got home to Piersville, that I was never truly enjoying the moment I was in. It didn't really hit me until I got to Vienna and slowed down a little. I think maybe because I wasn't thinking about where I was going next – hell, I didn't even *know* where I was heading next."

"Well, I can't tell you how much that kind of mind-frame has helped me over the years, Cal. I try to remember that there is only one moment, and that's the one you're in, so it's best to just enjoy it because you can't enjoy a moment you're not in. It's something I picked up in India – I spent some time with a man named Govinda, who changed the way I think about things in many ways. You should go to India, Caleb. It will blow your mind."

"You know what? That would have sounded like a crazy idea a year ago, but now it doesn't seem so out there."

"You're understanding the backpacker life," Kiwi Jas said knowingly.

"It's so nice to be free from routine and the expectations that come with it. The only expectation I have now is that there'll be somewhere to go next."

"There are always going to be expectations in life mate, there's no escaping them. You've just traded the ones from back home for new ones here. Tell me, what was expected of you back home?"

Caleb snorted. "Fuck. Well, let's just say I haven't quite lived up to them so far. But they're always there, hiding behind the people I see each day. Whenever one of my friends gets married or has kids, I feel that pressure weigh heavier on my shoulders. And this trip was just the icing on the cake."

"And what's expected of you over here?"

"Well, I don't feel any expectations over here, except for the one I already said about always having a new place to go, but that's one I embrace. I don't meet people long enough to have them expect anything of me."

"People always bring expectations to the table when they meet. They'll expect you to be interesting; they'll expect you to be interested by them; they'll expect you to fulfill some type of desire within themselves; they'll expect you to confirm what they already know about you and where you're from. Try this – the next time someone asks where you're from, tell them you're American. See if they treat you differently or ask you different questions from that point on. It's best to mess with people as much as possible – simple enjoyments you know. Call it a social experiment."

"I'll try it," Caleb said, reflected for a second and smiled. "Wait, so does that mean you're not really from New Zealand?".

"I wouldn't lie to you mate – I like ya. It's all those bloody boring bastards I try to mess with. And who would lie about being Aussie – fuck them!" he said and laughed loudly. The women at the next table looked up from their books and smiled politely smiles to keep their voices down.

"Well, mate, I've got to turn in early tonight on account I've got an early shift at the front desk, and you've got a date with the Sacre Coeur."

"That fucking thing?" Caleb pointed up at the sliver of white dome behind the scaffolding. "It's getting a makeover; plastic surgery; it's under the knife. I don't think they'll let me in."

"That thing's always under construction. Everything in Europe is behind scaffolding – Notre Dame, St Peter's, Big Ben – all of it. Fucking wanker's cover everything up so no one can enjoy it. No, you've got to hike up to the top and see the city from that view in the morning. It'll be worth it."

Caleb nodded and finished his drink.

"Meet me back here tomorrow evening and we'll wander the streets, try out our French on Parisian women."

They stood up and Caleb knocked the plastic chair over clumsily and then got his feet caught up in the plastic bag, but recovered well and set the chair back. Kiwi Jas slapped him on the shoulder and laughed. He looked back to the women, who were now staring in their direction, and in the soft light of the outdoor lamps, Jas gave them a wink before he turned and disappeared out of sight.

June 10, 1944

Dear Marie,
I don't have many words for you today. My hand is trembling as I write this, so I won't go into details. I made it. That's all I can say. Many didn't. Paterson - poor chap. I've learned a few important things over here, Marie, and one of them is that I have to keep moving. Those who stand still aren't going to make it, and I've got too much to live for now to even think of falling. I feared only for an instant that my son would go through his life with only a picture of me. But it was fleeting and I know that I can survive this. I went out with Jack to find some bread earlier, but all we found was wine. It'll do right now, but Jack's a whiskey man, so he's not happy. I told him we'll meet in Torquay after this whole mess is over and I'll buy him a whiskey then. I don't know what I'd do without him over here. A good friendship is worth more than all the cigarettes and honey combined. Not that I don't want you to keep sending them, love. I wouldn't suggest that, but it may be difficult now that we're moving. I'll be honest Marie, my hands are still shaking from this past week and I'm hungry, but I feel positive. I'm trying to at least. I've learned a lot over here – a lot about death. My candlelight is flickering, so I'll say goodnight. I'll be dreaming of your face tonight.

All my love,
Patrick

15

Caleb arrived onto the terrace carrying a six pack of beer he had purchased at the depanneur that afternoon. He chose a table along the railing overlooking the street and cracked the cap off one of the bottles and took a long, slow pull. It tasted bitter and he inspected the label for an alcohol percentage but couldn't find one.

"Drinking alone is the first sign of trouble!" Jas bellowed as he approached and startled him. Caleb stood to greet him. "How was your day at the Sacred Heart?"

"You were right! What a view. We need to go back up there at night sometime."

"Ah, too easy, mate. We'll do it tonight."

Caleb reached down and handed him a beer.

"What the fuck is this? You know they sell real beer here right?"

"Ya, it actually tastes a bit like ass," Caleb said.

"Tempting."

"Let's just say it's no Molson Canadian."

"Ya, you Canucks got some pretty fit beers in your country. I'll give you that. I've had a few Molson Exports in my day. Sign of a good country."

"Have you ever been?"

"Not yet, but I aim to spend some time there in the near future. I've got some connections in Whistler, and an ex-girlfriend in Toronto."

"Is she Canadian?"

"No actually, she's Irish, but living in Toronto. She was in New York for awhile trying to be an actress but New York got the better of her. I think Toronto's got the reputation as being a little softer on the human spirit. She likes it there, from what I hear."

"So, where'd you meet her then?" Caleb asked, intrigued – he had always had a thing for Irish girls; it was something about their accent.

"Coincidentally enough – in Ireland. I worked at a pub in Killarney for half a year shortly after I left New Zealand - one of my first long stays in a country. I guess I was eighteen. I ran out of money and Killarney was nice place to lay low for awhile. Anyways, her name was Naomi and she worked at the pub too. We had a good thing there for awhile, but as all good things end one way or another, we parted ways and both went on to see much more of the world than we would have if we stayed together. I probably would have ended up knocking her up and living out my years raising a pile of kids. Not the life for me, mate."

"I never would have thought to up and leave my hometown at that age," Caleb said. "Don't you ever miss home or wish you had a back yard or anything normal like that?" Caleb went to take a sip of beer and stopped. "Sorry, I didn't mean that you're not normal, just that it's what most people do I guess, but I'm realizing most 'normal' people are idiots, including myself."

"Hey, no offense taken, mate. And I do appreciate the admiration, but make sure to give yourself some credit too. You took a risk and came all the way over here. It doesn't matter how old you are." Jas tipped his beer forward and clinked bottles with Caleb. They both finished and Caleb pulled out two more.

"I think it's important to always put ourselves in the list of people we admire. Socrates talks about that. I definitely think he's onto something there, but admiration of the self is a little narcissistic in my opinion. I don't want to admire myself, just like you don't want to admire yourself. We want to admire others – that's a natural tendency."

He stopped and looked over to see three backpackers cross the terrace to their room. Caleb found it strange to imagine Jas admiring anyone.

"We should be *fascinated* with ourselves, but not in admiration of ourselves – that becomes dangerous. I would say this: no one person should be more interesting to oneself, than oneself," Kiwi Jas said and took a drink.

"That's an interesting way to look at things," Caleb said, fascinated with the outlook. Jas' voice was soothing and his sentences were woven together with a pleasing cadence.

"But that's the truth of human behaviour right there, mate. We are curious creatures, so why not be curious about ourselves first."

"I think we kind of are, aren't we?" said Caleb. Certainly, he had never considered himself the most interesting person he knew but he was curious about himself and his actions at times. He thought he had known himself until his decision to leave for Europe.

"But we push it back into our unconscious minds because we're too afraid to confront our own complexities – our idiosyncrasies – the things that make us unique," said Kiwi Jas. "Or better yet, what if we don't find any idiosyncrasies there? What if we we don't like ourselves? No, we would rather consume the complexities of others. That's why we love our distractions in Western society. We work long hours and then turn the TV on to delay that confrontation with ourselves. Shit, some people do it forever until they're lying on their deathbed and they have nothing to distract them from their thoughts and they're finally confronted with themselves. By then it's too late." Jas paused and took a long drink of his beer. The sound of car alarm went off below them for a few seconds and stopped abruptly. "And just think of what this Internet thing is going to do to our society. It's going to be a fucking travesty for the next generation who will devour it as distraction and make it almost impossible to know themselves. Email is just the beginning. It will breed false connection between people. It will change the world."

Caleb knew that Jas was right about the Internet and told him so.

"And you say you admire what I'm doing over here," said Kiwi Jas. "Well, in part, I'm doing it because I don't believe the current Western society has a future. Our civilization is headed for a collapse, so I'm selfishly taking what I can from this life while I'm young and full of piss and vinegar. I'm selfish, Caleb. I'm doing this for me. I'm what you'd call an ethical egoist. But at least I'm honest about it. I know the difference between right and wrong and sometimes I choose to do the wrong thing. This is why the moral people usually lose. They are restricted in life. You gotta learn to set aside some of your morals to live selfishly sometimes."

Caleb was turned around. "Why do you think we're headed for a collapse?" he asked. "What do you think will happen?"

"Well, mate." Jas' eyes sparkled. "First of all, consider the rate our population is growing. We are currently sitting around 6 billion on this planet. We were around 2 billion at the beginning of the century. That's a three-fold increase in less than a hundred years. How many people do you think this planet can handle? People need food, energy, water, and plenty of it. People consume and leave waste; people are not meant to be on this planet at this number. She can't handle us. And now we're gonna have close to 8 billion of us in thirty or forty years. But we're never gonna make it that far. Most of us won't see 2040. You want to know why?"

Caleb cleared his throat, not expecting to speak. "Why?"

"Have you ever heard of a guy called Malthus?'

"No."

"Well, he had this theory about natural checks to population, right. He argued that when population begins to get out of control, it will naturally check itself. Think of things like plagues, diseases, wars and that sort of thing. They've occurred throughout history. Just think of how many people would still be alive if the Black Plague didn't clear out Europe."

"I learned about that plague in history class."

"Ya, well we're due for another one real soon. I believe it's on its way and that's why I'm not dedicating my life to some out-dated notion of a career and a family and waiting for shit to hit the fan. No man – I'm enjoying life and living free. This all might sound negative, but it's actually really affirming – it's in the awareness that brings happiness. People aren't aware and so they live boring, pressured lives and say they are happy because they get a little slice of time to themselves each week. And why do they do this? Because they are promised a long, secure retirement where they get to watch their grandchildren grow up in a world they worked hard to make better. But they don't understand that they're not making it better by working for a system that adds to the lie of Western capitalism." Jas was becoming wild-eyed as he spoke and realized his passion was increasing his volume of speech; he stopped and smiled. Caleb lit a cigarette.

He could have been giving a speech in front of thousands, but it was only Caleb listening intently, ready to follow him anywhere.

"But let's not go down that road right now. To get back to my original point, in order to be interesting to oneself, one must do interesting things - spontaneous things – things one thought they were incapable of doing. In essence, one must live with no regrets."

Caleb looked back on his life and realized he had many regrets. He had stayed close to home and watched others do something with their lives while he worked the same job with the same people in the same town. His choices led him to a place he felt trapped in; only now was he really seeing it, the indifference to life that led him down that path. Why had it taken him so long to snap out of it and make a bold move? Even if coming to Europe had cost him the only good thing about his life in Piersville, he still didn't regret it. And there were even regrets he felt more immediately than losing Melanie. He regretted how things ended between him and Joss and he regretted ever talking to Skins; but he didn't regret ditching his bill in London with Jas, and he didn't regret coming back to Paris to meet him. He felt alive around him.

Jas withdrew from the conversation for a few seconds and then surfaced again with something to share. "I'll tell you one thing I've learned in my time over here, mate. There's something about a woman that can make you betray everything you stand for. They're wicked and yet I can't stay away from the whole damn lot of 'em."

Caleb smirked knowingly. "You had three on the go in London."

"I should know better, but I've resigned to stay in Paris for awhile to tangle with this bird I've met. She kind of tricked me into it like all beautiful women can. She's a crafty one; she keeps me on my toes, but let me tell you, she's got me believing in the almighty again. Her legs seem to stretch to heaven and the gate to paradise rests at the top of 'em." Jas raised his hands and looked towards the sky in reverence, before bringing them down and gently slapping Caleb on the back.

They laughed like teenagers and Caleb was feeling good with the glow of a warm, dusk buzz and suggested they go for a walk through the streets of Paris. Jas agreed and stood up to finish his beer. When it was empty, he rolled it across the terrace towards the garbage can and it slammed into it causing a loud bang; he turned, smiled and urged Caleb to drink up.

They wandered aimlessly through the streets until Jas motioned to turn down a quiet street that seemed steeped in history. The cobblestones made walking difficult. Caleb eyed a middle aged couple stretched back lazily into a shop window, hips entwined and stroking at each other's faces, intent on demonstrating their love. A motorcycle startled them as it roared past making only slight movements to avoid obstacles and turned sharply around the corner and out of sight. The turn was followed by a long, metallic burst of sound that turned everyone's head within earshot. Even the two lovers stopped kissing and turned their heads.

Jas started to run and Caleb followed. They could see a small commotion of two or three people in a panic hovering overtop the downed motorcyclist. Jas arrived first to see a mangled leg pinned between the bike and a guardrail, a car stopped in a precarious position, the bumper hovering over a figure clothed in leather and jean struggling to keep from screaming out in pain. One of the witnesses, a man with an overcoat and large beard, was trying to explain to a younger man in a tracksuit the urgency of the situation and kept making the symbol of a phone with his hand to his ear and pointing at the street. The younger man was in shock himself having witnessed the accident and he stood paralyzed until the man in the overcoat clapped his hands violently in front of his face, jolting him out of inaction. The driver of the vehicle was crying and running frantically between her car and the figure writhing in pain.

The motorcyclist's leg had been ripped open by the impact and looked like a stuffed doll's appendage hanging loosely. Both Caleb and Jas watched the blood slowly seep into the jeans until the whole leg was a thick purple, and the driver of the bike was repeating something indiscernible in a panicked gaze. It wasn't clear which he was more confused about, the state of his leg or the lack of help he was receiving. Suddenly, he became alert and yelled something as he raised his fist in the air. Jas reacted and knelt down to look more closely. The jeans had ripped in a few places but it was difficult to see exactly where the blood was coming from. The leg was twisted and the foot dangled loose from the ankle as if no sinew or bone existed. Caleb turned and vomited over the side of the barricade onto a female bystander's shoes and she yelled and swung her purse onto his back. Jas took off the bandana he was wearing around his head and proceeded to wrap it tightly around the wounded man's mid-thigh in an attempt to slow the blood supply to his lower leg. The man screamed but when Jas finished, he grabbed his hand and looked him right in the eye and assuaged him quietly, giving focus to the words he was saying: "My name's Jason, and I'll stay with you until the ambulance comes."

The biker looked into his face with full attention; they avoided looking at his leg or to the small crowd of onlookers. They kept their focus on each other as Kiwi-Jas grasped his hand and told him to keep his eyes on his. When it was clear the biker did not understand English, but was just happy that someone was tending to him, Jas shook his head and uttered: "The absurdity of life". The man didn't understand but kept his locked gaze and nodded. The sound of the words was comforting, regardless of denotation. Jas continued.

"One minute you're happy as shit on your motorcycle and the next you're bleeding to death in the street looking into the face of a stranger for comfort. Jesus. As flies to wanton boys are we to the gods. They kill us for their sport."

The minutes felt like hours as they waited for the ambulance to come roaring onto the scene, and when it did, the paramedics took over, giving no recognition to Jas' efforts and swearing and gesturing angrily to the bandana tied onto the leg.

Just as quickly as they arrived, they were gone and all that was left was a blood stain on the pavement. The police began to question the driver and take notes. They pushed the crowd back and signalled for Jas to stick around for questions, but he blended back into the crowd and nudged Caleb to come with him and they turned the corner out of sight.

"Hey slow down man. We didn't do anything wrong. It's not like we hit that guy," Caleb said.

"Do *you* want to sit around there for another hour answering questions while our buzz wears off? I'm not in the mood for hanging out with a bunch of cops right now. They always make me feel like I've done something wrong."

"I haven't had that many dealings with them," Caleb said. He slapped his hands together in excitement. "That was pretty messed up back there! I can't believe we just saw that. Stuff like that doesn't happen back home."

"So what kind of excitement does go on in Piersville?" Kiwi Jas asked calmly and looked back to see if anyone had noticed them leave.

"Well, I've never been in an accident or been arrested. A few underage drinking fines and that kind of thing," Caleb said. "I've been pretty good in that department."

"Getting arrested doesn't make you a bad person. And besides, there's no such thing as good and bad, mate. It's all relative – what one person considers harm, another might consider good. You'll find that out. The life of a backpacker has it's own rules. The longer you do this travel thing, the more you'll start to understand that mainstream rules don't apply to us blokes like they do for everyone else."

"Like stealing?"

"Yup. But we only do it when we need to. I was pretty bloody broke that night we met in The Weasel. I had to do it, mate."

"What about tonight?" Caleb asked.

"I've got a bit of money on me. Let's pop into that depanneur," Kiwi Jas said pointing across the street.

"Good. My buzz is starting to wear off. Let's get a bottle of wine and hike up the Sacre Coeur. I'd like to see this city at night," Caleb said.

They ran across the street darting between moving cars. One honked and hit the brakes at Jas' outstretched arm. He laughed and waved Caleb across.

The store was well lit and when they entered, the door signalled a noise that brought the clerk out from the back. Kiwi Jas asked if they had any Absinthe, and the clerk shook his head.

"In the back?" Jas asked. "I've got money," he said and flashed a wad of bills. The clerk put his finger up to signal he'd be back in a second and ducked into the back again.

Kiwi Jas opened his jacket and shot Caleb a devilish smile.

"I thought you said...."

Jas laughed and in one smooth motion took a bottle under the wing of his coat and started to run. Out of reflex, Caleb gripped his hand around the neck of a dark bottle and darted out behind Jas. His heart was beating fast as he pushed the door open. He didn't see the small lady as he leapt into the street and the force of his body knocked her over. She grabbed at his arm to soften her fall causing the bottle to loosen from his grip and smash onto the pavement in a dull crash that splattered red wine across the ground. The woman, stunned from the collision, regained her composure and jumped up to check herself for glass and red wine. It was running into crevices and pooling like blood in the street. Her reprimands in French were interrupted by the shopkeeper banging his fist into the window behind them. He was yelling from behind transparent glass to come back and pay. The glass held no reflection, so Caleb could not see how stunned he was, but he quickly snapped back into action and ran to catch up with Kiwi Jas who had not stopped and was already half a block ahead of him.

When he did finally catch him, they were at the base of Sacre Coeur.

"You're crazy, man!" Caleb said to him in winded breath.

"Maybe, but we've got wine don't we? Race me to the top," Jas said and started up the white Travertine steps.

When the wide steps broke off into separate flights they had both run out of breath and took a break on the grass. Caleb's lungs tingled from years of cigarettes, and he sat down to light one up. Jas crossed to join him and celebrate his win. "You gotta give those things up man. They're going to kill ya," he said.

"I thought you smoked, too."

"I dabble socially. Never got hooked. I don't have that personality, I guess. The only thing I'm addicted to is the truth."

"Man, that can be more dangerous than cigarettes," Caleb said.

"Knowledge is power my friend."

"The truth is painful, though. There's a reason why people are scared of it."

"Well, I'm scared of living my life in darkness, of not really knowing the world I'm in," Jas said and signalled them to keep moving. Caleb picked up the bottle of wine and followed him. Jas kicked off his shoes and walked barefoot to the summit where the white Basilica peered over the city judging all the sinners in Paris. A musician played to a group on the steps and his guitar swooned with slow, intoxicating renditions of American songs. His dread locks swung around his head as he moved smoothly in corduroy pants and a green army jacket and smiled at each handful of coins that were tossed in his open guitar case.

"Do you ever wonder what other people think about you?" Caleb asked.

"Not really. Should I?"

"Maybe I think about it too much," Caleb said.

"They probably think I just killed a guy judging from the blood on my pants." Jas shook his head. "Jesus that was intense, mate. Can you believe that? Here give me a drink of that wine!"

Caleb wiped the neck and handed him the bottle.

"I think I was in shock for a minute. Good thing you stepped up, though I don't think the paramedics were too keen on your bandana solution," Caleb said.

"Ah, fuck 'em!"

The musician launched into a Sublime song, which received some excited applause and a handful of coins from a young girl. Caleb took a long pull from the bottle and some dribbled down his chin and he caught it with his forearm in a slow, drawn out movement.

"Give me a few francs?" Jas asked with his head turned towards the musician.

"Here you are Socrates!" Caleb said as he reached into the pockets of his filthy jeans.

Kiwi-Jas stood up with the money in hand and deftly waltzed down the steps through clusters of bodies. His steps were light as he danced towards the figure holding a guitar and Caleb watched him closely, believing that maybe he wasn't performing at all; that maybe he had learned to abandon his self-consciousness altogether and let life move through him in whatever ways it chose. He seemed, in the moment, as someone who had given up on his agenda long ago and accepted the music of human existence to puppeteer his actions from some distant place Caleb had longed to understand and envied greatly. Slowly, as he watched this enigmatic figure caper through the steps of the church, his smile slowly waned from his face as he saw two policemen approach and survey the crowd. He kept an eye on them but hid his gaze when they looked his way. His heart began to quicken and his palms turned sweaty, but they soon disappeared into the night.

Caleb was admiring the view when Jas came back and settled down beside him on the steps.

"The cops just came by. Scared the shit out of me," Caleb said. "You don't think they'd be looking for us up here?"

"For a couple bottles of booze? I doubt it mate," said Kiwi Jas. "But we should probably head out soon. Let's wait a little while longer."

Caleb took comfort in Jas' suggestion even though he was enjoying the view and the music. He was happy they had come up to the church, but still nervous they might get caught. He felt far away from the city and loose from the wine they'd stole. Kiwi Jas began chatting to a woman beside them and Caleb turned to marvel at the old church.

When there was a break in Kiwi Jas' conversation, Caleb turned to him. "This sure is one unbelievable building isn't it," he said, motioning behind them.

"Bloody brilliant mate! All this money and time for a white hippie who turned good drinking water into alcohol so everyone could get wasted and write great things about him."

"I take it you're not down with Jesus," said Caleb.

"Oh, I have no problem with Jesus, mate. He seemed like a pretty hip dude. I'm down with his whole ethos. It's the institution of him I don't like. I don't need a book to tell me what's right and wrong, ya know?. I know it in here," Jas said pumping his fist into his chest twice to add emphasis. "I don't buy all this business of heaven and hell – I look up and I don't see heaven; I see stars" They both looked up out of reflex. "I don't have to imagine a heaven and hell; I've seen them both here on Earth. It's a mindset it is."

The Parisian streets were still busy below and the traffic sounded like a soft march through the warm evening air.

"Let me ask you: have you ever been in a moment that you wish could last forever? I mean, when you just felt perfectly happy?" Kiwi Jas asked.

Caleb sorted through years of memories until only one remained.

"There was one summer when Mel and I went to this folk music festival. I had been to a lot of rock concerts with my friends, but this one was different - it was just Mel and I. And there was such a great collection of good-hearted people enjoying music. On our last day, Sunday afternoon, I had one of these moments you're talking about. We were lying on the grass at the main stage. This duo was playing an alt-country set with this beautiful slide guitar; the music was just perfect for a sunny afternoon. I really remember the sound of the guitar. I had a beer in my hand and Mel was sleeping with her head in my lap. The sun was hot but not too hot, you know – just comfortable on my skin. About 20 feet ahead of us was this girl with a hula-hoop. She was wearing a long flowing dress and was slowly swivelling her hips to keep the hoop moving around her waist. The folds of her dress were moving in perfect rhythm with the song. Everything seemed to be in perfect harmony around me. It was a strange sensation. I remember stroking Mel's hair and sipping my beer and thinking, this is a moment I will remember forever. It was perfect."

"That moment is heaven. It's not some fucking place with gates and a guard deciding who gets in and who doesn't. Heaven is all the beautiful places in your mind. Don't let some human beings with an agenda distort such a beautiful notion for you."

"You know what's funny though – as much as I remember being in that perfect moment, I also remember realizing that it had to end; that it couldn't go on forever. The band would eventually stop playing and everyone who was gathered there would pack up and go home. As soon as I realized it had to end, the sensation was gone."

A few people shuffled past them and took seats next to Jas. The steps became more crowded as the musician played a rendition of Hey Jude.

"Well, there's no such thing as forever, mate. That's what gets us humans so out of sorts. Our brains can't even fathom the idea of eternity yet we're so scared by the notion it might be spent burning alive in some underground cave."

"But I think lots of people choose to believe in heaven and hell anyway, because it's comforting. It gives their lives meaning. Live a good life and there's a reward at the end. Do bad things and you'll pay for it after you're dead," said Caleb as he took a swig from the bottle of wine and passed it to Jas. Someone lit a joint behind them and the smell of marijuana filled the air around them.

"Of course they do – people want something to believe in so badly, they'll set aside everything that doesn't make sense for one simple message tucked away in there – that God loves them. If they're heterosexual and willing to obey him – he loves them. But the funny thing is is that deep down people don't want to *believe* in God, they want to *be* God. Us humans have pretty much eliminated the need for God when we started to control the planet with technology. When Nietszche said that God is dead, and that we've killed him, he was right. So, to answer your question: no, I don't believe in religion. I don't believe we need it either."

"But what about all the good it teaches us. I mean the Ten Commandments is a good list to follow. It keeps us from chaos. So even if there is no God, isn't it better that we have religion?"

"No man! It's insulting to me to think that we don't know the difference between right and wrong without religion telling us. We know what's right and what's wrong by our feelings of shame and joy. It's inside of us if we really pay attention."

"Sure, but maybe it's inside of us because we've been trained to feel that way," said Caleb.

"Let me ask you this: if one of the Ten Commandments said 'Thou Shalt Rape and Pillage' would that make raping and pillaging good?"

"No."

"But if God says they're good, then they would have to be, right?"

"Well, I guess I see your point. But we would know better."

"Exactly!"

Caleb admitted the point and shook his head. He had not been so engaged in a conversation in a long time. His brain was firing in a million directions. He thought of his grandfather in Europe and knew he must have considered that hell on earth. Did the soldiers feel like God had abandoned them for those years. Did his grandfather believe in God after that? Did he ever?

"Listen, mate, I'm not sure why any of us are here on this planet, but if I've been given this time, I'd prefer to spend it having fun," Jas said. I don't know how anyone could spend it in some stuffy church praying to a God to come solve their problems. There's so much to see in this world and if I'm wrong and there is some white, bearded man in the sky watching us, then I'm sure he'd be pretty happy that I've spent my life seeing all the cool places he's created. I think he'd be shaking his head at all the people who missed out on his creation because they spent their lives on there knees with their eyes closed."

"Sounds like a lot of people I know."

"But it doesn't just have to be church, you know. So many people spend their lives sitting behind a desk or staring at a screen and they call it living. Religion isn't just about sitting in a church. We all worship some pretty useless shit. And I can't really harp on religion, anyways. Nietzsche said that alcohol is just as bad. And look at me." Kiwi Jas lifted up the wine bottle to see how much was left but it was too dark to see through the glass.

"To be honest, I've been thinking about something similar since we saw that accident tonight. It made me think about how quickly things can change – just how fragile we are. One day we're walking down the sidewalk, and the next we're on our last breath. I don't want to waste my life and then regret it all on my deathbed."

"Well, I don't think that guy was dying. I reckon he'll be alright. But I know what you mean," Jas said.

"Something like that accident, as bad as it is, makes me kind of glad I took this trip. I could die tomorrow. Any of us could," Caleb said and motioned to the crowd on the steps.

"Maybe you're just an ethical egoist like me, mate. Welcome to the club. There's a lot of us," Kiwi Jas said and laughed.

The music started up again with a reggae version of Dead Flowers, and the chatter slowed to a hush again. Time slowed down, enough for Caleb to appreciate each note being played like drops of rain into a body of water. It was impossible to distinguish how each drop of water contributed just as each note was impossible to determine in a chord, but when transported by music, or buoyant by water, each singular part can be appreciated, even though it can't be sensed. For those who let themselves be transported by song or immersed in water, it is a feeling unified by many fragments of the whole. Transport comes to those who give up control. Caleb had spent a good deal of his life hearing notes but not understanding the larger significance of the song, how they could be played together to make something meaningful, but now he was listening, and there was a song to hear, a lake to dive into. He was learning to let himself go and give way to the refreshing currents of life, and in that release, he found beauty in simplicity masked by complexity.

Jas put his hand on Caleb's back and squeezed his neck fraternally. "There's someone I want you to meet tomorrow."

August 23, 1944

Dear Patrick,
I'm not sure if you're getting my letters anymore. They black out anything that might indicate where you are, so I can't determine much. The papers are saying the June attack has changed the tides of the war. It sounded horrible. I can't believe you had to go through that. I miss you. I pray each day for your safe return to me. I just hope you received the package I sent with the photographs of our son, Jack. Everyone thinks that he looks so much like you. I can't wait for you to meet him. He is starting to talk and saying the most adorable things. He said 'mama' the other day and it melted my heart. Phenon came by with his new wife, Margaret, and they give their regards. They just bought a cottage up north in the area of the Muskoka region. They said there are plots of land you can buy that aren't very dear and they're right on the water. Oh Patrick, wouldn't it be so lovely to have a cottage? I'm going to visit theirs this weekend and then we're all going to talk more about it.

Your mom received your letter the other day and she worries so about you but we keep each other company. We try not to read the news too much but it's all we have. It's so strange that we know more than you about what's happening over there. I wish I could hold you in my arms just once. I wish you were still training in Woodstock so I could drive to meet you for your furlough. I still go through our wedding pictures and I think you look so handsome in your suit, Patrick. I'm so lucky that you're all mine and I can't wait to wrap my arms around you when you get home. Be safe my love. Be safe!

All my love,
Marie

16

Caleb sat across from a German woman introduced as Lieselotte, a woman whose face rested in a natural smile and being the daughter of a fine arts professor, she was intellectual and curious. Her blonde hair spilled down heavily onto her right shoulder twisted once to hold it in place as the sun shone onto the back of her head in a luminous glow. She had a rather petite, triangular face that framed itself around two beautiful, brown eyes. Her lips were a natural red and framed with a thousand years of Prussian symmetry. She spoke English excellently, so the conversation wasn't victimized by repetition and over-pronounced syllables. She asked Caleb to call her Liese.

"So Jason tells me you two met in London whilst wetting your whistles," she said. Her choice of English idioms hinted at an upper class education and her command of syntax was impressive.

"Yes, he saved me from a night spent alone with Jack London," Caleb said, happy with his return banter, which he thought matched what she looked for in conversation.

"Well, I'd prefer a night with Jack London over a night with this schlump." She reached over and poked Jas in the ribs and kissed him playfully on the shoulder.

"So Jas says you're taking a break from school to work on your art," Caleb said.

"I find the whole scholastic realm rather pitiful right now – full of pedantic assholes. There is nothing I can learn right now except how to fail. I need some time to really narrow down my focus."

"What kind of art are you interested in?" Caleb asked.

"Painting. Everything else is just entertainment passed off as art. No one knows how to create real art anymore. Nothing seems authentic – it's either lacking originality or dripping with the desire for income. Of course, I'm lucky – my parents are well off, so I have the luxury to starve for what I do." She looked at him deeply. "I know that."

He wondered if she really did understand the irony of what she just said or maybe she knew it more than him. He could not read her. It was easy to get lost in her big, brown eyes.

Jas had perked up when she mentioned her parents and leaned forward, coffee in hand. "Her father is a professor at the Paris College of Art. Liese gets her talent from him. She says he's a genius. I'd say he's a genius just for creating something this goddam beautiful," he said and framed her face with his hands.

Liese accepted the flirtation by nuzzling her cheeks into his hands and then returned to sip her tea.

"My father is very generous. He helps his students out tremendously. In fact, I don't know if I have even told Jason this, but he purchased a loft on rue Letellier to help struggling students with a free place to stay. He even went and bought a number of mattresses and lamps for any artist who needs something for only a night or two. My father understands the expenses of the modern student. Housing alone could cost a student 7000 Euros. Tuition is dear, as well, but my father can't do anything about that," Lies stated matter of factly.

"Do students come and stay with him often?" Caleb asked.

"Many – up to twenty at times. They show up with their sleeping bags, their art supplies and a password. He uses word of mouth, which I find utterly irresponsible. He is too generous, in my opinion."

"How does he prevent people from taking advantage?"

"Well, he does change the password every month or so at least. I think right now he's having them say "Malebranche", who, if I remember correctly, is a Cartesian philosopher whose work is catalogued under Occasionalism. I *tried* to digest him but his whole premise is that there must be a God and so I lost interest," she said and took a long, elegant drag of her cigarette. "I'm an atheist."

Beams of sunlight came through the window, painting sections of the coffee shop with strokes of light. Her cigarette seemed heavy in her hand and released serpentine smoke in the air as her thin wrist dangled across her leg. The smoke hovered above her in a cloud and drifted slowly through the sunbeams.

Caleb wanted to say 'So am I', to impress her, but he wasn't sure. He thought he might be, especially after his last talk with Kiwi Jas, but he figured he lacked the conviction to fully believe there was no God. Maybe that's what Kiwi

Jas was attracted to in her, he thought. Maybe it wasn't her beauty, money, or intellect, but rather her disposition.

Caleb spent the next few days feeling like an outsider. He wasn't sure why they wanted him around; he felt it difficult to get to know Liese. She didn't give much away that didn't seem calculated as though she were constructing a perception she wanted people to believe. She had made it clear her family came from German money and they moved to Paris when her father accepted the tenured position at the college.

Kiwi Jas was a good match for her, but they lacked the passion that most new relationships boast of. They seemed more comfortable when others were around.

They had invited him to join them for an afternoon in the Latin Quarter, and Caleb enjoyed the colourful, narrow streets, but Liese was unimpressed.

"Where are all the bohemians? This place has been massacred by gentrification! It's gaudy," she said. "I need a drink."

"Give it a chance babe. I know a place a few minutes from here that will make us a couple Libertines that will be worth the walk through Times Square here," Jas said jokingly.

"Yes, it's all just so…..bright," she said. "Whatever happened to French despondency? Isn't this where Existentialism started? Sartre would cry if he saw how commercialized this place has become. And it's only going to get worse." She put her arm inside Jas' and turned away. "What are your thoughts, Cal?"

"I don't mind this place, actually. I can see what you mean about the commercialism, but some of these spots seem kind of soaked in history still. I mean look at this place – the Mediteranee, for example – it looks like its right out of a Hemingway novel." Caleb stopped and looked closely at the café.

"Well, let's hope that fat, drunk isn't inside," Liese said and laughed.

"Oh, you'd be swooning for ol' Hemingway I bet – he would have been a blast to be around," Kiwi Jas chimed in.

"He treated women like shit. I don't go for men like that. Besides, he only wrote one good book – Old Man and the Sea was a good read because it leaves out all his petty, ridiculous jealousies of the people in his life."

"I was told to read A Moveable Feast while I was here in Paris," Caleb said.

"Don't bother – it's basically a vehicle to slander Gertrude Stein, a strong, independent woman who he felt threatened by. But, granted, there are some nice passages. I do enjoy the explanation of Fitzgerald's talent, although it always left me feeling so sad for him. I think I would have really liked Zelda. I think I understand her," Lies said.

"I loved The Great Gatsby," Caleb said.

"The whole trope of the nouveau riche is one I see all too often, but it sparks an interesting debate. I just don't think some people are meant to have money. I mean, that sounds horrible, I know, but Gatsby stands as a character who embodies all the worst things about money – he can't handle it. Tom and Daisy are just so much more comfortable and its clear what Fitzgerald is saying about people. We need structure in society or it all dissolves into chaos. America is far too chaotic for my liking. I don't know how you live there."

"He's Canadian my dear," Jas corrected her.

"Hm. Interesting. Okay, seriously - let's get a drink soon; I'm dying of thirst."

"It's just around the corner. And for the record, I'm with Caleb on this – I like the way this place has changed over the years – it's nice to see some colours and some gaudiness. This city is full of melancholy; the Latin Quarter is supposed to be fun. And who says that Sartre would have hated to see this. Existentialism isn't really that despondent of a philosophy. It's actually quite uplifting when you think about it. When we free ourselves from some manufactured purpose, we're free to choose our own – that's celebratory, not sad. I rejoice as an atheist, and so should you my dear."

"Yes, yes, let's all rejoice please….over some drinks, sitting down at a table somewhere," she responded.

"I'm going to wander down this street to find a decent jewellery shop, but I won't be long. Jason, you and Caleb go get us a table and I'll come find you in a few minutes."

"Okay babe – it's Le Papillon just down to the right at this corner. I'll order you a Libertine."

"See you soon." As she drifted ahead, their hands were still clasped and Jas pulled her back and kissed her before letting her go.

When she was far enough ahead, he turned to Caleb to ask the timeless question that hangs on the mind of every man who has brought someone into his life: "So, what do you think of her?"

Caleb knew it wasn't his place to critique someone so far out of his league and so he used hyperbole to be safe, and a witticism to deflect.

"She's elegant, gorgeous, intelligent, classy….what do you want me to say? She's far too good for you, man! I'm sorry, but how did you convince her to take up with a Kiwi bum like you?"

"I pay her lots of money."

"I would hope so."

"Actually, it's the opposite. She's helping me out a little right now. I'm getting down to my last few Francs, so I need to find some steady work for awhile."

"The work at the Village Hostel isn't doing it?"

"Ha – not quite. That just covers my stay."

"So when will I start there? I could use some help as well, you know. Just want to keep taking advice from the Backpacker's Handbook, remember?"

"We do need to get you set up there. I'm just waiting for the owner to return from Greece to give you the okay. I'll get the paperwork sorted and he should be back in a couple days. Can you wait until then? Sorry, mate, I didn't think you'd arrive here so quickly when I sent you that email. I'm glad you're here, though. I can never get enough of you crazy Canucks."

They went inside to order drinks and then took a table outdoors by the sidewalk where Liese could find them.

She approached minutes later beaming with something in her hand.

"Look at this fabulous amulet I purchased," she said and stuck it out over the table so both Jas and Caleb could eye it closely. It was strikingly large, taking up a third of her palm, and the centre was deep purple, like a black mirror, surrounded by an intricate gold casing and leather strap. "Here, it's for you Jason. Put it on!"

Jas slipped the amulet over his head and let it rest against his chest. It was a noticeable piece of jewellery on a man. He stood up and embraced her, kissing her forehead in paternalistic fashion. "Thank you. I love it."

He turned to Caleb to show it off and Caleb commented on its prominence but felt unnerved by it's darkness; a mirror that gave no reflection. He excused himself to use the washroom.

When he returned, three more drinks had arrived and plans had been made.

"We're going to finish these drinks and then we're going to choose someone to follow," Jas said.

"To follow where?"

"Wherever they go," Jas said.

"I'm sorry – I don't understand." Caleb nodded thanks for the drink and took a sip.

"You're a people watcher right?" Jas asked.

"Ya. Who isn't?"

"Well, there's a game I like to play that takes it a step further. It adds a little more excitement. Don't you ever wonder where people are going when you watch them?"

"Don't you wonder what kind of lives they lead?" Liese added.

"Well, once in awhile when I'm in the mood, I like to just choose a person or a couple and follow them. It's even more fun to do in groups because you can make wagers on where you think they're going and see who's right," Jas said.

"That sounds kind of fun, actually. Sure, I'm in."

"Okay good. So all we need to do is decide on a person. It's much harder here because we don't know the area that well."

"Speak for yourself," Liese said.

The street was busy with a continuous stream of strangers in flux, some strolling languidly, some stopping every few feet to look in stores and read menus, and some walking briskly with a destination in mind.

"What about him?" Liese suggested as she pointed in the direction of a tall man in a cream turtleneck with long grey hair pulled back into a ponytail. He was carrying a brown leather satchel across his body and gripping it tightly. "He looks interesting."

"No, not him. He looks like a pedophile. I don't want to follow him into some child porn ring. What about them?" Kiwi Jas pointed at an attractive, young couple in their twenties who were both sharply dressed.

"Too boring. They're just going back to work," Liese said dryly.

Caleb was sorting through a sea of bodies until a silhouette stood out to him. He turned red instantly. He didn't believe it at first – thought his mind was playing a trick on him. But he kept his gaze on her. He watched her take a dark curl of hair in her fingers and twirl it as she stopped to look in a window.

"Her," he said.

Jas and Liese followed his extended arm.

"Who? The brunette in jeans?" Jas asked.

"Yup. Her."

Jas looked at Lieselotte and they signalled with their eyes they agreed.

"Okay, here's the game," Jas explained as they walked slowly allowing for an acceptable distance between them and their subject, "we all say where we think she's going and who she might be meeting. We follow her until she gets to where she's going and then we see who was right. The winner get's the others' first-born."

"Oh great – so I get stuck with a delinquent Kiwi kid? Fantastic." Leise said sarcastically and Jas poked her in response.

Caleb paid no attention to them; his gaze was focused on the familiar face in the crowd. How many times had he watched her movements and marvelled at her facial features, yet she seemed so distant from him now. She possessed her body fully; she owned it in a way that caused him to feel uncomfortable. He had wanted to be a part of it – to join her in its possession but he realized now that he never came close. Why did she have to be here, at this exact time? Fate was surely teaching him that he was not in control.

"Okay, I want to go first," Liese said and pushed Kiwi-Jas away from her to concentrate on the task. She eyed the young woman closely, from her small feet to her slender legs, past her small breasts and to her thick dark hair. "She's pretty." She looked back at Caleb for encouragement. "She's not French; she's not even European. I'd say she's American – about 21 years old. She's here with her family – parents and younger brother. They wanted a trip away together while she's young enough to still travel with them, but she is growing tired of them all and needs to take long breaks to walk alone in the city to contemplate her womanhood and be desired by French men. She is on her way back to meet them for an early dinner at a restaurant chosen by her father on advice he received from a business partner – somewhere that serves some American food but has a slight, calculated resemblance to a real Parisian café – one of those god-awful dives on the lower end of St Michel," Lieselotte exhaled.

"Well done Madame Goetschle. But you are wrong, my dear. This young, pretty thing is here alone. Look at the way she wanders aimlessly – she is in no rush to meet anyone. She is new to Paris – she just arrived today and this is her first experience with it. Look at the way she is eyeing everything like a child. She is sad because she has no one to share the beauty of Paris with. She will write postcards home to her friends to tell them of the Latin Quarter, but she will not be able to find the words to really express it. She will return to her hostel soon only because she does not want to eat alone and there will be people there who will invite her out because she is pretty and alone," Jas shot Liese a cocky smile, thinking he had outdone her.

"She's meeting someone," Caleb said confidently and touched the tattoo on his chest. "Her new lover and travel mate." It hurt him to say it but he was as sure of it as he was in his attraction to her. "She just parted with him for an hour so she could window shop and she knew he wouldn't be interested in all the pretty things to buy. He would be more interested in searching out the dirty streets of the Quarter, where the real people go about their day. He has dreadlocks and a thin beard. He'll be waiting for her at a small, dingy café that he will have chosen away from the tourists," Caleb said distantly, like he was pulling details from his memory.

"Jesus, mate, those are some pretty interesting details, but we'll just give the 'boyfriend' play, whether he's a bohemian James Dean type of guy or not," Jas said.

Caleb eyed their subject closely, and as they stood up to follow her, she turned their way and Caleb could swear that she looked right at him, and in this second he saw her again for the first time. Her face still had power over him. But she didn't see him; she was looking through him and he was just another body in the human liquid that surrounded her. She left the storefront and the three of them waited until she was far enough ahead before they exited onto the sidewalk and followed her.

Caleb felt like he was doing something wrong, but he wanted to see her with her new lover to turn the screw inside him one more rotation. He was starting to rely on the pain women caused him – a new pain in his life that had come with his desire to live for himself. The years spent comfortably with Melanie had only brought nuanced conflict, never the type of pain he had endured in his heart since their fight on the stairs.

She stopped again, this time to study a menu board. She looked like a tourist; her faded blue jeans and sneakers screamed of North American culture. Her small daypack rested over her flannel button-up shirt in stereotypical fashion. She pulled at her hair, which was greasy and slightly unkempt, and with her other hand stretched an elastic around a fistful and snapped it into a small pony tail. Caleb watched as she turned and kept walking. Jas nudged him to keep moving and they followed her as she turned onto rue de la Bucherie.

"Oh my. Is she going to Shakespeare's? Maybe we're all wrong," Liese said excitedly.

They were across the street as they watched her slow up and turn towards a green storefront with a giant yellow sign above the doorway that read SHAKESPEARE AND COMPANY. There were small crowds of people congregating outside, fingering through stacks of books and chatting idly. She sat down on a wooden bench resting against the exterior of the store and rested her face in the cradle of her hands.

"Well, none of us guessed this, but we still haven't seen who she's meeting. I bet her parents will be coming out the bookstore any minute," Liese said.

"There's no one. She just resting," Jas said.

"No, it's her boyfriend," Caleb asserted.

It took less than a minute for Caleb to know the game was over as he watched Ryan exit the store carrying a book in his hand. He walked towards the street and stopped. Joss saw him and ran up behind him.

"Holy shit, there's a dreadlocked kid," Jas said.

Joss slowed up as she approached the figure wearing ripped jeans and a green army jacket. He had a book tucked under his arm and his other hand placed in his pocket. She jumped up onto his back, and he stumbled two steps back to gain his balance and keep them from falling. Joss was laughing, but Ryan looked irritated at first as he let her down. When she wrapped her arms around him, he hugged her back and they walked on hand-in-hand.

Both Kiwi Jas and Liese turned and watched Caleb walk away.

Liese caught up to him and put her arm around him and told him he didn't have to talk about it.

He squeezed her hand and they kept walking but he couldn't shake the nagging feeling that it meant something. Seeing her this way was difficult but it forced him to finally see what Melanie had felt when he left her. He understood the pain a little better now.

He was struck with the realization that everyone on earth was just trying to be happy. Wasn't that why he came to Europe, why he gravitated to Joss? And wasn't Joss, and Ryan too, just trying to be happy together? How could he be angry with them when they all wanted the same thing? It caused people pain at times, but it was the only truth in life. He felt some of the weight in his heart lift for he knew deep down that he wanted Joss to be happy, just as he wanted others in his life to be. He had caused Melanie a lot of pain through his own struggle for happiness, and he wondered if she had ever come to the same realization he had. And he understood that it was through him that she had sought happiness. He was the thing she gravitated to when she was in pain. How hurtful it must have been for her to watch him toss it all aside, all her love. He realized how unconscious he'd been, and decided it was time to return to her and make things right. It was exciting, this feeling. Whatever it was he had come to Europe for, he felt he had found it in this moment.

September 22, 1944

Dear Patrick,
I received two of your letters at once today and so I'm writing in response to them both. I don't think you've received my last few, which makes me feel horrible. I hope they find their way to you or you can read them when you return. Say hi to Jack for me and feel free to share the honey and cigarettes with him. The papers are keeping us up to date with what's going on over there and we all take comfort in the good news lately. The ladies at the Church have been praying extra hard for you and for Ed Landon (he enlisted last year – remember Ed?). I'm so lucky to have the ladies at the Church – it's wonderful how dedicated they are. It's comforting to be able to go and pray with them. I'm realizing how important community is these days. I'm lucky in that way. Some people are all alone in this world. But not you and I, Pat. We have each other and our family and the Church and our friends. We are lucky even though it doesn't feel that way right now. I feel so good about our future together and think we are bringing Jack into a good world, one full of love. I miss you I'm sending you another picture of us. Everyone thinks that Jack looks so much like you. I can't wait for you to meet him. I visited Phenon and Margaret's cottage like I said and it's gorgeous. The sunsets are so nice across the lake and the people are so kind up north. The bugs can be quite a nuisance, though! I hope we can go and have a look when you get home. I do think you'd love it up there, Pat. We could invite Phenon and Margaret over for dinners outside. I can just picture it now. I hope that plants a wonderful image in your head, one you'd like to return to. Picture me in that yellow dress you like so much, the one I was wearing on the day we met. I've kept it, and I'll be wearing it again the next time we meet. I know that will be soon.

All my love,
Marie

17

Kiwi Jas stared intently as he talked.

"Time is a funny thing mate: it can heal you or it can bury you. But remember – time isn't real; only your choices are. And you can choose to let each day be a stitch in the healing or a shovel of dirt in your undoing, but ultimately it's up to you, even though it doesn't feel that way. The easy thing to do is let it bury you, because all you have to do is choose to do nothing and those shovels of dirt will pile up. The harder choice is to take action and find ways to enjoy life on your own terms."

The rain had held off all morning but was threatening now as the two sat on the terrace at their usual table. Jas' words reminded Caleb of the days spent after Melanie left him and the struggle he faced to negotiate the hours alone. The darkness he had experienced – that was the grave Kiwi Jas was talking about. He knew the pain. He understood the feeling of standing still for too long.

"I've seen men do drastic things to fill the void a woman's left behind. I know how hard it is – that loss, the feeling of watching someone go on with their life without you," Jas said with his hand on Caleb's shoulder.

"I just can't picture you being heartbroken," Caleb said. "You don't seem like the kind of guy who has women leave him. I'm sorry if that sounds weird."

"It's just not true mate – remember I told you about Naomi, my Irish ex? Well, what I didn't tell you was that she ended things, said she couldn't rely on me. It was her decision to leave for New York without me. I was heartbroken for awhile and I had to get out of Killarney – hell I had to get out of Ireland. To this day, an Irish accent still makes me think of her. That's real. But I used the time to get better, instead of to dwell. Sure the travel helps a lot – I think it would have been more difficult had I stayed in Killarney after she left. It's always easier when you're in motion. The one who stays put always suffers." A raindrop fell onto the table in front of them with a dull thud, followed by three more rapid knocks, and then a roar of thunder.

"Just keep moving, man, and you'll never get hurt."

The rain came down all afternoon retiring them to their bunks for a lazy day spent sleeping and reading. Caleb had debated telling Kiwi Jas he was going home to work things out with Melanie. He still had to convince himself it was the right decision, but deep down, he knew it was. He knew he could return to Europe again another time with her. They could go straight to Torquay for a week, the place he should have gone right away. He hadn't gotten any closer to his grandfather by traveling across the continent. Or they could spend a week at the cottage and reconnect there.

The following day, Jas brought up the job at the front desk and Caleb still couldn't tell him he was leaving soon. He figured he could work a few shifts for a few free nights and then change his ticket to fly out of De Gaulle airport.

And he appreciated the effort Jas put into getting him the position. He wanted to work, but just as the nature of most men prohibits them from seeking work when leisure is affordable, he found it difficult to force the matter.

"So, I gave the owner your form, the one you filled out, and he's just processing the paperwork, so your first shift will be Friday night – the late shift – are you cool with that? You'll be taking over for Jari – you know that Finnish dude who always pervs on the chicks?"

"Ya, okay."

"Well, he'll stick around and give you a hand for the first hour. You could always show up a bit early too and ask some questions. But Gregory, the owner, will only expect you there from 9pm on to get your free night."

"Where will you be at?"

"I'm going with Liese to a party one of her friends is throwing. Normally I work the Friday late shift but I took it off, which worked out perfectly. Look, the rain's letting up; let's go for a walk and grab a coffee."

"Lead the way. I'll buy. As a thank you," Caleb said.

"No worries."

"Everyone says you have to experience Paris in the rain, but it's just like any other city in the rain – makes me cold," Caleb said.

"Anyone who says they like any city in the rain is just being a pretentious twat."

"There's something I need to tell you," Caleb said. "I've decided to head home in a week and sort things out with Mel. I'll still work the shifts and everything...I really appreciate you doing this for me, it's just that..."

Suddenly, Jas stopped walking and turned as though he'd been startled. It was an expression Caleb had never seen on his friend's face as a deep concern settled into the corners of his mouth. He was watching a man cross the street towards them, too distant to make out his face. Jas turned his back to the street and changed his posture to a closed stance.

"Everything okay?" Caleb asked.

Jas darted a glance behind him to a man approaching and gained his composure. He turned to Caleb with a false tone. "All good, mate. I just remembered, I gotta make a phone call. Let's meet up later. And I understand about you wanting to leave. We'll talk more about it."

Jas slapped Caleb on the back and narrowed his eyes as though he were seeing him for the last time. It made Caleb uncomfortable but he nodded and said okay and watched him slip away into the cold, grey afternoon. The sky unleashed a downpour washing the street in blankets of rain. The man who seemed to have scared Jas off approached and offered Caleb shelter under his umbrella. The man wore brown leather shoes underneath the cuffs of his pants with dark water stains that reached half-way up his shins. He had dark Mediterranean features with a face that seemed approachable and full of candour. It was uncomfortable being so close to him, but he was happy to escape the rain. "Where did your friend go?" he asked Caleb.

"Who, Kiwi Jas? He said he had to make a phone call."

"Well, tell him I'll see him in a few days. He owes me some money."

"Why don't you tell him yourself," Caleb said abruptly, and ducked out from under his umbrella back into the rain. By the time he made it the café, the water had reached his scalp and was running down his face making it difficult to see. Thunder boomed like a cannon as he ordered a café au lait from a woman perturbed by the puddles he was leaving on her floor and all he could do was smile sheepishly back at her. The third round of thunder roared so loudly, it made him jump. It seemed as though it were coming through the door behind him.

Friday arrived and Caleb had not seen Kiwi Jas since his abrupt departure in the street. He took a shower to get ready for his shift and gave himself a quick glance in the mirror. He had let his facial hair grow and thought it might be appropriate to shave, especially if the owner was stopping by. When he finished, he packed up his small toiletries bag and went back to his room. He dressed in his cleanest clothes and went downstairs to start his shift. He had walked up and down the steps countless times as a patron of the hostel, but now he descended as an employee.

The lobby was empty and the only sound that could be heard was the rain. It hadn't stopped for three days. The young man at the check-in was reading Tolstoy and angled back from his stool so his back leaned against the wall. He looked in no rush to move, but Caleb introduced himself and announced that he was doing the late shift. The guy put his book down and introduced himself as 'Jari.'

"You've got the easy shift then, man," Jari said.

Caleb noticed his English was good, but the way he tacked on 'man' seemed forced like he had heard it in American movies.

"The busses all arrived here at three – so there won't be many people coming in during your shift." Jari pushed himself off the wall and then off the stool. "Anyways, we only have 10 beds left for tonight. Here – see." He opened the accommodation book, which outlined each room's availability. "Mainly, you'll be just overseeing things and making sure the front door stays locked and no one comes in without a key." He closed the book and looked at Caleb. "Is this your first shift?".

Caleb said yes and Jari offered to stick around for a little while to get him comfortable.

"Thanks. That would help. My friend Jas said he was going to leave a list of instructions for me, but I haven't seen him since Wednesday."

"Ahhh – Mr Kiwi Jas! The cool man. Actually, there is something here for you – it's got your name on it, but I don't know who left it."

Caleb opened the envelope and read the letter.

Hey you Crazy Canuck. If you're reading this, then I guess you're about to start your first shift. I'm sorry I haven't left you instructions like I promised. But more importantly, I'm sorry about the other thing. It's just who I've become. I don't know anything else anymore. You will forgive me when you're sixty-five sitting on your back porch taking stock of your life and feeling happy you lived adventures like this. How many people will be able to say they had an experience like the one you're about to have? Enjoy it. It will make you a better person when you return back to Piersville. But my advice is to never return; learn to be a real backpacker and maybe you'll run into me one day in a hostel in Peru and you can settle up with me then. And don't forget: it is never not right now. Be mindful and cherish what's real.

Kiwi Jas

The letter sent Caleb's thoughts running wild. 'What did he mean: the other thing?'

Jari interrupted his thoughts: "You said he was a friend of yours? How long you know him?"

Caleb was confused by the note and wasn't fully present when he responded. "We met a couple months ago in London. I've just met back up with him here in Paris. I guess I don't know him all that well, but he did offer me this position." He realized the scenario might have sounded strange to someone else. "Why do you ask?"

"Well, to be honest with you, I'm not sure you should have much trust in that person. I've been working here at Village for a long time now and things have been a little strange since he's started a few weeks ago."

"What do you mean - strange?" Caleb said.

"Strange like.....things going missing. Strange like that. I'm not sure. Never mind. He is your friend. I can tell. I am sorry."

Caleb eyed him suspiciously. He felt uneasy and wanted to change the subject. "So, you're from Finland, right?"

"Ja"

"I haven't been, but I hear good things. You guys have a pretty good hockey team"

"We won gold last year at the World Jr's. We hosted." The pride in his voice shone and he was happy with the change in topic as well, but the small talk wasn't shaking the uneasiness Caleb felt. His mind was still on the letter and its cryptic meaning.

A red umbrella pushed its way through the front door, held by a young man with a large frame and thick, black hair unkempt in a natural Mediterranean style. It was the same man who had shared his umbrella with Caleb days prior when Jas had left suddenly. He reached out and shook Caleb's hand.

"So, we meet again. I'm Gregory. This is my place."

"Caleb. I'm just starting work here tonight. Are you American?"

"Greek American. I run this hostel with my wife," Gregory said and then stepped into his role as owner and began to survey the place.

"Jari, can you make sure the pool cues are kept on the wall when not in use? I don't like them lying around. Remember we talked about this?" Gregory said and looked at him condescendingly. Jari nodded and walked over to comply with the request.

Gregory walked behind the front desk and called to Jari again: "And have you put the payment in the safe yet?"

Jari called back that he had.

Gregory disappeared into the back room for a few minutes and when he returned, he looked at Caleb. "Jari showing you how sings are done?"

"Yes, he's going to stick around for awhile and show me the ropes."

"Good. And the arrangement is that for each shift you work, you get free accommodation for one night."

"Yes, actually Kiwi Jas has explained a few things to me so far. I think he talked to you about me."

Gregory raised his eyebrow and looked at him curiously.

"Kiwi Jas huh? You tell Kiwi Jas he still owes me for his first week here. I believe you told me to tell him myself in a fairly curt manner. You were the one I met in the street the other day, correct? I don't care about that. I care that you're a trustworthy worker, but don't take that tone with me again, clear? Is Kiwi Jas around?"

"Clear. I'm not sure where he is actually. I haven't see him since that day."

"If you see him, you tell him to be here at this time tomorrow. He is a good talker, that guy, but I'm done with his talking. I need some money."

Gregory opened the reservation book and fingered quickly through the pages. "How many beds are occupied for tonight, Jari?"

"About forty."

Gregory mulled the number over in his head. Everything he did seemed to be in haste and his focus shifted from one thing to the next rather quickly. He reached under the counter and brought up a binder and fingered through it eyeing each document carefully until he came upon what he was looking for. He snapped the metal rings open quickly and shoved a piece of paper at Caleb. He didn't seem like the same man Caleb had met in the street the other day.

"Here, fill this out. It's not a paid position, but I ask all employees to fill it out. You can skip your banking info. That's just for paid positions."

Caleb recognized the form. It was the same one Kiwi Jas handed him a week ago.

"Oh, I've already filled this out. Jas had one for me. I gave it to him already."

Gregory looked confused. "Jason had you fill out a form that looked like this?" He asked and searched the air with his eyes. "Did you fill out your banking information and social security number?"

"Ya."

Gregory turned to Jari and asked for Jas' room number. He rushed out of the lobby and upstairs and when he returned, he asked Caleb: "Where's your passport?"

"In my bag" Caleb said nervously.

"When's the last time you saw it? Gregory asked.

"I don't know. It was there on Monday."

"Never leave your passport. Go quickly and see if it's there."

Caleb froze for a second

"Go!"

He raced back up the steps two at a time and fumbled the key in the lock before falling through the doorway. He ripped open his backpack, slid his hand down until he could feel the bottom. His heart was racing. Surely, it was still there, he thought, it was all a misunderstanding. His hand was searching the through dirty clothes and sundry items for the small booklet that would calm his heart down and bring everything back to normal. Nothing. He started pulling everything out and scattering it on the floor. He picked each item of clothing up and searched through it. His grandparents letters were there; thank God, he thought. But no money belt. It wasn't there. His heart sunk into his stomach and his skin turned to gooseflesh..

Gregory and Jari entered the room.

"It's gone isn't it?"

Gregory was looking at Caleb like a disappointed father. "Kid, I'd call your bank right away. It's likely that he's cleared out your account," Gregory said shaking his head. "Fuck. There was something about that kid I didn't trust."

He wasn't himself when Gregory entered with news that his new passport would take a week to arrive. Caleb threw his fist down on the front desk. "Why so fucking long?" he said irritably and Gregory took offense and yelled back for him to calm his tone, that it wasn't his fault.

"I don't have to help you, kid," Gregory said.

But Caleb harboured resentment and felt the hostel was partly to blame. When they started to argue, Caleb brought it up.

"Why do you have those banking forms around for anyone to take?" he said and pulled out the drawer where they were kept. He pointed at them but Gregory slammed the drawer shut with this foot and stepped into Caleb's face.

"You think this is my fault?" he yelled back. "Who's stupid enough to fill out his banking information for a stranger?"

Caleb's face was red, but he didn't back down. He had nothing and everything to lose. "He wasn't a stranger. He was my..."

Caleb turned away.

"Yeah, yeah. Kiwi Jas is everyone's friend. Listen kid. I'll help you get a new passport, but as for working here, I can't have someone in my employment who doesn't have a valid passport. It's the rules."

"Are you fucking kidding me? Where am I going to stay?"

"That's not my problem kid. I've got a family to feed and I'm not risking my business on a kid who's run into some bad luck. I still don't understand why you don't just call home and get money from your parents. Seems pretty easy to me."

"You don't understand," Caleb said. "My leaving was....I'll figure it out," he sighed.

"I'll hold your passport for you when it arrives, but it could be another week. Just call your parents, kid, and get a nice comfy hotel room," Gregory said as Caleb walked towards his room to pack. "This will make a great story someday," he yelled but Caleb was already in the hallway and had stopped listening.

He was in a philosophical mood as he sat on the cold steps by the Seine watching the river flow. The afternoon ushered in a cool wind, and as the sun jumped from cloud to cloud, it cast shadows on the street vendors along the riverbank. He felt depleted.

Skins had broken his body in London, and Joss had broken his heart in Prague, but Kiwi Jas had broken his spirit and it was the most damaging of all. Caleb got up and manoeuvred through the busy crowd to the bridge. He mustered little motivation, but worked his way to the edge and ran his hand along the stone barricade. The slow current was moving the riverboats along and he lost his orientation as he fixed his gaze on them. He stared across the river at the bridges stapled along it fastening the two sides of the city together. He contemplated each staple coming loose and the two sides of Paris splitting apart, drifting away in different directions with only a vast body of water remaining. He had never felt so alone.

He looked at his watch and realized he had nowhere to go. He thought about Franny and Daniel and where they might be – he was happy with them in Vienna, but he had abandoned the complacency of standing still for the gamble of flux. He had gambled and lost.

He was too ashamed to call home and admit he needed help. He knew his parents would offer him money, Melanie too, but his pride would suffer - he would have to admit defeat and he wasn't prepared to do it. He decided he would sort things out alone. He had a passport coming and was grateful for Gregory for taking him to the Canadian Embassy to sort it out and pay for it. He just needed to find a way to survive for a week while he got his passport in order. He needed enough money to pay for his flight change. Then, he could fly home to be with Melanie. One step at a time, he thought. Step one: find a place to sleep.

October 10, 1944

Dear Marie,
I wish I could write you one of my long letters, honey, but we've been moving so quickly that I don't get the time I'd like to properly tell you about what's been happening. Things are intense right now, but I can't say much in these letters, so I'll save it for when I get home. I'll tell you this my love, I've never missed you more than I do right now. I wish I had your arms around me. I wish I could just see your face. I love you so much, Marie.

Jack is no longer in our company, and I feel like I've lost the only true friend I have over here. I feel we will meet up again someday. I still owe him a whiskey, so maybe I'll get to repay my debt in the years to come. He flew more than fifty missions, which is unheard of, Marie. I'd say he's got the luck of the Irish alright.

I have to say that I feel quite lonely today. Some days are just worse than others. My legs are quite sore but there's no sense in complaining. I know how hard things have been for you and I hope you get to take that vacation to Niagara like you mentioned. You deserve it and it would be swell for Jack to see the Falls. I remember the first time I saw them as a child – the water was so powerful. I was barely tall enough to see over the glass and the mist came up all the way and soaked us. I wish I could be there with you both but there will plenty of time to vacation as a family. I like the idea of the cottage, Marie, and when I get home, we'll think on it together.

My legs are starting to cramp up so I better finish up. There are never any easy spots to sit down and write a proper letter but I promise I'll write you a longer one soon. I miss you so much, my love.

All my love,
Patrick

18

"Malebranche," Caleb said.

His heart was pounding and he wondered if he had pronounced it correctly. The young woman eyed him suspiciously as one does any stranger who is requesting something.

He looked too old to be a student, but his face looked sincere. His hair was greasy and unkempt. There were plum coloured bags under his eyes that signalled he hadn't slept in awhile. His Nike running shoes and Levi's jeans looked painfully out of place in any contemporary style of French fashion. The pack strapped to his waist forced him slightly forward and under his arm he was barely holding onto a case of art supplies that looked rather new. She paused and let him in.

"The loft is upstairs," she said. "You must wait here for Professor Goetschle first. He'll want to ask you a few questions. She looked him up and down again critically to let him know she wasn't sure of him – she looked like a woman who was naturally sceptical of everyone. She had thin lips that disappeared when she talked and her nose formed a small hook on her flat face. She was medium height and skinny with small dark eyes; her brown hair was cut neatly below her ears.

Caleb followed her into an apartment, which held a small, colourful kitchen and a doorway into a main living area with a window facing out into the street. She motioned him to take a seat at the table in the kitchen, which was covered in a mosaic of fragmented faces. The linoleum on the floor was dated and torn in places and a table sat in the middle of the room with two wooden chairs around it. He took one.

"Would you like a beer?"

"Yes. Thank you." He nodded a superfluous gesture. She moved slowly across the kitchen to the fridge, and pulled out a large bottle of beer. He didn't recognize the label and the first sip tasted bitter. The silence that hung between them was awkward, and he searched the room to avoid eye contact. The only window looked out to a brick wall across the alley. It was full of soft light. He noticed a large painting on the wall – it was of a child dressed in a suit and tie holding a gun. The young boy was staring out with apologetic eyes and a dour set of the mouth.

"You like it?" she asked.

"Yes. Did you paint that?"

"Yes. It is my son. What do you like about it?"

Caleb panicked. "I like the whole 'loss of innocence' theme and the contrast of images. It's powerful – what he represents."

"There's no symbolism – that's a true portrait. That's his suit and his gun," she responded plainly without blinking.

Caleb could not tell if she was being honest, and had nothing more to say but he remembered a conversation he had with Liese. "Well, I think you made the right choice to paint him instead of photograph him. Painting is the only real art form. Everything else is just entertainment passed off as art," he said.

The woman's small eyes narrowed on him, but she seemed satisfied with this comment and made a noise suggesting she agreed and then she reluctantly turned and left the kitchen.

Caleb took a large mouthful of beer and fought the urge to run. He wondered if she believed him. What would happen if they knew he was lying? Would they call the police? Could he be arrested? He convinced himself to stay, realizing he had no other choice.

The adventure Jas promised in his letter was beginning to unfold. The incident forced him into a defeated but empowered position whereby he felt compelled to gamble more – to keep moving. There are only some actions that can be taken when a person has nothing to lose. The more things a person accumulates, the less freedom he has to make desperate decisions.

He began to grow anxious as the minutes passed with no sign of the professor, but he used this time to go over his story. When the door opened again, a round, stout figure in corduroy pants and thin sweater entered the kitchen and stood over Caleb's hesitant frame slouched onto the table nursing the last few sips of his beer. Caleb stood up. The man reached out a large, soft hand and Caleb shook it. His face was red as though descending the stairs had worn him out. Professor Goetschle had a full head of white hair and his face was speckled with grey stubble. His eyes were penetrating and a smile formed unnaturally on his thick lips.

"So, I'm assuming you know who I am, since you came to us. I, however, do not know who you are and you don't look familiar to me. I know most of our students, and I cannot discern your face as one that frequents our campus," he said.

"I'm Canadian, Sir. I'm from Montreal"

The man repeated the city and it wasn't clear if he was questioning it or thinking aloud.

"Where do you study?"

"McGill. I'm in the middle of a fine arts degree. Just became uninspired with my classes – they seem too full of pedantic fools. I will return when I have created something I would proudly hang on my own wall."

The professor lifted his head slightly as though he were thinking and Caleb looked away. He shuffled his feet, leaned back against the table and tried to look sullen.

"Pride has nothing to do with art," he said in a booming voice that startled Caleb. "Do you feel defeated?"

"I'm hungry and tired. But I know there is something inside of me that needs to get out. I came to this country for a reason. I am standing here before you for a reason. The reason is coming from in here." Caleb pointed to his gut and the man nodded.

"How did you find out about us? How did you know to come here with the word 'Malebranche'? We don't use that word anymore. That was for last month."

"I met your daughter....Liese."

"My daughter? Where?"

"Here in Paris."

The professor said something in French and rubbed his forehead.

"How did she look?" The question caught Caleb off guard and he scrambled with an appropriate answer. "Well, did she look healthy?" he asked, slightly angered at the hesitation.

"She looked....healthy....yes."

"I don't see her very often anymore. She comes by here once in awhile, doesn't she Petra?" He looked back to the woman with the flat face who had let Caleb in. "She dances in and out of my life less frequently, but seems to spend more of my money." He paused. "Why did you come to this country with no money?"

"I had some, but it was stolen from me. Somebody I trusted. Right now, I have nothing. I would very much like to ask for your hospitality, but I will understand if you turn me away."

The man's gaze returned to Caleb's backpack and belongings. "So Liese told you what this loft is for I assume. I rent this place so my students can have a place to create. I don't care what they create so long as it challenges the way we look at the world. Some of my students even live here. I can give you a space to sleep and a canvas to paint on. It looks as though you have some art supplies with you, although they are very low quality – I don't know what you expect to paint with those." The professor paused for a second. "You can stay for a week, but I want a piece of art out of you while you're here. Petra will get you some better paints and brushes. And, I don't want to hear my daughter's name again. Do you have something to sleep on?"

"I'll make do with a spot on the floor," Caleb said with whatever stoicism he could muster. His excitement was hardly disguised.

"I only have one rule you must abide by here. You must respect the other artists. If there is any attempt on your part to undermine or compromise the other projects, you will be asked to leave. Some of the people who inhabit this space may not even speak to you and you must respect that. No one need explain their work to anyone but me, is that clear?"

"Yes, Sir."

"That being said, if anyone disrupts your progress in a manner you find inexcusable, you come to me first. You will be living in a place void of external conflict – the only real conflict lies within one's head." He put his finger up to Caleb's temple. "That is the conflict I want you to focus on. Respect it. You will tolerate things you do not agree with, things you do not like, people you do not find agreeable and art you do not find tasteful. If you can do these things you will fit right in here at this place. Find yourself a spot and sleep for a little while. You will not be starting anything today. You need to adjust to your new surroundings first. Let your work be what your body wills it to be, but do not confuse your body with the world it inhabits. They are two different constructs and art exists in both of them. I will come by in a few days and see how you are doing. I'm glad you are here. North America needs new ideas. I hope you can come up with one. There are some great things happening in this loft. Do you know why?" He stared at Caleb but didn't wait for a response. "Because everyone's hungry and poor."

"Thanks again, Sir."

He put his hand on Caleb's shoulder, lifted it and brought it back down with amicable force. He smiled quickly as though he had just accomplished something. Petra will show you upstairs. He left the apartment and Petra signalled Caleb to follow her. He collected his things and rushed to catch the door.

They ascended two flights of stairs and opened a large metal door into a wide, high-ceilinged loft lined with windows on each side that spread natural light into an otherwise cold and dull space, receiving little in the way of aesthetics besides the many canvases propped up onto easels and leaning against walls. The floor was concrete, cold and clinical. Caleb did a quick survey and counted more than twenty stations of people – some with futons set up in mock bedroom arrangements, but with no walls. A few screens had been set up between stations to give the illusion of rooms and as he looked closer at some of the work being created, he grew anxious. These were real artists. Some canvases stretched as wide as eight feet high. There were only six people in the loft that Caleb could see and none of them seemed all that interested in him.

"Here." Petra pointed to an empty mattress on the floor. It was a well-lit spot underneath a window. He set his pack down and rested the cheap art supplies, the ones he had stolen that morning.

Before Petra left him, she pointed out the washroom and small kitchen area at the far end of the loft, where the commons room was with a television, should he feel the need to watch some French programming to pass the time.

When she left, he walked back and explored – the rooms resembled the hostels he'd stayed in, only they were filled with real people, not spoiled, college kids taking a romp through Europe for the summer, commenting on how much their dollars were worth and stumbling around drunk every night. There were no groups of giggling American girls and Canadian boys showing off their hockey scars and talking about finding some good whiskey. It was not humming with travelers who could afford to act ignorant of real culture, making plans instead to visit every tourist trap in the city and collect post-cards and be gouged by restaurants that were catered to them by offering some American flair.

A few people eyed him as he rolled his blanket out onto an empty mattress and unpacked some of his things. He tried not to look at anyone as he spread his stuff out to mark his space: a thin blanket, his book, a flashlight and his toiletry bag. He tucked his art supplies out of sight. He had never painted anything, besides in high school when he fumbled his way through some landscapes, but if there was ever a time in his life to express himself creatively, it was here in Europe, in the loft, broken, hungry and scared.

When he awoke, there was no light coming in through the windows, only from a few naked bulbs hanging from the ceiling. He felt a sudden sense of aloneness. There was a note sitting beside him that read: 'When I was new, I needed friend. There is pub down this street. Kafka's. Come for drink when wake. On me.'

He scratched his head and looked around for the author. No one.

The pub was poorly lit and smelled like the body odour of old men. He forged his way between two bar stools and rested his elbow against the rail. The bartender looked his way between a long row of raised beer taps, boasting of a serious attention to craft, and cocked his head at Caleb's presence.

"Stella," Caleb said and pointed the tap handle.

As he waited, he felt the presence of someone behind him.

"Only foreigner would order Stella in a place as this. I see you found note." He gave a gigantic smile that stretched across a wide, chalk-white face.

"It was the only one I recognized," Caleb said. "Thanks for the invite. I'm Caleb."

"Hello Caleb. I am Peter. Thanks for coming. I have sitting alone here...for long time now. It is good to have other people to...drink beer!" His dark eyes lit up and his smile revealed a set of crooked teeth. His hair was black and thinly strewn across his forehead. There was an innocence to his face, but a shark-like hardness in his eyes.

The bartender returned with a pint of Stella and set it down quickly, spilling around the glass and leaving circles of beer on the dirty bar where coasters seemed like an afterthought. Caleb relished the first sip. It had been a week since he had a cold beer. Peter had quickly handed the bartender some money before Caleb could reach into his pocket and he thanked Peter, letting him know just how little money he had.

"I understand. No problems. I invite you. Beer is on me. I say this in note."

Peter signalled him over to a small table near the front door where he had been sitting. The tables were thick with narrative and could only be seen through a thin veil of smoke floating around them in rivers of sweet smelling tobacco.

Neither spoke as they got settled but sipped their beers nervously in place of conversation. Peter seemed harmless, but Caleb was guarded, having learned that getting to know anyone while traveling was dangerous.

"So, I'm getting better at accents. You're not from France are you?" Caleb asked.

"Russia," Peter said and thought for a second. "No. Austria as child. Then Russia. My father he is Russian."

"So, if you don't mind me asking, how did you end up at the loft?"

"Long story," Peter said slowly.

Caleb gave him a look that he wanted to know, so Peter stumbled his way through a story that Caleb understood very little of. He made out a few pieces of information - that when Yeltsin began liberalizing in 1992, his father moved the family to Moscow to capitalize as an entrepreneur and open his own hardware store, but he was over extended by the time the depression hit and he had to close up shop. Shock therapy didn't work and the people longed for the Gorbechev years again. Peter had received word of this in his second semester at the College of Art and subsequently his funding for school was cut off. He moved into the Professor's loft shortly after with the desire to continue in some artistic realm. He had little reason to return home to Russia.

"So you are not actually attending school then?" Caleb said slowly.

For the first time, Peter looked despondent. "No. I drop out last year. No money for my tuition. But I keep painting so Professor, he let me stay at loft."

Caleb nodded and said nothing. He could hear Peter say something to himself in Russian, but all Caleb could make out was a word he thought was 'perestroika'.

"So I see Canada flag on your backpack. You are from there?"

"Yes. I come from a city called Montreal. I attend school there."

"So why you here then?"

"I'm just taking a break. I was feeling......lost. Does that make sense?"

"Lost?"

"Sad"

"Oh, I see." Peter was struck by the comment, as though he did not equate Canada with sadness. Caleb took a big gulp of beer. Peter noticed they were getting low and offered to buy them another round. He insisted.

When he returned, it was obvious he had been thinking of topics to discuss. He was eager to know who Caleb studied back home. Caleb was ready for a question of that nature and drew on his visits to European art galleries and museums. Peter was satisfied with his answer of Degas, Rubens and Renoir, but not overly impressed.

"But who is the ones you really like?" Peter asked, itching to spill his own passions.

"I do love Van Gogh. His story is such a sad and passionate one, you know. I love art that comes from addiction," Caleb said and wasn't sure why.

"You North Americans don't know good art," Peter said with a smile. Caleb didn't take offense. He knew Peter was probably right.

"Hermann Nitsch. He is great artist – Actionist. He not just paint, but involves the people in his art. Some say he is pornography or blasphemy, but they don't understand what he is doing. He is exposing our silly beliefs – he hold a mirror up to us," Peter tapped a glass pane beside him that held the reflection of the bar in fuzzy lines.

Caleb was starting to feel out of his element and tried to contribute: "Well, at least he paints. Painting is the one true art form."

"Yes, but he also sacrifice sheep – he works with blood and flesh too. He is all your five senses in live theatre form. Yes, he goes to jail for this many times, but he is missionary." Peter wasn't sure if that was the word he wanted, and was finding it difficult to continue describing Nitsch's work in English, and blurted out "He is Austrian!" as a jovial closing to his description.

Peter indicated that he was out of money or else he would have bought them another round.

"We can order more – we will just leave without paying," Caleb said. "I've done it before."

Peter looked confused at this and shook his head. "No, this is not what men do. No, that is not right to do, to do something like this. No, we are done. We finish beers and go home," Peter said adamantly.

Caleb felt strange hearing the loft referred to as home, but he nodded his head, ashamed of his suggestion, realizing now what kind of a thing it was to steal to survive.

He knew he should be slow to trust anyone, but he trusted Peter for some reason. He looked Caleb in the eyes when he spoke and he meant what he said. And the earnestness in his expression assured Caleb that he had no agenda besides friendship.

"I lied," Caleb said. "When I told you I came from Montreal. I'm not an artist. I mean, I can play the guitar, but I don't paint."

Peter, confused at first, didn't respond, and in a moment of trust, something Caleb thought he no longer had any of, decided to tell Peter the whole truth – he told him of why he came to Europe; the beating he took in London; meeting Kiwi Jas; and Joss, and Miranda, and Ryan; his uncertainty about his relationship with Melanie; feeling that his best time was spent in the mornings in

Vienna; and how he made his way to Paris and what happened there. He didn't know why he trusted Peter, but he told him honestly that he just needed a place to stay until he could find some money to get home to Melanie

The feeling of being hungry and down on one's luck resonated with Peter and he nodded. "You do need friend," he said and smiled. "Like I say in note."

They finished their beers and exited Kafka's in good spirits. Caleb was glad he took the risk and came - the evening had taken his mind off his troubles, and he felt he had finally found something of a friend.

December 2, 1944

Dear Patrick,
I continue to pray for you, my love. This has lasted longer than all of us had imagined. Except for Phenon, that card. He somehow knew it. I'm horrified to read the newspaper accounts of what you're discovering over there. I hope you're not seeing what they're describing. I can't imagine how awful things have been over there for you, Patrick. I know you're lonely, and it makes me feel so terrible that I can't do anything about it, but I promise that when you get home, I'm going to wrap my arms around you and never let go. You deserve the world and I want to give that to you.

I'm so happy you think the cottage is a good idea. I think it would be so lovely to have a place to go with Jack and let him run around in the woods. You could teach him so much there. And just think about all the campfires we could have. We could toast marshmallows and you could sing songs and play the guitar for us. I just love that one Gene Autry song you sing. I do play that record from time to time and it reminds me of you.

It's difficult to know which of my letters are reaching you, and I pray that each one does in time. I'll continue to write as I know how important it must be to hear from us. I have so many plans for when you return and I can't wait to begin our lives together.

All my love,
Marie

19

A blank canvas stood before him as his second day in the loft came to an end. He had mustered very little artistic imagination and felt hungry for food and nothing for aestheticism.

He went to find Peter and when he peeked his head into the common room, a young woman with blonde hair and green eyes smiled and waved at him to sit down, but he declined and returned to his mattress.

When Peter returned, he appeared out of the dim light of the loft. He came and sat down beside him and crossed his legs. He had in his hands a packet of photos and began handing him one at a time explaining in great detail who each person was. The figures held stoic gazes, even the women, as though to smile was to show weakness. The clothes they wore were plain and tailored neatly around their neck; they reminded him of the pictures of his grandparents after the war.

When Peter was finished, Caleb showed him the photos he had with him. One was of Melanie. It was Caleb's favourite photo of her, one he often kept with him. In it, she was slightly drunk, but glowing from the alcohol and smiling unabashedly into the camera with her hand on her waist. She was wearing tight blue jeans and a black top that cupped her breasts well. She looked happy and full of youth.

Peter slowly handed him back the picture and asked if she knew where he was or that he had run out of money. Caleb said that she didn't and placed the picture back into his bag.

Peter stood up and signalled that he'd be back in a minute. When he returned, he had a guitar in one hand and a paint brush in the other. He handed Caleb the guitar and then, looking around to make sure no one was watching, proceeded to send his brush across the empty canvas in a few long strokes that challenged what Caleb thought about the power of a few brush strokes. He said good night and Caleb said thank you in an honest declaration of gratitude. He felt a little closer to him, and a lot closer to returning home to Melanie.

Holding the guitar by the top of the neck, Caleb searched the park for a spot to practice. He wanted to be invisible until he was ready to perform, so he settled against a tree off the beaten path and danced his fingers up and down the frets, stretching his memory for the three or four songs he used to play waiting for his night shifts to start.

A John Prine song started to come back to him. Slowly, a few more returned and he spent another half an hour going through each one, ensuring his strumming was on and his lyrics were right. Nervously, he stood up and walked back down the path to the mouth of the park that was swallowing a steady stream of people.

He had forgotten to bring the case and realized he had no receptacle to place before him, so he fished through the closest garbage bin and picked out a dirty paper bag. He dumped the pieces of bread out and folded down the rim, making small rips where necessary so it sat on the dirty ground flopped over like a pathetic jester's hat. He took his place again, and, as some eyed him with disdain and some with curiosity, he began to play the Prine song and at first he sang quietly and those who passed by hardly noticed him. He received nothing. He moved on to a Pink Floyd song that required a little more of an advanced intro and lyrics that might catch more recognition. He sang a little louder this time but still made no eye contact with anyone. When he finished his second song, he looked down to see one coin in his bag. After the fourth song, he began again with his four song rotation, realizing that each person would only hear a few seconds and his four songs would carry him through the afternoon. After his third rotation, he began to care less about those who dismissed him and started to feel a simple freedom. He was playing music for money. It was pure. If people felt entertained, they gave him something, but the less he cared about the money and focused purely on doing the best rendition of the song he could, the easier it became. He was soon playing for his own enjoyment.

When hunger overtook him, he packed up the bag of coins and worried it would break through the bottom, so he put his other hand underneath to support it and hobbled over to a nearby tree with the guitar tucked under his arm in an awkward shuffle. He stuffed three handfuls of coins into his pockets and tossed the bag back into a bin. He went and bought some bread, cheese, meat and red wine, and returned to the loft. He found Peter lying on his mattress reading a letter with great, sullen intent.

Caleb sat next to him and put down the things he carried. He wanted to ask if he could make him something to eat but instead he asked if everything was alright. He could now see that Peter had been crying.

"My father is died," he said.

Caleb put his arms around him and hugged him as Peter buried his head into Caleb's shoulder but he didn't cry. Neither man spoke; there was nothing to say.

With little communication, they found themselves back at Kafka's and Caleb spent the money he had earned that day on vodka and beer and listened to the truth about his father's death in the dim light of the pub and what Caleb realized was that Alexai had taken his own life in likely fashion for a man in turmoil.

"Things bad in Russia," Peter said after a long silence. "I know that. This Yeltsin no good. He too close to Americans. Gorbachev at least had vision for country, but Yeltsin just puppet. So many rich people now but poor people suffer so. Why? For what?" Peter paused and hung his head close to his beer. "But, I didn't think this to happen. I am responsible. My sister thinks so," he said matter-of-factly.

"You couldn't have saved him," Caleb said. "You need to be here, pursuing your passion. You've got serious talent and you need to continue. Hell, even the thing you brushed onto my canvas is better than anything I could ever create."

Peter seemed affected by this and said thank you while looking into his beer like there was an answer to life in there somewhere. He was holding onto it with both hands.

They sat at their table in the corner until both of Caleb's pockets were empty and wandered back to the loft with heavy heads that would leave them lethargic for the entire next morning.

Throughout the day, artists stopped by Peter's station with gifts of food and vodka. They huddled around him, awkwardly shifting their eyes to avert direct contact. Caleb had not seen many of them in the loft before; it was though they had come out of the shadows. They appeared for the news of death.

The crowd flickered like a flame around Peter. Caleb had little luck making conversation with anyone, but gave a sympathetic smile to the blonde with green eyes he had seen in the common room. She smiled kindly back at him and asked his name.

"Caleb."

"Cay-leb?"

"Yes, and yours?" he asked.

"Nimara," she said.

She was attractive from a distance, but up close she was intimidatingly beautiful. Her olive-green eyes rested softly on a honey-coloured cheekbones. When she spoke, her upper lip danced over her front teeth that slanted towards her tongue, and when her expression rested, the corners of her lips curled towards her eyes.

"Do you know Peter well?" he asked her.

"No, but I respect him. He...pure talent. He do something great one day." She paused and smiled to someone who waved to her. "What you do here?" she asked.

"Learn" Caleb thought it sounded stupid but he didn't know what to say.

"We all here to learn. Are you?"

"Am I.....?"

"Learning," she said and laughed.

"I'm learning a lot about life," he said and worried about sounding cliché.

She curled her lips into a smile and touched his arm before moving on. Caleb took the opportunity to slip away from the crowd. He tucked Peter's guitar under his arm and took the exit to the stairs. He returned a few hours later with a bag from the depanneur. Peter was lying on his bed in a supine position staring at the ceiling. A woman with dark features and long dark hair was sitting cross-legged by his head; she was softly stroking his forehead. She looked at Caleb and smiled, signalling to place the groceries on the table against the wall. He unpacked the bag, and carefully laid out some crackers, cheeses, pickles, and vodka.

A few hours later, he returned to see more people congregated around Peter's station. What started as a rather reserved reception for Peter grew into a party. The crowd seemed more relaxed than the rigid reception that occurred that afternoon and there were many bottles of wine and vodka placed amongst dishes of food. A tall man with a thin, dark beard and cleft lip was playing guitar in the centre of the group and Nimara was singing a French ballad. Caleb walked over put his arm around Peter, who was singing along to Nimara's ballad and received a smile. He couldn't understand what it was exactly that made him feel comfortable around Peter. As they stood, swaying to the music, Caleb thought about the mortality of his own father and felt lucky he had him in his life. He would be there when he got home, but there would come a day when he would be placed in Peter's position. His thoughts grew deeper until they silenced everything around him. The vodka was taking hold. He looked around and caught Nimara in an innocent glance as she sang. He surveyed the rest of the space, but what caught his eye in one of the last things he remembered of the night was Petra and professor Goetschle standing by his station, turned towards his canvas in discussion. Petra was pointing at it and the professor was nodding.

He woke up in his bed with a strong headache and a dry mouth. He forced his body up off the mattress and made his way to the kitchen for a glass of water. He passed Peter's station, where half empty glasses and bottles were strewn across the floor. Peter was fast asleep, fully clothed and snoring. He looked peaceful.

He couldn't find any clean glasses, so he stuck his head under the tap and let the water pour into his mouth, inhaling large gulps and letting the water teem down his throat.

"Is that how to cure hangovers in America?"

The voice caught him off guard and he swallowed quickly and choked. Nimara was standing behind him in jogging pants and a worn red t-shirt.

"Did you leave some for me?" she asked.

Caleb laughed nervously causing his head to throb.

"I can wash you out a glass if you like?" he said.

"No. If tap is good enough for American, good enough for me."

Caleb moved out of the way to let her take a drink. "I'm not American by the way."

"Canadian?"

"Yup."

She turned the tap back on and gathered her hair to one side as she bent over to take a drink. Her shirt slid up and revealed her lower back. He noticed a tattoo of a symbol he'd never seen before in black ink.

"What are you planning to do today?" he asked her.

"Go for walk. Paint. Cry. The usual," she said.

"Would you like to come to the park with me to busk?"

"Busk?"

"Play guitar for money. You can sing. You're very good. I liked your song last night."

"Oh, I understand. Thank you for the compliments! I like to sing."

She thought for a second and agreed.

It began to rain as soon as they walked a few blocks, but it was only a light drizzle, so they continued onto the park and sat under a tree waiting for the rain to stop. He leaned the guitar against the tree and sat next to it with his back against the trunk. Nimara kneeled down beside him. She had on a pair of faded jeans and the same red t-shirt.

"So, how did you come to the loft?" she asked.

"I have a suggestion. Let's not ask each other that. I imagine neither of us is happy about the circumstances that led us here."

"You are right, perhaps. But I have nothing to be ashamed of. Do you?"

"I do have things to hide, yes – regrets. I'm full of them actually. But I'd rather ask you about where you're going than where you've been. What's next?"

"I'll finish a few more pieces, and the professor will help me get my first exhibit. Then I'll be famous and buy my own loft and make great work. That's where I will go. And you?'

"Home, eventually. But right now I need some money."

"We all need money."

"Yes, well I'm not much of a painter but I will try to produce something while I'm here. Peter's helping me."

Nimara's eyes dropped. "I feel so bad for Peter. He is good person. I want success for him."

"He's been nice to me."

"What do you want success at Cay-leb?"

"Forgiveness, I guess."

"You want to succeed at forgiving? For what?" She let out a puzzled laugh.

"I want to succeed at being forgiven."

"Oh, I see. You've been a bad boy."

"Yes."

"Then I hope you get forgiveness too. You seem like a good boy to me, even if you have done bad things. All you can do is ask."

They both sat in silence for a minute looking at the sky, trying to figure out if the rain would stop soon and then it did and the sky bled yellow through an opening in the clouds; the sun reflected off the puddles and hovered in the mist across the grass. The rain had come and gone and Nimara reached across him and took the guitar in her hands.

"Let's go," she said.

Caleb followed her to a spot along the main path between two benches and sat next to her on the wet ground.

"I'll start. Then you. We split all money," she said matter-of-factly.

Caleb agreed. "Just make sure you sing louder than me."

She played a few songs in French and then a few in English so he sang along when he could. Her voice was beautiful he felt confident beside her and he closed his eyes as she played.

She peered into the guitar case.

"I'm rich!" she said as she combed the bottom of the case.

"Hey!" Caleb reached out his hand to stop her. "We split it all up at the end. Busker's code."

She acquiesced and handed him the guitar. "Yes, of course. I'll just count."

He had gotten into the habit of keeping his eyes open while playing, and watching people's legs shuffle by in a dizzying parade. It seemed more patterned the more he watched- a thin knee followed by a stout knee followed by a pant leg followed by a briefcase followed by a cascading sun dress. Even the tossing of coins seemed to start following a pattern. Every few minutes, they landed with a thud, rolled against the side of the case and stopped. Each sound sparked a tiny burst of joy that slowly became a means to move again. He realized he would survive without calling home for help and it filled him with a joy he had not experienced before.

He exchanged a smile with Nimara and gazed back into the pattern of legs moving passed them until one, a thin set of female calves falling from a pair of blue shorts, stopped and disrupted the calming shuffle. He followed the legs up thin torso, past a small set of breasts forming mounds from a thin, white blouse and a up a long neck to a face he had not seen for awhile and one he had nearly forgotten about. He stopped playing.

"Caleb?"

"Miranda?"

"Holy shit. What are you doing? I mean, why are you...." She put her hand on her hip to signal she was thinking. Her mouth had descended at the corners as though she were concerned for a young child.

Caleb put down his guitar and stood, his face was flush with embarrassment. He didn't know what to say. He put his hands in his pockets and looked up to her. She was slightly taller than him and it always made him feel self-conscious.

"I'm just playing music with my friend. This is Nimara," he said. She stayed seated but waved a friendly greeting. "She's trying to make some money."

"I see. How have you been? *Where* have you been," she asked dutifully.

"Let's go grab a coffee."

"Will your friend be okay without you?" she asked in a voice that reminded him how condescending she could be.

"Nimara, is it cool if I take off for a few minutes?"

"Yes, of course. Go with your friend."

They walked a short distance and Miranda offered to buy.

"Are you sure?"

"Ya, it looks like you could use one. And a shower."

"I'm just hung over."

"Not much has changed I see."

"Listen, Miranda, I'm not in the mood to put up with an attitude. If you're still upset about Prague then that's your problem – I'm done apologizing. I don't have the energy to argue."

"I don't want to argue with you either Caleb. I'm sorry. It's good to see you. Seriously, is everything okay?"

"To be honest, no, not really. There have been some ups and downs. I'm surviving though."

"Is that why you're begging? Do you have a place to stay?"

"We're not begging. It's called busking."

"Where are you guys staying?"

"I forget the name. It's on rue de Latelliere. What about you? Are you still traveling with Ryan and Joss?" It still stung him a little to say their names together.

"No. We came to Paris together, but things got complicated. Actually, things changed after you left, to be honest. Dammit Caleb, why did you have to act like that in Prague? Why did you say those things? Everything was fine until then."

"I act like an asshole sometimes. I don't know why. So let me guess – Joss and Ryan ended up getting together?"

"You guessed it. Big shocker. You could probably see it coming, but I didn't. I'm not good at seeing that kind of thing I guess. I thought he liked me."

"He did like you. Just not the way you wanted him to. Guys are fucked up like that. They always go for the wrong girl."

Miranda smiled in consolation.

"Honestly, do you need some money?"

"Yes, I do, but not yours. I'm earning it by playing guitar. I'll make enough to get home. I don't think I've ever been so broke, but it's kind of freeing in a way."

"You're going back to your girlfriend?"

"I'm going home to see if she'll take me back. I can go see Torquay another time."

"What's in Torquay?"

"It's a place that my grandfather went after the war. It had a big impact on him and I guess I thought it would allow me to get closer to him or something. It was the only place he wanted to return to in Europe. This continent was a different place for his generation."

"It's just a playground for our generation," Miranda said.

"And you know what's funny: my grandpa saw so much death over here. For me, death is happening back home in Canada."

"The shooting?"

"Ya, my friends are dying at home while I'm in Europe. The places we find safe change over time I guess. Who would have thought that someone would open fire in a public place in Piersville. A kid too. He had barely turned twenty-one."

"It's happened before in Canada– Polytechnique in Montreal. It'll happen again. There's no such thing as a perfectly safe place."

"There are many needless ways to die I guess."

"But, the war wasn't needless," Miranda said. "Our grandparents' generation didn't die for nothing - we all know what they sacrificed for us. But, I'm starting to think this isn't the place for our generation either. I mean, what are we all doing over here?

"Escaping from our lives," said Caleb.

"Yeah, exactly. People just use this continent to escape their problems, their relationships. They wander from place to place getting drunk, hooking up and finding some time to visit museums to justify the trip. Look at us two – we didn't face anything; we ran away from our life. So did Ryan and Joss. So does everybody, I guess. If you want to call it a vacation, go for it, but I think our generation doesn't know how to handle the banality of real life so we find a way to escape it by racking up a debt we can't pay off. Sure we're going to have some great memories, but there is a life back home that both of us could have spent the energy trying to make better instead of coming over here."

"I know a guy who would have a great time arguing with you about that. But at least you guys are all trying to escape from painful situations. I had everything and took it all for granted. I was just running away from complacency. Who does that?"

She raised her eyebrows reflectively. "Being complacent doesn't always mean you're happy" she said and took a sip of her coffee.

"You know, I saw Joss and Ryan in here in Paris," Caleb said.

She searched his words for meaning and her mouth turned down at the corners again.

"Did they see you?" she asked.

"No. I didn't say hi. I figured it'd be better that way."

"Hmm. Maybe."

They finished their coffees in awkward silence and said goodbye.

"I'm sorry about everything that happened between us," Caleb said earnestly. Miranda reached out her long arms to offer a hug.

"It was good to see you, Caleb," she said and they parted ways.

When he returned to Nimara, she was laying on her back with the neck of the guitar resting on her stomach. The case had been emptied. Caleb stood over her and called her lazy. He had the urge to lie with her.

"Lazy is good for my life. Was that past lover?"

"No, just a friend."

Nimara offered a contemplative look.

"You like her or something?" Caleb asked and laughed at her inquisitiveness.

"She's cute," Nimara said and sat up in a puerile position. She was looking up at him with her legs crossed. He leaned down and grabbed the guitar off her lap.

"Be careful with that Mr Cay-leb. Peter paid big for that."

"Peter paid for this? I thought it was his?"

"He trade Petra one of his paintings for it. So you could use it to get home," she said.

Caleb was struck by Nimara's revelation and it made him smile.

"Ah, that is the Peter effect," she said. "He has way of making people smile." She patted him on the shoulder as a signal she was ready to go. "Here is your share of our millions, Mr Cay-leb."

She pulled a fistful of money out of her left pocket and put it into his cupped hands. It was just paper and metal from strangers' pockets, but it was the only thing that would get him home.

December 25, 1944

Dear Marie,
Merry Christmas, sweetheart! I haven't received a letter from you in a long while, but they may all come in one bunch. It's hard to reach us here and if they don't make their way to me, they'll be returned to you and I'll read them when I get home. Did Jack enjoy the train set? I look forward to playing trains with him when I get home. It pains me to be away for another one, but next Christmas I expect we'll all be together and every Christmas after that. Did my parents come by and spend the morning with you both? They said you were doing dinner at Uncle Walter's. Don't let him drink too much rum as he likes to do!
    I imagine you're reading the papers so you might know as much, if not more, than I do about what's going on. I don't know how to express the things I've seen the past few months. I have been trying to find the words, but they fail me. My mind wanders. I can't help but think so many Canadians waited so long in England just to die so fast in France. The scene is still quite vivid in my mind. The water was so cold. I just want this to be over. I thought the victory at ▮▮▮▮ would have moved things along more quickly but these Germans just won't give up. We've been moving ▮▮▮ towards the ▮▮▮▮ and pushing these damn Jerries back slowly. The fighting here has been bitter but the end, I believe, is in sight.

Love always,
Patrick

20

He spent his mornings busking in the park with Nimara telling her many things he hadn't told anyone before. She asked about Melanie often and he found it comforting to talk to another someone about her. Nimara helped him understand his situation by listening. He was surprised how helpful it was to say things out loud that had been housed in his mind for so long. It gave life to the healthy thoughts and put the harmful ones to rest.

They learned new songs together and performed them in the park and talked about them over coffee after. He even began adding paint to his canvas with her insistence. And the next time the professor and Petra came by, he felt proud that what they saw was his own work. And while they didn't seem that impressed, it didn't bother him: he was creating something of his own.

It was important he finish the painting before he left, but he hadn't told them how close he was. He had enough money to change his flight and even a little extra for some gifts for Mel. He was getting back on his feet and it was all thanks to Peter. He had offered his help when it was Peter who really needed it, and there was nothing more selfless than that. People needed to rely on each other, that was how the human race had survived. It wasn't everyone for themselves as Kiwi Jas had thought. The truth was that happiness was found in the connection with others. Why had he not valued the connections in his life more highly? Why had he tossed them away so carelessly?

After spending an hour deliberating over a few final brush strokes, Caleb decided it was good enough to hang on his wall and packed up his things. He counted his money, placed it all into a plastic bag, and stuffed it deep into his pack, all the way to the bottom.

He wrote a note and pinned it to his painting:

Dear Professor Goetschle,

I am happy for the opportunity and still hungry. This is not my best work but it's a place to start. I consider this painting a portrait even though the face is turned towards the window. It's a comment on the power of a window to both reflect and offer a glimpse of what's out there in the world. I think people are the same as glass sometimes.

Say goodbye to your daughter, Liese, for me if you see her, and tell her I have no hard feelings. I have gone home. I want you to know how important your loft has been. It helps people take hunger from their stomach and put it into their art. For me, it has helped to trust people again. I've realized the importance of friendship when I was starting to question it. Connecting with people is the only true thing in life.

Thank you,
Caleb.

Peter had been distracted by his own work, a painting he had started after the news of his father, whose sudden departure had magnified parts of his life, parts he had ignored for years. The painting was full of dark tones and crisp edges: it was what he saw when he looked in the mirror, he said.

When Caleb found him, he was sitting on his bed with Nimara looking through a book of photographs. He was glad to see them both together.

"You look packed up like you leaving," Peter said.

"I am leaving. I wanted to give you your guitar back. You don't know how important it's been for me."

"I do know. That's why I gave it to you. That's what friends do. They give the most important things. But that is different for all people."

Peter and Nimara stood up. "You leaving us Mr Cay-leb? But we made such a good team, you and me. Like Sonny and Cher," Nimara said and smiled.

Caleb laughed at her reference and nodded that he was going and signalled for hugs. Nimara reached out first and gave him a generous one that lasted a few seconds and she kissed him on the cheek.

"Don't be a bad boy anymore, okay?"

Peter, with his chalk-white face full of solemnity, was sad to say goodbye.

"Good luck with your life. I'm glad you came to stay with us for little while. It was nice to have a North American come see what good art is all about."

"I know what you did for me, Peter. Thanks for everything, but especially for helping me trust people again."

"The world it needs trust...and good friends who help each other in hard times."

"Well, don't go sacrificing sheep anytime soon, like your idol Hermann...."

"Nitsch! No, I leave that to him. I just paint," Peter said.

"I wish I could have helped you more with everything you're going through."

"From great loss comes great art," Peter said forcing a smile that didn't form correctly. They exchanged emails and Caleb left. As he walked out into the bright afternoon sun, he threw his art supplies in the nearest trash bin. He felt closer to Kiwi Jas, as though he were able to touch his existence somehow. He had proven that he could live a lie, for a little while at least. But it was the trust he placed in a friend that really helped him survive. He could have kept deceiving Peter, but that would have kept a distance between them. He had never really known Kiwi Jas, and that made him sad. Jas would go through life without truly knowing anyone. Had Naomi in Ireland even been real, or was she a lie too? Real happiness had been in front of Caleb the whole time in Piersville – he had good friends and family he could be honest with.

It was something his grandfather had learned in Europe as well. His letters had emphasized his friendship with Jack and how important it had been for him. It was then Caleb realized it was the distance, and not the place that would connect him with this grandfather. Places change. Europe had changed. But the effect of distance on a person never changes. It helps them reflect on what they've left behind. It puts into perspective what's important. Patrick had not been blind to what he had; he loved Marie and didn't need to leave to realize that like Caleb had. But Patrick's sense of obligation was strong and so he was torn between love and duty. Distance did make him miss Marie more, love her even more because he knew what life was like without her. Caleb had left the ones he loved because he wasn't sure he needed them anymore and he was learning now that he was wrong.

He wanted to surprise Melanie by coming home early, but couldn't resist calling her one last time before he left for the airport. He'd have lots of time as he stood standby, but he felt a strange sense of happiness and urgency to hear her voice.

He found a pay phone and dialled her work number.

"Bayview Clinic"

"Is Melanie Hazen there?"

"Just one second. May I ask who's calling?

"It's Caleb."

"Oh hey Caleb, I'll grab her."

As the elevator music kicked in, he wondered if it had been a mistake to call her at work.

"Hi Caleb." The tone of her voice indicated she wasn't excited to hear from him.

"I've got good news. I'm coming home."

"Why?"

"Because I want to make things right with you. Because I miss you."

There was silence. It hung between them like a noose.

"Say something, say you're happy I'm coming back, that you'll pick me up from the airport."

"I don't want you to come home."

"But you don't know what I've been through. I've been trying to get home for a month now. Something happened. I'll tell you about when I get back. Listen, I've realized some things over here. I've taken you for granted. I know that."

"It's too late, Cal."

"No, don't say that. I'm on my way to the airport now."

"No really, it's too late now. I'm with someone else. I have been for a few weeks."

"I don't believe you."

"It's true. I'm sorry. Maybe if you had have come home a month ago, we could have sorted things out, but I've made up my mind now and I'm not turning back. I need someone dependable in my life."

"But I was coming home a month ago. That's when everything happened. I couldn't leave."

"But you're so good at leaving. You left me and Piersville behind without a second thought. But when it was time to come home, all of a sudden you couldn't leave. Seems funny to me. Listen, I have to go. I'm working. Stay in Europe. I'm doing fine."

"Who is it? You know I'll find out eventually."

"You don't know him."

"Bullshit."

"Goodbye Caleb."

The phone went dead and he let it drop and dangle by its cord. It swung into the glass wall and wrapped around his leg. He kicked it away and punched the glass until his knuckle split open and blood spread across his fist. It felt like he was going to be sick as he wandered out into the street aimlessly. He lit up a cigarette and it tightened his stomach around the small amount of food he had eaten that day and the truth settled in that Melanie might be gone for good. He had waited too long. There was no reason to go home now and there was no reason for him to stay. He felt as though he were back on the Seine River watching the land being torn apart at the seams and drifting alone in a body of water. He searched for something he could use to make him feel better, but nothing came to him, except Torquay and the way his grandpa explained its calming waters in his letters. He could picture the beach, the marina, the Ferris wheel and knew he had to go. He had little money, but lots of time. He could hitchhike and sleep in parks. And if things got bad, he had enough money to change his flight and go home.

    He pulled out his map and plotted a course to the coast where the ferries crossed the English Channel from Dieppe. He first walked to The Village Hostel and picked up his new passport, and thanked Gregory for his help. Gregory eyed him suspiciously but smiled and told him he was a good kid. Then Caleb walked for hours until his legs were sore, and he was far enough away from the city that he could stick out his thumb for a ride. The cars passed him like waves setting into the shore of the night. Each headlight blinded him as it came within a few feet of his outstretched arm, holding stiff and stubborn while cars wheeled loudly passed with a brief clap of noise until out of sight. He couldn't help but think he had gambled the most important thing in his life and lost. What was once something he had never thought he could lose was now something he was cavalier enough to lay on the line and it made him question who he'd become. He was angry with himself for being so naïve, but proud that he had survived the attack on his spirit. He had survived France.

September 5, 1945

Dear Marie,
I'm on my way to home to you soon darling. The war is over. What a horrible, goddam confusion. I can't wait to leave this place behind and never return. I have missed your face, but your picture has brought me comfort in the darkest of places. I don't know why any of this happened - the atrocities confound me. I can't even begin to tell you about the things we've come across over here. England's pretty bombed out too – what a horror.

They have postponed my departure, but given me a short leave to pass the time. I'm heading down to Torquay on the southeast coast of England that Jack told me about. He said he planned to retire there and I'm going to go find out why.

I'll spend a week there in November and then I'll finally be coming home. How is our son? I haven't received your letters in some time as I've been moving too much, and I've learned it was difficult to get them to us on the front lines. Many others have missing out on letters from home, but no one misses them more than I do, my love. You don't know how warm it's made me feel inside to receive your letters over the years. I have relied on your caring words when I've been in the darkest of places. The mind can be a strange place when left up to its own devices too long. I've tried to make a heaven of hell in my mind thinking about you two, but it's been difficult. I know I'm coming home to a beautiful life with you and Jack.

I'll see you both soon my love.

Yours always,
Patrick

21

He sat against an empty cargo box at the ferry terminal waiting to cross the English Channel. He could smell the salt in the air when the breeze passed and swung the cargo door gently enough to emit a throaty moan of hinged steel.

He checked his watch. It was 2:30.

The next ferry didn't come until 4:10 and he thought about sleeping but feared he'd miss the boat. Since leaving Paris, he'd slept very little. The last ride up the N27 to Dieppe was the worst of all. He had waited hours before being picked up and the car had a horrible smell coming from the trunk. "Frogs" he was told and he wasn't sure if the woman was joking. He spent the ride with his face towards the window.

He lifted himself up by his legs and scoured the platform for a safe place to explore. The thought of sitting in a ferry terminal depressed him, so he walked from the port and headed northwest through a block of the city, across the busy Boulevard du Verdun and along an expanse of grass where bodies were strewn about, laying peacefully in the sun. There was something important about this place; he recognized the name from history class and knew it was tied to WWII. He wondered if his grandfather spent time here, but it wasn't mentioned by his father. He knew that his grandfather landed on the beaches at Normandy and moved north to fight in the Battle of the Scheldt, but there were many mysteries surrounding his time in Europe. He wished he had done more research before coming to the continent. Torquay was the one place that brought his grandfather joy, and that was the place he needed to get to.

He continued along the grass, passed a sign for the Square du Canada and onto the pebble beach. The rocks twisted his feet as he managed his way to the water. A sharp cliffside sprouted from the lush green landscape in the distance and towered menacingly over the water. The beach stretched infinitely beneath it. Caleb had been to many beaches in his life, but he felt so far away from this one. The sun shone off the water in a familiar way, and the waves kissed the shore with the same slow embrace as Lake Ontario, but he felt it haunted with other men's memories. He imagined men running towards him, pushing against knee-high tides, their guns swinging from their shoulders as they tried to keep their packs from toppling them forward. He saw them reach the shore and crawl along the beach. He saw them gunned down by phantom shooters. He saw their blood stain the beach red and turn the froth pink in the undulating waves. But it was all pieced together from movie's he'd seen. He had nothing authentic to use other than Hollywood. The ones who knew it, rarely talked about it.

He thanked the driver for the ride and stepped out of the car. He watched it melted back into the traffic of Torbay Road. Torquay was vibrant with colourful lights along the boulevard, and a Ferris wheel in motion. The sun had just disappeared, but a trail of red haze was scattered across the horizon Evening-swimmers bathed in the shallow waters; he felt like he was dreaming, like he had stepped out into a memory.

The park across the street was lush with intricate designs carved out in bushes and well-manicured lawns. A couple could be heard playing tennis in the near distance. He walked down the concrete steps to the beach and took off his shoes and wriggled his toes into the sand. It cooled his feet. He set his bag down and walked to the water. A group of adults were drinking wine on a blanket in the sand. They were chatting idly keeping an eye on their children playing at the shore. The three kids were splashing water at each other and laughing. Caleb walked past them until he was knee deep. The water felt good after a long car ride and he walked until his waist was covered and extended his arms above his head and dove. When he fell below the surface, every sound disappeared. He held his breath for as long as he could, but the years of smoking forced him to resurface early. The sun was low enough in the sky that it reflected off the water and blinded him as he opened his eyes. Treading water took more energy than he could afford, so he swam gently back to shore staying submerged as long as he could. He used his hands to push him through the shallow waters to shore and raised himself like a swamp monster in front of the children, who were startled for a second, but went back to playing in the sand.

He was dripping wet as he hovered over his pack, and removed a dirty towel to dry himself and shimmy back into his jeans. He hoisted his pack onto his bare shoulders and made his way across the intersection in a line of pedestrians on their way back from the beach. He walked through the park and stopped to watch the couple play tennis, lobbying the ball playfully back and forth across the net and calling to each other in French. He stood watching them with his hands clasped to the gate until they noticed and stopped playing. He lingered for a second longer and moved on. The pathway took him north to a quiet street lined with manicured shrubs. The salt in the air followed him up the ascent as the wind blew gently past.

It was getting darker, but the street was well lit. At the end just passed an old tire shop, he came upon a dark green entrance in a white, spanish hotel block. He peered into a brightly lit bar boasting libations on glass shelves lit from underneath. It was too fancy to be called The Hole in the Wall. The name on the glass said The Torquay Inn. The bartender eventually looked up and waved. She had one hand on a beer tap beaming a toothy smile. He reciprocated but when she motioned him to come in, he stepped back and continued uphill.

The city lights illuminated the speckled vessels below; they looked like toy boats in bathtub. He walked the cobble stone street through an alleyway until he came to a fork in the road, and a dull, red door with a sign above like a bloody gash that read The Hole in the Wall, and he entered.

The floor was tiled and ceilings sat low with thick beams stretching lengthwise across the pub. The beertaps sat in the centre of the space with benches built into the surrounding walls. Glassware hung above the taps with gold lettering outlining the types of draughts. A sign on the wall said 'Torquy's oldest pub. Circa 1540' and a few old men sat along the bar rail smacking their lips and grumbling over the weather.

The bartender was a large man, clean cut with combed black hair, dusted with a few streaks of grey. His chin was long and formed a canoe-shaped countenance.

He spoke loudly and welcomed Caleb. "What can I get for you lad?"

Caleb surveyed the shiny taps, trying to choose carefully. He asked for an Otter Bitter and saddled onto an empty bar stool, resting his pack awkwardly against a thick, wooden beam descending from the ceiling. The bartender moved sluggishly as he wiped down glasses and placed them on the rack. The wall behind him was scattered with old pictures, some in frames resting in front of dusty bottles, some pinned to the wall, faded with time.

The bartender returned with a full glass of beer and a frothy head pillowing the top so one unsteady movement might spill it over, and Caleb cradled it in his hands and took a first sip to remove the head. He paid with a handful of coins and received an eyeful in return.

"You Canadian?" the old man beside him asked as he turned his head slightly.

Caleb looked back to see his flag was turned out on his pack.

"What's a young Canadian kid doing by himself in an old man's pub in Torquay? Surely your hostel didn't send you here."

"Just looked like a good place to buy my last British pint."

"The saddest sentence I've ever heard," the man said through a thick moustache that tickled the underneath of a wide, red nose. His eyebrows were thick and wild on a face that was small but with prominent features like he never grew into them.

"Well, I'm heading back home soon and I've only got a little bit of money left."

"Well, you picked a good lager there, mate. And a good town to visit. People come here for the tourist attractions – beaches, marina, parks and that, but this town's rich with history. It's more than just a fancy Ferris wheel."

"Well, that's kind of why I'm here. My grandfather spent time here after the war and fell in love with the place."

The old man eyed him carefully and took a healthy drink of his beer. "He storm the beaches?"

"Ya. He stayed here on his way home to Canada."

"Well, this town was kept pretty much intact during the blitz, you know. Germans didn't have much interest. Many fled here during the messy stuff." His eyes lost focus and he seemed to be staring at something beyond the wall. He regained focus and smacked his lips. "And before that in the Great War, this town was a medical outpost. It wasn't until after that we became Monte Carlo or whatever. Eh Tom – is that what they call us? British Monte Carlo?"

The bartender responded without turning around. "The English Riviera."

The man snorted and started watching the television again.

Caleb looked around and wondered where his grandpa had sat. He felt his presence and couldn't wait to tell his dad he had made it there.

He took another swig of beer and noticed one of the pictures behind the bar – it held a face he recognized, one he'd known since he was a child: a pair of eyes that he had stared curiously into through his life. He knew those eyes, the cropped hair cut, but he didn't know that smile. This was the same young man who had stared out to him in uniform, with eyes that sunk back into the war. But this man was smiling in a bar with friends enjoying a beer – a different man.

He flagged the bartender down and asked to see the picture. When he held it in his hands, he looked deeply into it like it wasn't real. It was the same face but the eyes. He knew him as a soldier and as a grandfather, but it never seemed real to him that at one point he was a man who spent time in bars, telling jokes and laughing with friends.

Patrick was standing between two men, who looked roughly his age; he had his arms around them. They were all smiling, but their eyes held a secret.

Caleb placed his fingers on the glass of the framed picture. He had only known this person through his father, but it's never possible to understand someone through stories, or pictures, or other people. It's in flux that people reveal themselves.

He knew there was nothing in his life that equalled the war for a generation of men who must have wondered why God abandoned a part of the Earth for six years. It was not something meant to be understood – a horror beyond the fingertips of language, packaged neatly for his generation in a two hour Hollywood movie that resolved at the end, but there was no possible ending to such a thing. If there was, it was death. Every story, if left long enough ends in death.

And every one who's been to war knows that hell exists on earth, and hopes that heaven is out of reach from the dark hands that orchestrated such evil, that they will no longer have to hold up the wall that kept everyone else outside. His father knew of this wall, it was made of glass and men lived behind it after the war.

It was easy to forget it was there. One of the functions of glass is to disappear, to vanish into the very world that it separates them from. It can keep the world out while giving a clear picture of it. A window can let the light in while keeping the world away - to watch life happen without being out in it. They lived behind glass walls that no one could see. It was comforting, like a piece of clothing, like a gun.

But glass has other functions than clarity. It has a reflective nature that evokes vanity in many and curiosity in some, but when there is the proper contrast of light between the two sides – the viewer and the world – then glass awakens from its silence, becomes a part of the world again and takes form to throw one's shape back onto them. Some men, the men who have known true horror, the basest of human conditions, live with this glass always around them so that the world appears and disappears with the contrast of light and sometimes when the world looks in it doesn't see them, only itself reflecting back and that is when things are darkest. And sometimes when these men look out to the world, to the ones they love and things they are lucky to have, they don't feel lucky at all for they can't see anything but their own faces distorted in the reflection, in memories they are sure can't be of this world. Yet they exist in a place they fight to hide. They live in two worlds, and glass keeps them apart.

"What's with the picture, son?" the old man beside him asked. He looked to the bartender who shrugged.

"Can I take this?" Caleb asked

The bartender gave him a puzzled look. "Not bloody likely!"

Caleb nodded in acquiescence.

"Why would you want a picture of my father from the '40s?" he asked.

"Which one is your father?" Caleb asked.

The man reached over and placed his large hairy finger on the figure to Patrick's right, a husky dark-haired man with freckles down his face and shoulders. He was wearing a white t shirt and he had his long arm raised high with a beer in his hand.

"Who is the other man?" Caleb asked.

"Which one? There's two," the bartender replied.

"That one on the far left," Caleb pointed at the man staring calmly into the camera, fair skinned and tall. His hair was cropped neatly to one side and his face looked soft and affable, but his eyes were stern. He was leaning forward into the camera craning his neck to bring his head to the level of the other two.

"I believe his name was Jack. A gunner in the RAF."

"And the other one was actually a Canadian bloke. A seargant in the Queens Own Rifles."

"The Chaudiere to be exact," Caleb said. "That's my grandfather."

Both men stopped what they were doing.

"Bloody hell! Are you shitting us kid?"

"I'm not. That's my grandfather, right there in that picture. In the middle. That's him."

"Jesus H. Christ. You walk in here off the street looking like a godamm ragamuffin and you're trying to bullshit me in my own pub. Get the fuck out a' here."

Caleb went to his backpack and rummaged through it under the careful eye of the bartender and returned with a picture of his grandfather and a letter. The bartender studied it until a smile crossed his lips.

"Bloody hell, you're not fucking with me," he said. "Paul-y look at this picture. The kid's not fucking with us." He handed the picture to the old man beside Caleb.

"Patrick Edmund Arthur," Caleb said proudly to himself.

"My father never talked much about those years, but he talked about that picture sometimes," the bartender said. "Those two guys had met during the war. They both ended up here afterwards and spent nights in this pub with my father, who had just returned himself, with a leg missing, mind you. They were some of his first customers. The picture was taken right behind you." The bartender pointed to the beam behind Caleb.

"So, that's Jack," Caleb said and studied his face. "My grandpa talks about him in his letters. This is unbelievable. I can't wait to tell my dad."

"Pretty amazing stuff kid. You want another pint, there?"

"I've just got enough for one, thanks."

"This one's on me."

"Shit, thanks! I'd love to stay and talk more. Did your father ever tell you what my grandpa was like?" Caleb asked.

"Like personality-wise?"

"Ya"

"He liked to laugh. He was generous. He was kind. He was respectful. I can't tell you more than that kid." The bartender set a full beer down in front of him and took the empty one away. "But what more can you say about a man? My father remembered him, and my father doesn't remember many people. Did he ever tell you about the war?"

"He died after I was born. His heart."

"Sorry to hear that." The bartender raised his glass.

Caleb jumped up from his stool. "Hey, do you think I could get a picture of us? It'll mean a lot to my old man."

"Of course. You sure you want us in it too? Paul-y's not that photogenic - poor, ugly bastard. Me on the other hand, I'm a gorgeous fucker."

"I want all of us in it. And the photograph. Is there someone who could take it?"

"Reg, get out here for a sec," the bartender bellowed and teenager popped out from the kitchen.

"Caleb held the photograph in front of his chest and the two men stood on either side holding up a beer."

"To Patrick and Jack," the bartender said as Reg steadied the camera.

They all chimed in as the camera snapped a shot: "To Patrick and Jack!"

November 5, 1945

Dear Marie,
I'm on my way home to you darling. The war is over. I can't wait to leave this place behind and never return. They have postponed my departure, but given me a short leave to pass the time. I've come down to a town called Torquay on the southeast coast of England that Jack told me about. He said he planned to retire here and I can understand why. It's beautiful, quiet and peaceful. How I've longed to feel the calmness of the water. It's one of the deepest blues I've ever seen. Today, I sat and watched the boats come and go from the marina. There is a stillness in my heart here that I haven't felt since I was in your arms. How you'd love it here. I have missed your face, but your picture has brought me comfort in the darkest of places. The atrocities confound me. I can't even begin to tell you about the things we've come across over here. England's fairly bombed out too – what a horror. Being here in Torquay feels like I've escaped the war for a time, though. The Germans left this place alone, thank God. It's rather odd to see all the cobblestone streets intact, and every building erect. I do look forward to taking walks through town, and maybe even take a ride on the Ferris wheel in the centre.

      How is our son? I haven't received your letters in some time as I've been moving too much, but I long to see his face as well. I think the idea of buying a cottage is a splendid one, and I can't wait to talk to you about it when I return. It could be a place we feel the calmness of the water together and watch our children grow.

See you soon my love.

Yours always,
Patrick

22

The cool October air hit him as he stepped off the plane. His stomach felt tight and he was nervous to see his father. An unmistakable feeling of panic hit him like he had just woken up from a dream. As he waited for his bag to appear on the carousel, he looked around for someone to connect with, someone to share a gaze with to acknowledge the melancholy of being home from an adventure.

His father was waiting for him at the terminal, his back against the glass partition. When he saw Caleb, he kicked off the wall, walked over and hugged him.

"Good to see ya, pal!" he said and held the embrace longer than any other time in Caleb's life. He felt weak in his father's arms; somehow his stature was larger, more powerful than he had remembered. Jack took the pack from him and carried it out of the terminal. He had the sudden sensation of a child following his dad to the car. It reminded him of walking back to their station wagon after a weekend at the cottage when he was growing up.

The smell of the family car made him instantly sentimental, and he fell silent. They struggled to articulate something they had never been able to say to each other.

"Life doesn't make sense sometimes, Caleb," Jack said looking out the windshield of the parked car.

Caleb nodded and tried to avoid eye contact. A tear fell down his cheek. He wiped it away quickly, but his father saw it. Another tear came and Caleb tried to talk and gave up when his voice cracked. His father took his right hand off the wheel and placed it on Caleb's shoulder.

"Did you find what you were looking for over there?"

Caleb stared out the passenger side window into the rain. It was coming down harder now. "I want to show you something," Caleb said and pulled out an envelope full of pictures from his pack. He flipped through them as his father looked at him curiously. When Caleb found the one he was looking for, he handed it across the console.

Jack examined it closely but was having difficulty understanding its significance.

"That's him. In that picture I'm holding," Caleb said. "Grandpa."

"Where did you...?"

"And that's Jack beside him. *The* Jack"

His father examined it closer until he was convinced. He looked back at Caleb, astonished. His gaze fell back upon the picture and he moved his thumb across it to feel its texture as though it would make it more real. Caleb realized how odd it must be for his father to finally see a picture of the man he was named after.

"You found this in Torquay?"

Caleb nodded. "In that bar he writes about."

His father nodded and held his gaze on it.

"You should have seen the look on the bartender's face when I told him," Caleb said.

"It's funny. We never got a picture of you two before he passed," Jack said. "It was always something I regretted."

"It was an interesting ending to an interesting adventure," Caleb said and accepted the picture back. "I've got a lot to tell you about, Dad."

Jack paused. "I think we're due for a really long chat," Jack said. "I've never told you much about my travels when I was your age. Maybe it's time."

"That was the trip you took through Asia before meeting mom?"

"I was a bit younger than you, but I still felt the need to see some of the world before settling down. It was a different time back then."

"Do you still remember the places you went and the people you met?"

"Of course. There were a few people I met who impacted me deeply. Sometimes it's the people that only come into your life briefly that change you the most. It's important to pay attention to them. Jack was that person for your grandpa."

"Did they ever meet again after the war?"

"They lost touch and never saw each other again as far I as I know," Jack said and paused. "I imagine you also met a few people over there who left an impact."

"I did," Caleb said and got lost in memories of the last few months. "I think I learned a lot about myself. And it turns out I don't know much about anything."

"None of us really do," Jack said giving him a sympathetic look. "Well, I can tell you're tired. I'll let you get some rest and we'll talk more later. "

"I'm thinking of going up to the cottage for awhile when I get home," Caleb said. "Would that be alright?"

Jack looked surprised. "If you're willing to do some work while you're up there. Sure, I think that's a good idea." Jack turned the ignition and let the car idle for a few seconds. "And thanks for bringing me that picture. It means a lot."

Caleb nodded and felt the lethargy of his long flight kick in. He rested his head against the window.

"I think it's time we start being more honest with each other about our lives," Jack said.

Caleb looked at him and nodded. The sound of the rain was soothing and he rested his head against the window again. He let his heavy eyelids drop and fell into a deep sleep that lasted the drive home.

November 14, 1945

Dear Marie,
You won't believe who I've met here in Torquay: Jack! I'm not overly surprised. We planned to meet here, but never believed it would actually happen and that the timing would be the same. We've been spending the days sitting on the beach and walking the streets for hours chatting. I've almost convinced him to move to Canada. He's off to teacher's college and I think he'll make a fine teacher wherever he goes.

    He's been taking me to a place in the evenings called A Hole in the Wall, and it's just that! A hole! But a Brit named Lenny has just taken it over and is planning to make some improvements to the place. Lenny lost his leg in Belgium when the Germans surrounded his slit trench. He thought he was a goner and so he considers everyday a gift. I think we all do. The three of us spend the evenings drinking scotch (too much!) and sharing some stories. It's difficult to open up about the last few years, but not with these two. They've both lived quite the life. I've been realizing how lucky I am, Marie, and I know I've told you I feel lucky, but I truly know what I want in life now. I want peace. I want to raise a family with you.

    One night Jack told me one about an uncle of his who walked out on his family one day. Just left. But then returned ten years later out of the blue and wanted his family back. His wife barely recognized him but the sons did instantly. They still felt that bond, even though he had abandoned them. It struck me that a man could ever leave the ones he loves on purpose. Now that I have a family, you're all I can think about. I can't imagine leaving you, but I then I worry I did that very thing by coming over here.

    But what struck me about Jack's story was that the man came back. No man is meant to live alone no matter how free he feels. The aloneness will eat you up. Even though I have never met my son, I feel tied to him because he's part of me. Distance doesn't' change that. Neither does time. When I look into his face in the pictures I have, I see more than just my son. I see all the generations that led to him and all the generations that will follow him. It's difficult to explain, but it's a feeling I cherish over here. Thoughts like that have kept me going, Marie.

    I'm running out of page here, but I have so much to tell you about when we meet. I guess you will hear all about the parade that's being planned for us and as soon as we're dismissed, I'll be over in that crowd like a flash of lightning to find the prettiest girl in the whole crowd – my beautiful wife. I love you more than anything,

Your husband,
  Patrick

23

Caleb had goose bumps as he drove down the lane. He wondered if the cottage would look as he remembered it. The trees had grown out over the lane and brushed up against his car causing soft clunking noises as he passed them. When he saw it at the end of the lane, it looked small and isolated. The lake was marshy and unfit for swimming but had always attracted wildlife. Beavers conducted their business in silence waddling in and out of the lake with their prizes in tow; birds flew the perimeter chirping mating songs and surveying the trees. It wasn't all that rare, he remembered, to see a deer come to the water to drink.

The paint had begun to crack and peel away and the wood was rotting on the deck railing and some of the floorboards needed replacing. The roof had begun to sag on one side and sprouted a thick green moss. Each year that passed added more repairs to an already lengthy list until it almost seemed impossible to fix up, and the only option would be to sell. But they never did.

When he opened the front door, he felt like he was eight years old again with his sleeping bag under his arm and his fishing rod in his hand. He remembered feeling so happy as a child to finally open that door after the long drive. The first thing they would do was claim their beds and run out to the back deck overlooking the lake. They'd fly down the stairs and out onto the lawn, over the little bridge to the trails that Patrick had blazed fifty years earlier. Caleb loved wandering those trails as a child, amongst the towering trees and still water.

The sweet, musty air filled his lungs as he pushed the cottage door open with his shoulder. The cottage looked abandoned: the table against the window with the old bread box on top, empty and open; the paintings of sailboats on the walls thick with dust; the laminate countertop covered in mouse droppings; the sink dense with spider webs and dead flies. The small living room still looked cozy with old books under the boarded up windows, and the fireplace, wise with stories, still stood as the centrepiece, the backbone of the cottage. He peered into the bedroom that he and his brothers had always shared, often sitting on the top bunk all afternoon playing board games; the beds now sunk low and the covers were torn to shreds; a quick rustling made his heart jump and a squirrel leapt up onto the top bunk and disappeared through a hole by the window.

    He rolled his sleeping bag onto the floor by the old fireplace and read until he fell asleep.

Walking through the woods, he had learned, was a way to recharge his spirit. He often felt alone in the cottage by himself but never while he was on the trails surrounded by the trees. They had a way of soothing him and taking his mind off his troubles. He enjoyed finding a soft, flat spot off the trail and lying supine with his gaze upwards to the canopy of foliage. Each branch burst thick with green fingers reaching towards the sun; they swayed and shifted with the wind like a crowd waving their arms in concert. The trunks that rooted each tree firmly in place were bare and told of a long history. It struck Caleb that everything has a past, even trees. What is the sense in trying to ignore it? His past, his time in Piersville, was as much a part of him as the low trunk is to a tree. Even further were the roots that kept each tree planted. How deep they ran, he thought, and how invisible they were. He looked out to the tips of the longest branches, knowing the roots of a tree extend as far underground, and realized these trees were dependent on the concealed origins beneath him. They are what allowed each one to reach so far, to stretch so high. How important they are yet easily forgotten. The past is what keeps things in place; he had finally understood it, and accepted that Piersville was important. It was his roots.

    It became clear that the only real struggle was to be conscious of the moment. He laid back and closed his eyes, felt the northern breeze cool his skin. Two birds conversed in song across the nearby lake. His mind cleared. There was only a thin consciousness that kept him awake.

When he opened his eyes, he couldn't tell if he'd slept. He moved from the forest floor back to the cottage to gather wood and prepare kindling for a fire. He was surprised Melanie had accepted his invitation to visit him. He wasn't sure what to expect, but knew they had a lot to talk about. He knew she was dating someone new and he wanted her to know he was happy for her.

When he heard her car pull up and the door slam, he went to meet her.

"I always enjoyed it here," she said in a tone that signalled she was happier than the last time they'd spoken. She handed him a bottle of wine and a grocery bag of food. "It's the quiet, I think."

Caleb took her along the trails he'd blazed. They began at the back corner of the property through the rocky boulders of the high ground and navigated through the dense pine trees down to the lake. The trail lined the water for half a kilometre before the banks rose too high over the marshy water's edge.

"These were all the original trails your grandfather blazed when they bought it?" Melanie asked stepping over roots and trying to keep pace.

"He blazed them all in '48" Caleb said. "After the war. Did I tell you I found a picture of him in a pub in Torquay? The one in his letters."

Melanie shook her head.

"Well after the Kiwi Jas incident, I wasn't able to travel to some of the places I wanted to in Holland and France, but I did make it to Torquay, which was really the most important for me. I found the Hole in the Wall where he spent so many nights with Jack and there was a picture hanging behind the bar. It was him, Jack and the bartender all smiling away like the war had never happened. I asked the bartender if I could have it, and he basically told me to fuck off," he said and laughed.

"That's really nice, Cal – about the picture. I'm glad you found a piece of him over there."

"Europe would have been a lonely place for him, but he found comfort in friendship," Caleb said. "That's something I realized over there – I had been a bad friend to pretty much everyone I cared about. Including you. I took everyone who loved me for granted."

"People are important. You shouldn't push away the good ones," Melanie said.

"I think it might be too late for that advice," Caleb said. "I've lost you haven't I?"

Melanie stopped to take a rest and look out over the lake. The sun had set low enough that it reflected off the water in a sparkling white line stretching towards them. Caleb remembered the summer nights as a child watching the sun go down behind the lake after his parents took them for a hike on clear evenings.

He remembered the warm cup of hot chocolate in his hands and feeling of being part of a family. It was simple then.

He gazed on the outline of Melanie's face as she looked over the horizon of trees. She looked statuesque and he wanted to keep her there in that moment. She was more beautiful to him than ever before. Possibly it was the way the sun was setting on her silhouette, or the way her hair had fallen around her face; maybe it was her resolve, or her unselfishness that he noticed in her; but no, he knew it was something to do with him. Something in him had changed and he was seeing her differently now.

It was shattered when she felt his stare and turned to him, smiled and stood up. She reached out her hand and helped him up. They wandered back in the low light of dusk. They ate a late dinner and sat by the fire.

"Cal, there's something I have to ask you," she said as she leaned forward in her lawn chair. The fire illuminated her face against the darkness behind them. "Why didn't you ask me for help?"

He took a deep breath and sighed. He knew the question would come up at some point, but he expected it from his parents before he expected it from her. The truth was, he didn't know why exactly, but it was hidden behind a sense of antagonism he felt at the time as though he were out to prove something to everyone. He had later realized that he did it to prove something to himself and he told her so. He told her how shameful he felt at that time.

"Europe really opened my eyes," he said.

He could tell she wasn't satisfied with his answer and he struggled to give her what she wanted. "I was too proud," he continued and left it at that.

"Do you want to talk about the shooting?" he asked as the fire began to dwindle. He stood up and took some more wood from the pile. He placed one log carefully across the embers, and kept one log in his hand. He waited. A flame appeared and licked at both sides of the wood. He placed the second one and sat back down. He had been thinking about the difference between his experience and his grandfather's. Patrick had traveled there to meet death, to look it straight in the eye; Caleb had traveled there for pleasure, while death and violence were happening in his home town. He had run away from death, a different kind of war being waged by kids, not for territory or hegemony, but for recognition of an unhappy life. He apologized for bringing it up and stood next to her stroking her hair as she wiped tears from her eyes.

"Can you play me a song," she said and picked up the old guitar they had found inside.

"It's probably out of tune" he said, but accepted it and strummed it once to find that he was right.

"I don't care. I just want to hear you play something. Like you used to."

"Wish You Were Here?" he asked and she smiled sarcastically at him and laughed.

"Sure."

He played her songs like he used to sitting around their house on lazy Sunday afternoons, and she sang along with him until an hour had passed and they realized it was getting late.

"Thanks for inviting me, Cal. I've always liked it here. I'm sorry I was so mad at you last time we talked. I don't want to be angry with you anymore."

"I hope you can come visit me again," he said. "I'm going to spend more time up here. There's still a lot of work to do on this place. You know it's funny – I went all the way to Europe to find my grandfather, but all I needed to do was to come up here. I never realized how much of him is in the cottage. He was happy here too, until. Well, you know."

"Is this where it happened?"

"The heart attack? Ya, right here in the cottage"

"Was he alone?"

"No, we were all here. I was just born. We were all down at the water when it happened. That's what my father says. My grandma was with him. She held him as we waited for help. It just didn't come fast enough."

When they arrived at her car, she admitted she'd had too much wine to drive home.

"Just spend the night here, Mel. The cottage is a mess but I'll give you the bedroom. I'll sleep on the couch."

She nodded and in an impulsive act, kissed him. It turned into a long embrace and ended with a kiss on her forehead.

"You were right earlier, Cal. Things are over between us. I've started seeing someone new."

Caleb nodded and kissed her on the forehead again. "I know," he said. "I know about you and McDonough. I don't like him much, but I'm glad you're happy. We're all just trying to be happy aren't we?"

She smiled and followed him into the cottage and he made up the bed for her. He rolled his sleeping bag out again by the fireplace and removed his clothes. Melanie entered the living room to say goodnight. "When did you get that?" she asked pointing at his tattoo.

"It was a mistake," he said. "I'm getting it removed."

"No" she told him. "You should keep it. Removing it will only leave a scar anyways."

She walked over and ran her fingers across his chest before tracing the word and mouthing 'Europe.' She said goodnight and slipped back into the bedroom.

When Caleb awoke in the morning, she was already gone. A note sat on the counter addressed to him. He recognized Melanie's handwriting instantly and felt sentimental for the notes she used to write him in the early years.

Dear Caleb,

It was good to see you. I'm really glad you're fixing up the cottage. Your grandpa would be proud of you. I think you need to be alone for awhile, and figure out what you want in life. I'm not going to wait for you because I don't think I'm what you need. I think I was for a long time, just as you were the person I needed. I don't want us to hurt each other anymore; but I want us to be friends. I'll always love you and be there for you when you need someone to talk to. I know there are more things that happened to you in Europe than you're telling me and I hope someday you can feel open enough to explain them. But there are just some things we can't give each other. I've found them in someone else and I want you to be happy for me. I know you don't like McDonough, but he's a good man. He's good to me and I hope you can accept that I've moved on.

I hope you understand.

Love always,
Mel

December 1, 1945

Dear Patrick,
I am writing you with the awareness that you may, in fact, be home before this letter reaches England, and I pray that's true! I've received your November letter and to be honest my love, your words made me cry. I feel the same way about the bond that you and I have. Distance and time cannot change it. When we see each other at the parade, I know our love will be stronger than ever. I can't wait for you to meet your son. He's heard all about you and seen pictures, but I want him to touch your face and hear your voice. I long for him to feel the warmth of your smile, the same warmth that I've felt so many times.

Your parents and I will be at the parade early and we'll be the ones clapping the loudest. Pastor Hagan has encouraged the whole congregation to attend, and you know how they all respect Pastor so much. He's been a big support over this past year. I even convinced Phenon to come, and he'll bring Margaret. We're all so proud of you, Patrick, and what the Queens Own has accomplished over there. The papers have been publishing individual stories, and I want them to write something on your contribution. I mean, becoming a sergeant that helped lead the attack that won the war. You must be so proud. And they should write something about Jack. I can't believe he flew over seventy missions! That is truly remarkable and there should be a record kept of it. You are both so lucky. I hope you feel that way.

It sounds like you're having a swell time in Torquay and I'm glad you're able to finally buy Jack that glass of whiskey you owe him! Poor Lenny – I know this will sound selfish, but I'm glad you're coming home to me in one piece, my love. I know many men weren't so lucky. I hope you have let Jack know that if he comes to Canada, he is more than welcome to come stay with us. I would love to meet the man who's become such a good friend to you.

Get home safe. And get home soon!

All my love,
Marie

25

When he had finished the roof and re-built the deck, Caleb turned his efforts to the inside of the cottage. It would need more than a coat of paint; some framing would need to be done and he'd have to replace the flooring room by room. Everything would need to be moved and he struggled on his own to lift the cumbersome cabinet that sat in the corner of the master bedroom. He decided to unscrew the hinges on the back to remove the top half first and then move the lower half, which held four long drawers. Taking the drawers separately would remove some of the weight, as well, and as he pulled them out one-by-one, he noticed they were still full of old bedsheets and pillow cases. They would all need to be tossed, he thought. As he pulled them out, he recoiled at the musty stench that filled the air, but he noticed an envelope that remained at the bottom of the fourth drawer. He recognized the style of paper and the handwriting on faded ink. It was one of his grandfather's from the war, but one that had been kept separate from the others, one that Caleb had never seen.

June 8, 1944

Dear Son,

I'm writing to you from a place I hope you never find yourself. I'm far away from the ones I love, the roots I had laid, and the life I was happy with. I am surrounded

by death, and yet there is new life to celebrate: yours. You belong to a place I hope to return to. Someday, we will meet and I will forget the evils of man when I look into your eyes. There are things I hope you never see, things that no man should. It has made me realize how important family is. It has made me cherish friendship above all else. I have made a good friend over here, a man for whom you were named after. Without his company, and without the letters from your mother, I don't know if I would have survived this war. No one can be happy alone, but sometimes it takes being alone to realize that. I hope you don't find yourself alone very often in your life, son. Surround yourself with the ones you love and you'll find happiness. Stand up for what you believe in and never take anything for granted. There is a lot of good in this world if you look for it.
You will always be loved.

Your father,
Patrick

He put the letter down and walked out to the deck to watch the sun go down. He listened to the water lapping against the shore. Frogs croaked throaty moans as the sun dropped behind the trees colouring the sky a blood orange. He was tingling with reflection.

 The wooden railing creaked as he eased himself onto the ledge that was the last barrier between him and the grass below. He could see himself in the sliding glass door and as dusk approached, his reflection waned and he could begin to see through the glass and into the cottage. He pictured his grandfather inside and tried to imagine what his evenings were like up there by himself. Was he lonely?

 It was then that Caleb realized he belonged to that universal struggle his grandfather wrote about. He had had to be alone to realize what loneliness really was.

 He had taken the people in his life for granted and now he understood how important it was to have people to depend on and people to love. Everyone on earth was fighting against loneliness.

 Kiwi Jas was right: heaven and hell did exist on Earth. There were choices and there were consequences and no guarantees that anyone could be happy, but one could choose to surround themselves with the right people. He knew how it felt to be free and alone; he knew the consequences of it. It meant floating dangerously between pleasure and regret. It was a gamble, a toss of the dice. He knew now that he could make mistakes and the people who truly mattered in his life would forgive him, but it wasn't without consequence.

December 3, 1945

Dear Marie,
I expect that you may have me in your arms before this letter arrives home, and I hope that's the case, my dear. I have decided to write you this and race it home. We'll see which arrives first. If it is this letter, I want you to know that I've had much time to reflect in Torquay and I realize that nothing that I've done over here will make me more proud than being a good husband and father to you and Jack. I know you are proud of me for what the Queen's Own has accomplished but it's more important that you're proud of the husband I will be to you, and the father I will be to our son. Any man can enlist in the war and head off to Europe, but it takes much more to be a strong man at home.

    There were some nights I couldn't sleep and I lay looking at the stars and realized that we all had different reasons for coming to Europe: some came to seek adventure (and they certainly found that); some came out of duty to their country and the commonwealth; and some men came to escape poverty. But we were all in this together and now that it's over, we are all left to deal with the consequences of it alone. I worry for some men, Marie. I don't know what they have to go home to. I don't know what they'll have to keep them company but their memories of war. Surely their thoughts in conjunction with their aloneness will lead them back to hell. The mind is it's own place, Marie, and I'm glad I have you and Jack to occupy mine with. When things get dark, you two are my light. You bring me back from the places I fear. A man without loved ones is in a hell of his own making.

    There is nothing I'm more excited about than seeing your faces and holding you both in my arms. I am a lucky man, my love. I don't doubt that for a second. I was torn between love and duty for so long but I'm no longer conflicted. It is love that brings me home and it is love and community that will bring me happiness.

All my love,
Patrick

26

Jack arrived on the afternoon Caleb was working on the eaves troughs. Caleb turned his footing on the ladder to see the black Volkswagen Jetta coming down the lane, and stepped down slowly to greet him.

"The place is looking good, Cal," Jack said as he closed the car door and approached him. "I'm glad you decided to take this on."

"Where's mom? I thought she was coming too?"

"Had to work. She'll be up tomorrow," Jack said and led them into the cottage. He ran his hand along the drywall that separated the kitchen from the living room. Caleb watched nervously as his father inspected the work. They walked around the cottage checking angles and sturdiness. When he was pleased, he looked at Caleb and gave him a nod.

Caleb cracked the caps off two bottles of beer and handed his father one. Jack accepted and they both took a long swig and acknowledged each other by lifting their bottles upwards slightly.

They both took a seat at the table. The wind picked up outside and rattled the windowpane in the kitchen. Caleb was happy his father had come and told him so. He had been lonely at the cottage. The only people he'd talked to since Melanie's visit had been the clerks at the hardware store and it was only a few words about the weather.

"I found the letter grandpa wrote to you in '44. It was tucked away in a drawer in the old hutch in there."

Jack looked surprised.

"I can't believe he went three years without meeting you," Caleb said. "It must have been so hard for him knowing you guys were at home waiting."

"It was tough for your grandma too. They kept each other going with those letters. I don't know who relied on them more."

"They were really in love weren't they?"

"It's a rare thing."

"You've never talked much about his life after the war," Caleb said.

Jack looked uneasy and stared out the window. He remained silent for a few seconds. "Your grandfather had a tough time after he got home from the war," he said. "I think most of those guys didn't know what kind of shit they were bringing back with them. He retreated back into himself a lot. I wasn't sure where he went, but I was too scared to ask. And he certainly wasn't interested in telling me about it."

"Did he talk to grandma?"

"I don't think he talked to anyone about it. Not even your grandmother. He seemed distant at times and I thought maybe he wanted to talk but I don't think he had the words," Jack said.

"This cottage must have been good for him."

"Buying the cottage was important for both of them," Jack said. "I think Mom figured it would be a peaceful place he could make new memories with his family. Replace the ones from the war. It doesn't work that way, but she tried. She loved him. I think you can see that from the letters. I know you took some with you to Europe and I was upset with you at first, but I understand."

Caleb nodded and wiped away the condensation his beer bottle left on the table. He took a sip and thought about his grandfather alone in the cottage for so long.

"Do you remember coming up here as a kid?" Caleb asked.

"Sure. But not until I was older. When he first got the cottage, Dad spent the whole summer up here working on it and getting it ready for the family to use," Jack said. "He put a lot of himself into it. I don't remember him being gone for that summer, but I do have a vivid memory of coming up here to pick him up. Mom took Catherine and I in the old Chev. I can still hear the brakes on that thing. Surely Dad would have heard us a mile away coming down the lane. But he wasn't anywhere to be found when we got out." Jack fell silent and gazed out the window until he remembered the beer in his hand and took a long sip. "We walked all through the cottage and around the property but we couldn't find him. I remember the sound of Mom's voice as she tried to act normal but I could tell she was really worried."

"Where was he?" Caleb asked.

We eventually found him sitting in the woods. He was crying. I still remember that moment. I had never seen him cry before. Mom went over and took him in her arms and they spoke a few words. She told us to go back to the car, so I took Catherine and we waited in the backseat. I stared out the window for a long time and eventually they came back and went into the cottage to gather Dad's things. When they got to the deck, he fell back down to his knees and cried again." Jack leaned forward on the table and clasped his hands together in a reflective state. "Mom stood over him rubbing his back with her hand. He was holding the hem of her dress to his face as his tears dampened small circles around her knees. I stared through the window at my father, the hero, who was in all this pain." Jack paused and took a sip of his beer. "We never talked about that day. We never brought it up. But every time I left the cottage from that time forward, I always looked back to that place on the deck where I first saw my dad cry. When I first understand that he *could* cry. You don't often think of your father that way.

"I've never seen you cry," Caleb said.

"I did at both your grandparents' funerals. You were just a baby then. And I've cried many times after that. Life can be hard sometimes Caleb. But you surround yourself with the right people and it makes the hard times easier. Your mother has helped me when I wouldn't have made it alone."

"I've learned to rely on people more too," Caleb said. "Mel and I are done. I think we were a long time ago."

"I wondered that. I figured she wouldn't forgive you for leaving," Jack said. "I don't agree with what you did, but I understand it. You're my son, and I'll love you no matter what stupid things you do. The thing is, I've done plenty myself. It doesn't discount the good we've done."

They shared a smile and a moment of pause.

"What is your earliest memory of you and I?" Jack asked.

Caleb was surprised by the question and had to think for a few seconds. "I'm not sure if it's the earliest, but I do remember driving along a big body of water one evening with you. I don't remember how old I was. Must have been Lake Ontario, I guess."

Jack nodded. "I used to take you for drives in the evening when your mom worked night shifts. You were only five or six then."

"I remember the sun coming in through the windshield. We pulled over at one of the rest stops for a swim. I can still remember the sound of the waves against the shore. They formed all these little pools on the rocks," Caleb said remembering the freedom he felt as he danced across the rock beaches, splashing around the water while his father looked on. "We wrestled and you let me throw you in. I distinctly remember that." He pictured his father sinking under the surface, sprawled out lifeless as Caleb stood triumphantly overtop. Caleb could see him through the water, but in the obtuse angle of the sun spreading a thousand points of light, he could also see his own reflection moving with the rippling surface of the water. It was an image more powerful than the circumstances that created it for those long five seconds were seconds in celluloid – they served the arc of a higher purpose. He knew he was part of something that he would never fully understand: the possibility of seeing both images was imprinted on his mind forever like a photograph.

"It's funny the things we remember," Jack said.

Caleb nodded and smiled. He was still very much back on that beach in his mind. After their swim, they had gotten into the car and driven home. His gaze was set out the front windshield with the wind blowing through the passenger side windows. He watched his father's hand on the wheel – his large knuckles in steady grip steering them home. He snuck glances at his father's profile, studying the side of his face, and from time to time his father would catch his gaze, turn and smile. Caleb smiled back and returned to watching the passing landscape out the window. It put him at ease to know his father was in control. He just needed to feel that way sometimes. Every boy does.

Made in the USA
Middletown, DE
02 May 2019